Her Beast in Brighton

BASTARDS OF BRIGHTON
BOOK 1

TANYA WILDE

Dearest Reader;

Thank you for your support of a small press. At Dragonblade Publishing, we strive to bring you the highest quality Historical Romance from some of the best authors in the business. Without your support, there is no 'us', so we sincerely hope you adore these stories and find some new favorite authors along the way.

Happy Reading!

CEO, Dragonblade Publishing

Prologue

L ADY CALLIOPE BALFOUR rubbed her bare arms to ward off the chill, ignoring the sting of pain as she shrank deeper into the corner of the dark, dusty attic. On her lap, curled in a ball of white fur, lay Prince, the snowy greyhound puppy she had found cowering in a flower patch beneath the library window. He was the only warmth she had left, the only thing in this forsaken place that made her feel needed and alive.

She knew all too well what had brought her here—the latest in a string of punishments from her stepmother, Duvessa. This time, her crime had been compassion. Finding Prince and hiding him in her room had stirred an anger in Duvessa so fierce that the heavens nearly shook with her wrath. But not even the sting of the cane had persuaded Calliope to abandon him. She'd endure anything, even her growing hunger and the bruises that throbbed beneath her skin.

She would not give him up.

"I'm sorry, Prince," she whispered, tucking her face in his soft fur. "This is the only way I can keep you."

It was a miracle already that Duvessa hadn't torn the puppy from her arms. But Calliope knew the puppy would be used as a tool to keep her in line, a weakness her stepmother would surely exploit when it suited her. Still, she would fight to keep Prince by her side, whether she was locked in the attic for a week or a month, with nothing but a thin blanket and old portraits of her father and his ancestry stacked against the walls.

I shall not give in.

What was the worst they could do to her?

Her gaze fell on the proud face of her father, the late Honorable Viscount of Balfour. What would he say if he knew his brother had abandoned her to Duvessa's whims? Her uncle, the current viscount, barely acknowledged her existence. Would he care that his niece was being locked away like a prisoner? That she should be learning to dance, cite poetry, or play the piano like other girls her age and not cowering in the shadows?

She stroked Prince's head.

She had no family in this house. But she did have friends—silent, unseen allies among the servants, who would sneak her extra bread when they could and empty the chamber pot her stepmother had left for her. They always offered the same words of encouragement before leaving: *"Just hold on a little longer, Miss Calliope."*

And she would. Duvessa and her daughters had always been darkness to her—draped in black like the night, cold and cruel as winter winds. Even in sunlight, they cast long shadows.

They were the reason she hated the dark. The dark meant punishment. The dark meant pain. The dark always whispered their names.

She gathered Prince more tightly into her embrace.

Hold on a little longer . . .

Her gaze drifted to the small window, its glass covered by wooden planks. How much time had passed? How much longer did she need to hold on? No, it didn't matter. She could endure as long as she needed to. She could hold on forever.

Calliope smiled against Prince's soft white coat. She didn't need to hold on forever—just until her eighteenth birthday.

Four years.

Only four more years. It sounded unbearably long, but still

not as long as forever.

She shut her eyes, allowing her mind to drift to a future she had created in her dreams. She'd escape. She'd make something of herself. And she'd live a quiet, peaceful life in the light.

Her mother once said she had a face like morning light—soft and fair, with eyes too curious for their own good. A constellation of freckles danced across her nose, and her golden hair always tangled when she was nervous.

"A dreamer's face," her mother used to say, "but with a fire hidden underneath."

She clung to those words now.

Some things could only be escaped through imagination, and Calliope did that quite well. In her future, everything glowed bright and smelled fresh. She wouldn't be ridiculed or beaten anymore. She wouldn't have to fight for every scrap of food. She wouldn't be locked in closets. She wouldn't be cold.

She'd live a peaceful life, away from Duvessa, her vile stepsisters, and the family that didn't claim her after her father's death. The family that had never saved her. But most importantly, she would find a loving husband and build a true family—one that resembled a time before her father married that woman and everything fell apart.

The creak of wooden steps startled her out of her daydream, and her arms tightened protectively around Prince. She held her breath as the footsteps grew louder, stopping just outside the attic door. A few beats of silence followed before a snicker came from behind the door.

"Still not ready to give up on that mutt?" Victoria, the oldest of her stepsisters, sneered.

Calliope dug her toes into the floorboards. *No. Never.*

"Not speaking? How long do you think you can stay in that filthy attic this time, heh?" Morgana, her second stepsister, taunted.

However long it takes.

"Do you think she's finally dead?" Morgana's shrill tone

asked, but Calliope still ignored them. Responding only made it worse. They believed themselves above her because their father had been an earl, and Papa merely a viscount. She had long ago given up trying to understand why that mattered—why they must treat her so cruelly.

"Oh," Victoria scoffed, "the little rat won't die so easily. Even though it would be better if she were dead, it would cause Mama too much trouble. She will still be of some use in the future."

Calliope's brows drew together as she stared at the door. What use? What was the use of living this way? Being treated this way? Was she truly that unlovable?

No, Papa loved you. He did.

Yet those memories felt so far away, almost as if she had dreamed them.

"Oh, right," Morgana said. "Mama promised that old dodger she would marry this brat to him when she came of age. What's his name again?"

What old dodger? What marriage?

"Lord Flemming or something," Victoria answered.

Did they mean Lord Flemmington? The smelly old lord who had been calling on Duvessa in recent weeks and whose stench lingered long after he left? He could have been her grandfather! The mere thought of being shackled to him made her stomach churn. Surely her stepmother wouldn't do such a thing. Surely her uncle—

"And the viscount agreed." Victoria snickered.

Calliope's hands balled into fists. She didn't know if the girls were lying, but let them try to marry her off to that old man! She would rather join her father in the afterlife than allow that to happen!

The door suddenly opened, and Calliope shielded her eyes as flickering candlelight intruded into the attic and made her squint. Once her eyes adjusted, she lowered her arm to find the unwelcome sight of her two stepsisters in the doorway.

"What a pitiful creature you are," Morgana said before laughing. "How entertaining to watch you cower."

Just a little longer . . .

"Yes," Victoria agreed with a sly smile. "What a pitiful creature. Shall I be merciful today?" A piece of bread was tossed her way, landing at her feet.

Calliope didn't rise to their taunts. She wouldn't waste her already-depleted breath on these girls. She'd save it for surviving the darkness. And for Prince. Whatever breath was left, she'd give to him.

"What are you girls doing here?" A chilling voice cut through the air like a knife, cold and commanding. Her stepsisters' expressions faltered, their smugness vanishing in an instant.

Duvessa.

Calliope's whole body went stiff.

She held no love for this woman who had married her father exactly one year after her mother passed away. Within the next year, everything had fallen apart. Duvessa became with child, her father passed away shortly after, and a few months later, the viscountess suffered a miscarriage. Calliope didn't know much about those things, but she understood through the beatings she'd received that she was blamed for it all. The screeching of her stepmother still echoed in her nightmares: "You wretched creature! This is all your fault! If I could have given birth to a son, my position would be secured! You shall stay at my side until I have used all you're worth! I shall see to it!"

The door of the attic slammed shut again, jarring Calliope out of that horrid memory.

"We merely came to see whether our little sister had reflected on her actions, Mama," she heard Victoria answer, a sickening sweetness clinging to each syllable.

"Come." Duvessa's tone brooked no argument. "Don't disturb her punishment, lest her insolence rub off on you. You have dance lessons in an hour."

Calliope listened as they descended the steps, only breathing a sigh of relief when the shallow creaks of the stairs faded into silence once more. She reached for the piece of bread, too hard to be enjoyable, breaking off a small piece and feeding it to Prince.

"Keep your strength up, little one," she whispered. Young pups needed plenty of food to survive, and Calliope could skip a meal or two if she must.

Her gaze turned to her father's portrait once more. *I shall survive too, Papa.*

She just needed to bide her time a little longer.

Chapter One

Brighton 1817
Six years later

CALLIOPE HATED THE night. She shivered, pressing herself tightly against the wall of the building she hid against. Why on earth had she ever thought it a good idea to pick up her package in the dead of night? Not that she had any choice in the matter. Mr. Rollings had sent a request to meet at this location at a most ungodly hour.

Midnight.

What an unfortunate change of schedule.

And what ought to have taken ten minutes had stretched into thirty, leaving her twenty minutes late, thanks to the winding streets of the Lanes, which all looked the same at night. It had taken a while to orient herself.

Nevertheless, she ought to have known better.

This did not fit the quiet, uneventful life she had envisioned. All she wanted was peace, which begged the question, whatever prompted the man to ask this of her? She tugged her cap lower, clutching her satchel tightly over her pounding heart.

Deep breaths, Calliope.

Thank sun and stars she'd purchased a male outfit for this meeting. She might have to run. Fast.

She peeked from behind the wall to where her Mr. Rollings

was conversing with two very large men, dabbing at his brow with a handkerchief. She couldn't see his expression clearly, but she could practically feel the tension flooding from him. Other customers, no doubt, since she'd been late. She wondered what the problem was that led him to meet with them at this hour. And how long it would take them to go away so *she* could talk to Mr. Rollings.

Something about the exchange set her nerves on edge. The looming figures seemed to be one with the night. Carved from the shadows themselves. Their features were even more impossible to distinguish with their caps pulled low over their heads, nor did their statures seem even remotely familiar.

I should have brought Prince.

But then, it was probably a blessing that she hadn't. He'd growl and perhaps even attack when threatened. No, she should have brough her pistol, but she'd completely forgotten about it!

Stars.

All this over some French oil. Very well, *orange blossom* oil, plus some other scents, distilled in the French manner, finer than anything she could source at home. More than that, she loved using this particular oil to create her own uniquely scented candles. It made her feel closer to her mother, who had enjoyed the art of candle-making and favored French scents. After her passing, her father had arranged lessons for Calliope. She had loved those lessons. However, she didn't love meeting at this hour to collect her oil.

And she hated the dark.

Loathed nothing more.

Darkness reminded her of them. Duvessa and her daughters. Black as sin and just as merciless.

Nothing good ever happened when all the lights blew out. A sentiment once again proved right in her current predicament. But this was no attic. Every shadow here posed a potential threat.

She should never have come.

But she had placed explicit trust in Mr. Rollings even though she'd only known him for a few short months. After all, Mr. Fitz, her father's solicitor and her guardian angel who had helped her escape, had made the acquaintance. He'd handled all the terms beforehand, and he would never put her life in danger. So when she'd received Mr. Rollings's message, she had ignored all the "the Vikings have arrived" bells echoing through her bones.

Fie. Fie. Fie.

For the love of wax! How did I get myself into such a horrible situation?

A blistering curse rang out, followed by a dark voice filled with fury, "What the devil do you mean the shipment is missing?"

Calliope flinched.

Exactly what she feared. Nothing good happened in the dark. Ever.

"I do not know, my lord," Mr. Rollings stuttered.

"Don't bloody call me that," the same man snapped, dangerous, and way too close. "I'm not a lord. I'm Death if you don't spill the truth about my shipment."

Case in point.

The other man just watched silently.

And what are you just standing around for, Calliope?

Run!

But her feet couldn't move. Could she just leave Mr. Rollings to his fate?

"What do you want to do with him?" The furious one asked the silent one.

A beat of silence, then, "Deal with him."

Calliope shivered at the low, gravelly voice that carried over to her. Like he hadn't used it in years, or only ever used it to growl threats. Calm. Deadly. Final. The impact lashed across her nerves and lodged beneath her breastbone, driving in deep.

Even worse, she felt marked by it.

He was the leader here. His words were law.

The furious one stepped forward and a fist shot out. Mr. Rollings dropped to the ground, the bone-jarring echo joining that of her gasp.

Her hands flew to cover her mouth as two heads swiveled her way.

Sensation deserted her limbs.

The man who'd watched Mr. Rollings being knocked senseless, the one with the deeper voice, stepped forward. "Who's there? Show yourself. Obedience begets lenience, resistance begets wrath."

Like you showed Mr. Rollings? Not in this lifetime!

Her body snapped into motion, and she bolted in the direction—she hoped—of her shop, only to snag on her own steps and pitch forward. Then to her horror, she promptly tripped over her feet, crashing to the ground hard. The impact jarred her bones, a low *oof* escaping when her palms scraped over loose stones, biting through leather gloves.

Calliope! You foot-clod!

She scurried back to her feet, snatched up the satchel that had landed beside her, and dashed down the alley with all her might, ignoring her aching knees.

Curses ripped through the dark.

Do not *look back.*

She clenched her jaw and pushed on.

Who were these men? She hadn't been in Brighton long. Almost three months in total. The first two were spent in small, rented lodgings, planning and preparing every detail of her new life. The past fortnight had at last seen her open the doors to her shop, above which she now lived. Before that, it had taken years of whispered schemes and secret hopes to reach this point—to flee Duvessa and her despicable plan to wed her to the loathsome Lord Flemmington. Calliope had learned the hard way that people don't rescue girls like her. If they, *she*, wanted freedom, she'd have to claim it for herself.

Only with the secret help of a few loyal servants and the ever-resourceful Mr. Fitz had she managed to escape and begin anew in this seaside town.

Now her lungs burned.

Why did she decide on Brighton again?

There were other, more remote towns Duvessa avoided with a passion, too. *Just admit it, Calliope. You wanted to live near the ocean.* And since she never debuted, and rarely met others, she didn't need to worry that she'd be recognized. Even her own family had abandoned her to Duvessa since her father's death. Some she hadn't seen since her mother's.

A quiet life.

A comfortable life.

Hidden away and free from Duvessa and her horrid stepsisters.

Not dashing through the misty, dark streets from brigands who might harm her if she were caught! Fortunately, she had already regained her sense of direction, and didn't dare slow until she reached her shop. She nervously glanced over her shoulder while she fished for the key and jammed it into the lock with trembling hands.

Come on!

The key rattled as she attempted to unlock the door, joined by voices echoing somewhere through the streets, followed by approaching footsteps growing closer.

The beat of her heart sped up.

Don't look.

Fie this! She should have ignored Mr. Rollings's request!

The door gave way, and she staggered inside, nearly sprawling in her haste. Calliope slammed it shut, and the moment the bolt slid into place relief struck her, dizzying. She leaned back, spine pressed to the wood, breath coming fast. A second later, she slid to the floor.

She'd evaded those men. By some miracle.

Her attention caught on the flickering candle on the counter.

Drat! She scurried forward on her hands and feet to snuff out the light with the tips of her fingers. The room plunged into total darkness, wrapping around her like a well-worn cloak.

It's all right, Calliope. Just a little longer.

Her gaze flicked to the narrow-curtained doorway leading to the workroom, where a stairwell spiraled up to her private rooms. She didn't know how, but her legs made it to her living quarters in two parts determination and one part daze. Not until her arms were around Prince did her mind begin to clear.

He licked her face, and a bubble of laughter escaped from her lips. Just short of hysterical. No, most definitely hysterical.

"Dear God," she breathed between the bouts. "What did I just witness?" A kidnapping? A *murder*? Surely not. And yet she could not deny the sight of Mr. Rollings falling to the ground. Utterly terrifying! Was Mr. Rollings still alive? And what about her oil? She hated to even entertain the unbidden thought, but if those men found her goods, they'd find her, correct? If they found her . . .

Do not even entertain such a thought!

But the image of those men, *hounds*, sniffing at the package and allowing others to sniff and track her, still burst into her mind.

What would they do to her if they caught her?

They hadn't.

Yet.

Her ears strained for any noises that might indicate the two big men had caught onto her and her shop. What had Mr. Rollings said when he'd delivered her first purchase?

Take care, Miss Turner. Brighton is run by beasts.

She'd laughed it off then, believed the older man an overly cautious tradesman. But now . . . now she wasn't laughing.

She had escaped the night. But it had seen her now. And she had a horrifying feeling it would not forget her.

Was it true? Was Brighton run by beasts? Had she encountered them tonight? No matter how much she wished she could unsee what she'd witnessed, she could not.

"It's fine," she said to Prince after the beat of her heart finally started to settle, rubbing his back. "They didn't catch me." Her gaze moved to the window, and she slowly rose, padding over to peek through the window to the street below.

Not a soul stirred.

She let out a deep breath of relief. So far, she'd been remarkably lucky. If they didn't know who had witnessed their deeds, she was in no imminent danger. However . . . "Should I move to another town?"

No, that wouldn't do. Mr. Fitz had paid six months' rent in advance, and apparently her landlord had made it clear that the payment would not be returned no matter what. Plus, her secret inheritance was generous, but not an endless pit of wealth. She and Prince were stuck here for the time being.

But what about Mr. Rollings?

You can't help him, Calliope.

She studied the street below. If there was one thing Calliope had learned from her time with Duvessa and her daughters, it was that the world favored those who looked out for themselves. She couldn't afford to dwell on Mr. Rollings. Her life, her survival, depended on her focusing solely on herself. However, she couldn't do nothing at all. Her conscience would haunt her forever. So, she'd pen a letter to Mr. Fitz. He might be able to assist Mr. Rollings where she could not.

Her breath hitched as two shadows moved into the street. She jerked from the window, pressing her whole body against the wall, heart leaping several beats. After a moment, she cautiously craned her neck to confirm that she wasn't imagining things.

Oh sun and stars, she wasn't.

Two men tracked the street below. She recognized the caps on their heads instantly. The air froze between her lungs and throat as her gaze remained fixed on them until their silhouettes cleared the street.

Calliope wanted to scream into a pillow.

I'm sorry, Mr. Rollings, but there is nothing I can do for you right now.

MAXEN FURY LOVED the night.

Darkness wasn't just where he thrived, it was where he ruled.

On the other hand, he hated trouble.

And trouble always occurred in threes. They caused complications. And if there was one thing that he, one of the seven bastard sons of the Duke of Crane, wanted to avoid at all costs, it was complications. They had a way of turning deadly. He'd learned that the hard way, long before he'd been old enough to understand the cost.

Damn it all to hell.

He should have known this night would gather into a pile of shite the moment he caught sight of the new shop right next to his bolt-hole this morning—all bright and *sweet*.

Dagger, that arse, who managed all their properties, had rented out that blasted one without his permission while he was busy setting up a warehouse in Worthing for the past fortnight. His brother also hadn't given him any additional information other than he'd been too gloomy and should enjoy some freshness.

He still wanted to throttle the man.

How could the arse be so careless? That shop—*that space*—was where they hid their barrels. What would happen if they required the gunpowder?

He pushed the thought aside with a curse. No use lamenting over it now. The deed was done and could not be undone for the time being.

Maxen scowled at the man sprawled on the ground.

Now *this*.

What the bloody hell had he done to deserve this bloody mess?

And what the hell had he just heard? His sharp gaze followed Dagger's to the shadows beyond the buildings where the unmistakable sound had come from.

"Someone is watching us," Dagger said darkly.

Bloody fine.

"Who's there?" Maxen called out, and then added for good measure, "Show yourself. Obedience begets lenience, resistance begets wrath."

Silence.

Maxen motioned to the man sprawled on the ground. "Keep an eye on him. I'll go have a look." He set off in the direction of the noise without waiting for his brother's response, cursing his luck. He hadn't wanted to come out tonight to meet this fool, Rollings. But he'd had no other choice. He ran these streets. *He* did the sweeping if there were messes to clear. Especially missing cargo messes.

And when there was proverbial blood in the water, Maxen always hunted.

He strode briskly through the dark, his whole body on high alert, a scowl forming when he heard another sound. This one almost like an *oof*, followed by footsteps fleeing, confirming they hadn't been mistaken.

A little rat.

He broke into a sprint, a slew of curses filling his mind as his joints suddenly protesting the sudden charge. He couldn't let some gutter-born sneak slip into the cracks. Not when the possibility existed that it might be an enemy spy.

"Stop!" Maxen growled as a small figure in the distance came into view.

The sneak showed no signs of heeding his warning and continued to scurry away. The darkness obscured his vision, but they appeared to be a lad—a *child*—who probably hadn't even sprouted facial hair yet. That didn't mean much. Children growing up on the streets oftentimes couldn't be considered children at all. Boys and girls grew up fast in the gutter. Sly. Cunning.

Just ask him.

No, this wouldn't be *just* a boy.

A spy.

They had to be.

His gut had never been wrong before. Shite. Where the hell was Reaper? He should have been in the shadows, keeping an eye out for any unwanted nuisances. How had his brother missed this little pest?

Another sibling who could use a good throttling.

The shadow vanished down an alleyway, and a blur shot beneath him. Bloody hell! Maxen jolted, boots slipping as a hellish cat streaked underfoot. He barely avoided stumbling and planting his face into the dirt. Another foul curse left his lips when he whipped his gaze up again and could no longer tell which alley the lad had darted into. "Damn it!"

He dragged a hand through his hair, frustration forming a poisonous pit in his stomach.

A low chuckle filled the street.

Reaper emerged from shadows, amusement animating his entire face. A dark cloud instantly pulled at Maxen's brows. "What the devil are you laughing at?"

His brother shrugged. "You lost your prey. A first."

Ah, yes. Trouble always occurred in threes.

Confound it. The last thing he had time for was a little rodent on the loose. "The thing was slippery," he said begrudgingly.

"You're getting old, brother."

Maxen scoffed. "Do not talk about my age. Where were *you*? You were supposed to have our backs. *You* missed the boy before I did."

"I did have your back. No harm came to you, did it?"

"You call a rat escaping no harm?" Maxen started forward and chose an alleyway he thought the lad might have darted into, but there were so many he was blindly guessing at this point. He hated guessing.

"Don't be sour. That specific spot was cut off from my vi-sion."

Not good enough. "You should have scouted the area. Patrolled it."

"I did. There was no one when I passed that section. Your mouse couldn't have been here for long."

Meaning they shouldn't have overheard or witnessed too much, but they still overheard and witnessed enough. "Is that supposed to reassure me?"

"So we silence the person." Reaper said with another careless shrug, following him with silent steps. "Are you sure this is the correct alley?"

"You tell me. I stumbled."

"My apologies, *frère*, I was watching you stumble."

Maxen grunted, fingers itching to wrap around his brother's neck. As if calling him brother in French would spare him his ire. Fine. It might. But to silence their little crack-crawler, they had to find him first, and there were too bloody many cracks and all of them were dark.

"Is now the time to admit I can't claim to regret not keeping an eye on the alley since I got to catch you in a *cat tangle?*"

Maxen glared at this brother, who flashed him a grin. The arse lifted a hand, a shoe dangling from his finger. "They did, however, leave this behind."

His brow shot upward. "A shoe?"

"A woman's slipper to be exact."

His gaze fixated on the feminine item. "So it wasn't a lad after all."

Reaper tossed the slipper over and Maxen snatched it midair. He turned it over in his palm grimly, the imprint of a heel barely fading.

A woman. A bold one. A foolish one.

Something in him, something primal, something absolutely foreign, whispered: *Find her. Find her right now.*

"A girl would be my guess, yes, but what girl creeps around in the shadows in the dead of night?"

Even more guesses. He hated guessing. "One from that

wretched club of aristocrats playing at smuggling."

"They were dealt with."

"Organizations like that aren't always fully handled. There are always foxes that wish to become wolves." As if he needed any more hindrances. He was building an untouchable empire. For that, he needed more power and more blunt than any enemy. He could not have weaknesses. Could not have rats slipping through cracks.

"I don't know. The way this person fled, perhaps they weren't wearing it," Reaper pointed out. "It could have slipped from the bag they carried."

Maxen grunted. "You don't think it was one of those blue-blooded feather heads?"

Reaper stepped up to meet his pace. "Those women are aristocrats. Could they give us both the slip like this?"

Good point. "So a spy, then. But who would send a girl?"

"*Him.*"

A shiver shot down Maxen's spine.

Him?

No. It could absolutely not be. He wouldn't meddle in their affairs. It would mean war if that were the case. Again. The late Duke of Crane, their father, had been the cruelest blackguard alive. The current duke, their half-brother, was a recluse, and no obstacle to them. He might even become an ally, albeit a reluctant one, in the future. "It's not Crane."

Reaper shrugged, a silver coin appearing between his fingers. He rolled it lazily over his knuckles. "Could also be the *other* him."

Sirius?

That man, their uncle on their father's side, had been "reported" dead ten years ago. Only they knew it to be a bold lie. Their uncle was as bad as the late duke. Certainly cunning. An outright coward in Maxen's view. He had never coveted his brother's title. No, that would have placed him under the scrutiny of the man he feared most, the Crown, and society as a whole. So he set his sights elsewhere.

Sirus Faiththorne didn't have the spine to build an empire of his own. He was a vulture who fed off the work of stronger men. What he wanted, he took in the dark and had no qualms hiring cutthroats to do his dirty deeds. The man stood for the one thing they stood violently against: killing as a means to an end.

Maxen felt a throb in his temples coming on.

They'd shipped him off in a crate years ago, bound for the East and never meant to return. It was the fastest way to deal with persistent pests without crushing them beneath a boot. Without blood.

But if he had found a way to claw himself back . . .

God help them all.

If there was one thing Maxen had learned in all his thirty-two years of life, one couldn't fight a phantom in the shadows. Until he saw the blackguard's face with his own damn eyes, he would not believe their uncle had returned.

"Let us hope it's not him." Maxen's grip tightened on the slipper. "I want this girl found."

Chapter Two

CALLIOPE BREATHED IN the comforting brightness when she entered her shop, The Whispering Wick, the next morning after a quick stroll, Prince trotting beside her, his claws clicking on the hardwood floor as he padded around the shop, sniffing the rows of candles stacked neatly on the shelves that lined two walls—his ritual before settling in the corner on his pillow.

Sun poured through the large arched window.

Ah, daylight.

Calliope could scarcely believe she wasn't shackled to a hopeless life anymore. She had claimed this little piece of the world, and it didn't belong to anyone but her.

She swept a quick gaze over the snug space.

Real. It was very much real.

The left side of the shop held simpler, more affordable, day-to-day use candles wrapped in paper and tied with ribbons. Even simpler ones were arranged in glass jars. Along the right, finer, more exotic scented candles were carefully arranged. Beneath the shelves, drawers held more stock. She had spent the months in her former abode creating them, and if it hadn't been for Mr. Fitz, this would not have been possible.

Her shoulders drooped.

Mr. Rollings as well . . .

She strode over to the counter and slumped over it, her eyes landing on the leatherbound ledger, a quill resting beside a small inkpot. Right, she should pen a letter to Mr. Fitz sooner rather than later.

Prince nudged her hand, his dark eyes filled with canine affection, and she reached out to scratch behind his ears. "Everything is going to be fine. More than fine."

The words, spoken aloud, soothed the anxiety left by last night.

Not fully. But some.

After all, the bruises on her knees from the fall served as an annoying reminder. Who would have thought that only hours ago, she'd been racing down the dark streets of her new neighborhood. She'd barely escaped with her skin intact—it certainly felt as such!—and while she would like nothing more than to forget about the entire affair, those ruthless men were still out there somewhere. Perhaps still searching for her.

Calliope only hoped that during their pursuit of her, Mr. Rollings had managed to slip away. How lucky that would be! However, she now knew he had dealings with dangerous people. Could she do business again with him again knowing this?

She didn't believe so.

But that didn't mean she wanted the man to die.

"I should just forget about it." She glanced at Prince, now stretched out lazily at her feet. "There's no reason to ever encounter them again." She certainly wouldn't venture into the streets at night again!

Prince lifted his head to look at her before dropping his head to his paws again with a heavy sigh, as if exasperated by her constant misadventures. Hah! A dog's sigh truly did embody the truest air of disappointment.

"Oh, don't act so put upon. I'm still here, aren't I? And you had some extra snacks last night because of my fortunate escape. Be grateful."

Prince twitched one ear in response, as if to indicate he'd

prefer his treats without the threat of mortal peril next time, thank you very much.

She smiled, shaking her head.

The doorbell jingled, and after last night, the sound pierced sharp and jarring. She turned. "Good . . ."—her smile faltered and a prickling awareness skittered over her scalp—"morning."

A man filled the doorway.

But not just your average, everyday man. This one was tall and unmoving. A shadow carved in black. Not merely *dressed* in black, though he was, he wore the color like midnight had chosen him. Hair. Eyes. The gloves on his hands. A jagged scar split his lip, sharpening his look into a promise of feral danger.

Everything about him seemed sculpted from the night.

Call it instinct, since she hadn't met many men in her life, but he wore himself with the ease of one well acquainted with domination. But it wasn't this that thoroughly unsettled her, rather, the way he stood, still as a predator, danger clinging to him like a second skin, and all his focus trained on her.

Also, he was absurdly handsome.

Calliope!

Right. Danger.

How was she supposed to respond to a man staring at her with the air between them crackling akin to thunder?

"Good morning," he finally returned, his tone a low, hoarse growl that barely qualified as civil.

Her blood turned to ice.

That voice. She knew that voice.

She felt the cadence in her bones before she placed the sound in her mind. Her stomach twisted, not just in dread, but with something deeper. Something far too complicated to dissect in this space and time. Perhaps in any space and time.

The memory of the previous night surged back in vivid, terrifying clarity.

No.

No, it couldn't be.

Instinct howled warnings to the pulse beneath her skin.

This was the man who'd chased her last night.

Calliope's breath trapped between her heart and her lips. She forced her face into what she hoped was her carefully crafted shop owner's smile, trying her best to keep her tone as unruffled as possible. "Can I help you, sir?"

He took a step inside, his sharp gaze sweeping over her shelves with a detachment that almost raised her hackles. The door shutting behind him sent another shudder through her, and she shot a quick glance at Prince, but the hound merely lifted his head at the man and dropped his muzzle back onto his paws.

Some help you are, you big traitor.

"A candle shop." His dark eyes circled back to meet hers. "Interesting."

Er, what could possibly be so interesting about a candle shop? Unless he suspected she was the person from last night? But how? Had they glimpsed her enter here and allowed her a false sense of victory? Questions flooded her mind, each one more terrifying than the last.

No, Calliope.

She couldn't lose her nerve. Not before the axe fell on her neck. Only then.

"Indeed," she murmured. She could feel the strain around the corners of her smile, so she moved behind the counter to distract herself, placing a rather obvious amount of distance between them. He seemed unbothered, but she sensed amusement from him, though she couldn't be sure. Humor certainly didn't show on his face. Or his eyes. "Would you perhaps like to purchase a batch of candles?"

Not even a twitch. "I'm not here as a customer."

Lord, oh, lord.

"Oh?" Prince, seeming to pick up on her discomfort, rose to his feet, staring the man with ears pricked. *Good boy.* "Then what brings you to my humble *candle* shop?"

The dark devil didn't waste any time in reaching into his coat, and a jolt of fear dashed through her. How could it not? The man was . . . something else. A being of his own. Would he pull out a pistol? A dagger? But instead of a weapon, he withdrew something small and delicate, holding the object up between his fingers.

A slipper.

Her slipper.

But not just *any* slipper. The satin footwear was the only item she still owned from that house. A symbol of the girl who had escaped a nightmare. The girl who dreamed. The girl who claimed her freedom. The sight hit her like a stone to the chest, and she nearly snatched her shoe from him in horror.

Fortunately, she caught herself just in time.

Do not reveal yourself!

The man's gaze sharpened nonetheless.

Urgh. She couldn't be sure for he said not a word. Just stared.

And stared.

No. *Studied.*

She cleared her throat. *Get hold of yourself, Calliope.* "Why are you showing me a shoe?"

"It's my hope that you might recognize who the slipper belongs to and point me to its owner."

How casually framed. And stars, she hated the way the roughness of his voice threaded along her nerves.

Focus!

How had her shoe ended up in his hand in the first place?

Calliope racked her brain. It must have slipped from her satchel when she tripped. She could find no other possible explanation. What rotten luck was this? She wanted to groan at this colossal error. "That, unfortunately, I cannot do." Or else . . .

He smiled without smiling. More a feeling than a sight, and not a pleasant one at that. Black pools bore into her. "Are you certain you don't recognize this?"

"Why should I? Because I'm a woman?" She didn't give him time to respond. "What a hopelessly insufferable thing to imply."

"So, you do *not* recognize it, then?" he pressed without so much as acknowledging her remarks.

This man! "I do *not*."

He arched an equally insufferable black brow. "Perhaps you could try the shoe on. Just to be sure."

Calliope's jaw slackened. Surely he had not asked her that? "I shall most certainly not do that. Who knows where that slipper's been." She knew exactly where. She only prayed he didn't.

"No need to bristle, Miss Turner. It's just a shoe."

The adopted last name was still jostling to hear. Wait. "How do you know my name?"

He slid her slipper back into his coat, eyes never leaving hers. "I didn't come here just for a shoe, Miss Turner. There's another matter between us."

Impossible. "What else could there possibly be between us?" *Except distance. A lot of distance.*

"The matter of property," he announced. "I am your landlord."

Her eyes flew wide. "No, you are not."

"Yes, Miss Turner, I am."

But if that were true . . . A horrible realization settled over her. *He* was Mr. Fury? He, as in the man, the *beast*, from last night? Her landlord?

"You are . . ."

"Maxen Fury. The arrangement your solicitor made was with my brother. Without my permission, I should add."

Her lips parted but no words formed.

Mr. Fitz handled her secret inheritance, helped with her lodgings, and all the matters of setting up her shop while she adapted to her new world. All the new possibilities open to her.

Escaping that household had taken priority over everything else.

But even now, even free, it seemed that others still held the keys.

"I see."

Those two words spoke volumes. She could see much. He was far from being pleased by the prospect of her being his tenant. And she hadn't thought to question Mr. Fitz about the arrangement after they'd discussed her options. She'd trusted him, forever grateful for being her ally.

Well, she wasn't pleased either! Who would want a criminal for a landlord? It might, as much as she was loathe to admit, be best to find another place. "If you wish to nullify our arrangement, all you have to do is return my rent."

"I don't." His expression didn't change, but something flickered in the depths of those fathomless eyes. Reluctance? Suspicion? She couldn't tell. But it made her stomach twist in a strange way.

Her brows snapped together. "Didn't you say your brother rented us this space without your permission?"

"I don't return blunt."

How . . . blunt.

But of course, he wouldn't just be an ordinary villain. He'd have to be a greedy one, too. Urgh! She didn't want to live in apprehension for the next six months.

You can do this, Calliope.

It was just six months.

She'd been through worse for longer.

"Very well."

A curt nod. "I'll stomach your perfumes till your contract ends. Then I want you gone."

Rude beast. "It's candles, and you don't have to stomach anything if you don't visit my shop."

His black eyes stared at her steadily. "I am your neighbor."

"You live next door?" The question snapped from her tongue before she could swallow it back.

He inclined his head, the first spark of real amusement glinting in his gaze. "Yes. I do."

What on earth was happening? What world had she stepped into? She did not want to live next door to a Beast of Brighton!

And why show her the slipper at all if he did not suspect her? But would he be speaking with such ease if he were certain? Wouldn't he have dragged her off to a dungeon already? In all likelihood, he would probably visit all the shops in this neighborhood today to find the owner of that slipper.

"Well, I appreciate you introducing yourself." That might have been her only luck. Now she could put a face to the local villain. Her gaze swept over his scar again. A dangerous villain. Yet another she would have to escape at some point.

Prince cocked his head at the man, whose lips twitched. "Quite the guardian you have there. Should I feel honored that he's deemed me worthy of his boredom?"

His mocking tone felt like earth wrapping around the soles of her feet. She ground her teeth, glaring at the man. "He saves canines for the night."

His gaze seared a path over her body then met her eyes again. The contempt rolling off him was palpable. "The worst monsters walk in daylight, too, Miss Turner." A shiver traveled down her spine, the faintest hint of menace flaring in his gaze as he assessed her. "I imagine you don't know much about me, Miss Turner, but I don't like trouble in my territory. If you keep to your own affairs, I'll keep to mine."

"Well, I certainly don't plan to cross into yours." Ever. Again.

In fact, she wanted to stay very, very far away.

THIS WOMAN COULDN'T hold a convincing face if her life depended on it. And she had the kind of face that didn't belong in Brighton.

Or at least not in *his* Brighton.

She was too damn *delicate*.

And yet, she hadn't trembled when he loomed, and he had done so deliberately. She hadn't stuttered when he pushed. She hadn't folded under his gaze. That unsettled Maxen more than her perfumes ever could. Or candles. Ridiculous.

Even more damn ridiculous, he'd stood in bloodier rooms, faced men who'd slit throats for two coins, sharp blades as smiles. But when her eyes had locked on his, he'd felt unnerved. Peeled back. As though she might glimpse something he'd never dared show another soul, should his guard slip.

The tips of his fingers twitched.

His new tenant was small, slight in frame and graceful in posture. She wore a simple day dress of a pink, though not the bold shade. The softer one. Whatever it was called. Nothing out of the ordinary. But something still struck him as off. She felt wrong for the Lanes. Her golden hair was too golden. Like the sun. Even her voice sounded spun from sunlight. She was running a candle shop for Christ's sake—sunshine turned to business. She looked like sunlight turned flesh. And for one cursed second, every damn rule he lived by deserted him.

Her green eyes, bright enough to blind. Behind them?

Storms.

Secrets.

She hadn't so much as flinched when he'd pulled the slipper from his coat. However, he had caught a slight hesitation. Not overt. But enough to set his every instinct on high alert. As a man trained to spot a blade in a glance and a lie in a heartbeat, his senses had detected something but also not a bloody thing.

A first.

And it could mean just about anything under the damn sun.

She might be lying. Might be she didn't trust him searching for a woman with nothing but a slipper. Might be a possibility he hadn't considered. Despite that, she met his gaze with chin held high.

His hand flexed. A flicker of instinct. To reach. To touch. To feel. He curled his fingers into a fist against the absurd urge instead. To feel he'd have to remove his gloves, and he never removed them in front of anyone.

"I will hold you to that, Miss Turner. Let's not meet again, then."

Her eyes blazed at him. "Agreed."

He strode from the shop, pausing with his hand on the door, casting her one last glance at her before stepping out completely. He didn't go far, however, leaning against the cool stone wall of a nearby building across the street, his eyes trained on the woman's shop. Every nerve in his body felt pulled tight, sharpening his senses as he turned over what he had learned from their brief encounter.

Calliope Turner.

A vision of sunlight.

Could she truly be the same woman who had slipped through his grasp last night? Had he chased her through the dark alleys, her shadow just a whisper against the cobblestones as she evaded him with skill?

Bloody troublesome.

He didn't do loose ends. Didn't do sweet scents. Didn't do women like her. Polished edges. She practically gleamed with them. A finish the Lanes could never scuff away. That spine. That poise. She was not from his world, hadn't scraped her way from the gutters. And he hadn't crawled his way to his position now to end back there because he lost focus. For that reason, he needed to determine his new tenant's true intentions in Brighton. Young women didn't just open candle shops and run them by themselves without a guardian.

Ones with secrets might.

He should never have left Brighton. Should have sent one of his brothers. Perhaps then he wouldn't have a merchant bleeding in the bloody dungeon beneath his tavern. And her.

Drake, his right-hand brother and second oldest of the Fury brood, appeared beside him, sliding his hands into his pockets. "Is it her?" he asked in a murmur so low it barely rose above the clatter of the growing streetway. "Your little spy?"

Maxen didn't respond immediately, his gaze remaining fixed on the shop's window where Miss Turner once more arranged her candles. Was she? He wasn't entirely certain. And he wanted to be certain. If it was her, she might just be an expert at hiding.

Or she might just be a normal, polished young woman.

Still, a nagging suspicion burrowed into him.

"I'm not sure," he finally said. She was hiding something. But he didn't know what. Yet.

"You have a suspicion."

"Of course. Why else would I be keeping an eye here?"

"Lurking."

Maxen merely shrugged. "Call it what you will."

Drake crossed his arms over his chest. "We can't afford any wild loose ends running around Brighton."

The slipper burned against his chest. It was not a decision he wanted to make, but for now, "We do nothing."

"That's not like you."

Maxen shrugged. If it was indeed her, which he was about ten percent unsure about, this innocent-looking Miss Turner with her golden spun hair and bright, piercing eyes would have to be watched closely. Something Maxen wanted to do even less than he wanted to deal with her in the first place.

"If you want me to handle the chit—"

"No." He turned to his brother, gaze hardening. "She's on my territory. I will handle her."

His brother's brows furrowed. "She seems to have caught your interest."

"Interest?" Maxen turned the word over in his mind. That couldn't be. He'd only just met her. And she was everything he avoided. Everything delicate and soft and *light*. She barely reached his damn shoulders, for Christ's sake.

"Is she pretty?" Drake asked, his voice laced with amusement.

"No."

Pretty could not begin to describe her. Her golden halo framed a face that held a unique beauty. A few freckles danced across her nose, her lips pink and fiery. Her eyes, however, were what claimed and held his attention.

They sparkled with a life force all their own.

Even so, whatever interest might gather died with the stench of uncertainty that clung to her. Aye, she smelled of entanglements he didn't need or want. A puzzle he had no desire to solve.

He wanted her gone. Right after he turned any uncertainty to certainty. If she was a spy . . . Which reminded him. "What happened with Rollings?"

"Still not talking much."

Damn it. "What's your judgment on his involvement with the shipment loss?"

"Not involved."

"This isn't good." Maxen didn't question his brother. Drake had his ways to pull the truth from people. All his brothers had. Drake, however, had never failed before. Frustration slashed at him.

Another bloody mystery.

Nothing ever slipped passed him, yet in the span of twenty-four-hours, two mysteries had landed on his doorstep. "Who else would know about our shipment? Our routes? Our damn timelines?"

"No one." Drake rubbed his temples. "Except perhaps the ring of women dabbling on our margins that the Duke of Mortimer took down. But unlikely."

And yet nothing ever stayed down forever. Just look at the Furys themselves. No matter what life dealt them, they always rose back up. "He cut off the head, but we both know another one will soon appear. Perhaps it already has."

"We've filled the vacancy thoroughly," Drake reminded him.

"That doesn't mean someone else won't try." In the gutters, survival favored the strong. And he'd spend his whole life strengthening his family, their connections, and their place in the world. There was little that could topple them, but that didn't mean there was *nothing*. And it was his job as the head of the brood to eliminate those things. "And there is the duke himself."

"You believe Mortimer and his men could be behind this?"

"We have history."

Drake snorted. "We were never his aim."

"Doesn't mean we won't become it."

"And we'll know the moment we do, but this isn't his style."

"True." He supposed.

"And *her*?" Drake motioned to the candle shop. "It could just be a coincidence she appeared here."

"Maybe." He hoped for Miss Turner's sake that was all it was, or he would have to dispose of her the only way he knew how. He'd rather not tread that path, not unless he was left no choice.

"Wait—over yonder. Isn't that . . .?"

Maxen's brows furrowed as his gaze fell on a tall man striding up the street and entering her shop. An egotistical posture he knew all too well.

Well, well, well.

Promises were only as good as the people who made them.

As were their words.

And every single one of hers just became more suspicious.

Chapter Three

HER HANDSOME-AS-SIN LANDLORD was a criminal.

A criminal.

Her landlord.

Criminal.

The thought kept churning in Calliope's mind like a vexing song she could not rid herself of. *A handsome criminal.*

Maxen Fury. Even his name made her skin prickle. With unease, of course. Nothing else. He even walked like he had no natural predator. Like the very air stirred differently around him.

Let's not meet again, then.

Perhaps the wisest words ever spoken.

Still, why hadn't Prince barked at the man? The hound had keen senses, but he'd simply remained curled up, unbothered by her landlord's presence.

Unlike her.

Prince nudged her hand, and she stroked his head. "Very well, I shall forgive you this time," she said her gaze on the door the man had disappeared through, leaving a coldness in his wake. The question remained: Did Mr. Fury believe her?

He was everything she *had* to avoid in her new life.

Dark, dangerous, and an unprecedented threat to her mission—a peaceful life free from those who would hurt and control her.

And he would be a threat.

The mere knowledge of his existence was an incomprehensible disruption. Not to mention the man himself. His overbearing presence. He carried himself like someone accustomed to control, to bending things—and people—to his will. Just like Duvessa. And his eyes seemed to observe more than anyone had a right to. Calliope couldn't allow anyone to discover her secret.

And her slipper!

Now she must get rid of the matching one in her possession before he somehow discovered it with her. Though the idea seemed inconceivable, she couldn't take the chance. But where? Somewhere *far* away from her shop.

On her way to post her letter to Mr. Fitz?

Calliope would most certainly have to rid herself of the thing during the day. There was no way she was moving about in the dark streets again! She would also have to start looking for another shop as soon as possible. A place far from his *territory* as he so ominously called it. Moving would be bothersome. After all, while this shop was not the best neighborhood in Brighton, her first concern had always been staying out of Duvessa's line of sight. Her stepmother might send people to inquire after her, and she'd wager they would never think to search for her here. Besides, the shop was not meant to make her rich. Her inheritance could last her a lifetime. This life was meant to give her independence, and she'd chosen candles because they reminded her of home. Her true home.

However, Calliope didn't want a villain as a landlord and the looming threat of danger dangling over her head. All her worries were reserved for Duvessa or her uncle.

She didn't need this, this perilous position.

So, until she could relocate, she'd make herself as invisible as possible. She was good at that. Fortunately. Inhaling a deep, steady breath, she let the soothing scents of her shop fill her lungs.

So good.

No sooner had she allowed herself to relax than the chime of the bell struck her nerves full force. Bah! Should she replace the bell with another one? Something softer. Something that didn't sound like doom swinging on a hinge.

She quickly smoothed her skirt and summoned a smile for yet another tall man who stepped inside. His eyes crinkled at the edges as he returned her smile with one that made her feel instantly at ease. So unlike her *first* customer of the day.

"Good day." His gaze swept over the shelves with interest. "I'm in search for a gift for my niece. She adores sweet-smelling things."

Calliope almost laughed at his twitch at the word *things*.

"Of course." She indicated to the display on right. "There are more exotic scents such as poppy and rose, pear and peony, cucumber and honey. The ones on the other side are more simple scents like vanilla and such."

He nodded thoughtfully, his gaze flicking to the bundles before back to her. "I'll take each of the combination ones you mentioned."

She nodded once and turned to the shelves, gathering each of the requested bundles quickly and brought them back to her counter to wrap.

"You've quite a charming place here," the man noted. "How long have you been open?"

"Not too long," Calliope replied while she slipped open the cabinet beneath the counter and drew out wrapping paper. In the short time since she'd escaped Duvessa, she'd learned to be vague, to deflect questions without ever truly answering them. She told him his total and added, "Just a few weeks."

He fished the coins from his coin pouch and set them down. "Do you hail from these parts?"

Such a simple question, and yet the hairs on the back of her neck rose. "You mean England?" She carefully wrapped the items and pushed the parcel toward him.

He chuckled. "Forgive my curiosity." His gaze lingered on

her for a moment, thoughtful. "I quite enjoy Brighton myself. It's the sort of town where one can be anyone or no one. I asked only because this shop has been unoccupied ever since I can recall."

It has?

The doorbell tolled as she was about to respond, and the air seemed to shift, growing tense and almost electric.

Maxen Fury.

Again.

His presence filled the room instantly, his dark gaze sweeping over her with a look that was equal parts curious, assessing, and flat before turning to the other man. He looked at *him* with the kind of cold calculation that made Calliope's skin prickle.

Was her customer a criminal as well?

For the love of wax, spare her, please.

"Mr. Fury," she greeted politely, as if he were just another customer and not a dark cloud looming over her life.

Her landlord's gaze didn't waver from the stranger. "Peregrine. What brings you to Brighton?"

Such calm.

Such danger.

Such . . .

No. Do not get distracted. This man . . . He had done something to Mr. Rollings. *Such danger* was not the way to describe him. As though it was to be awed.

"Shopping," the other man replied smoothly, his friendly demeanor now edged with a hint of challenge. "Is that a crime?"

Mr. Fury's eyes narrowed. "Did I not tell you to steer clear of my territory?"

Territory.

There was that word again. It sent gooseflesh over her body. And from the look of it, her first real customer for today was not so simple either.

Her customer, Mr. Peregrine, glanced at Calliope, his expression softening slightly as he gestured toward Mr. Fury. "You should be careful of this man, miss."

So forward.

Of course, she already knew this. Yet something about this warning unsettled her, sending a prickle of doubt up her spine.

That devil's gaze turned to her, a hard glint in his eye. "And you, Miss Turner, would be wise to be wary of *him*." He glanced back to her customer. "After all, he's the one wandering into places he has no business being."

I do not want to deal with this.

She looked between them, feeling trapped between two growling dogs. She didn't trust either of them, quite honestly, so forcing herself to remain calm and ignore them, she nudged the man's parcel closer to him a bit pointedly. "I'm quite capable of taking care of myself, Mr. Fury, thank you. Now, if there is nothing else, please refrain from causing a stir in my store and settle your scores outside." *And far away from me!*

That mouth curved into a humorless smile as he took in her defiant stance. But there was something in his gaze that made the skin of her scalp prickle once again, an interest that she had no intention of encouraging.

"Very well, Miss Turner," her landlord conceded.

She didn't look at him again. Couldn't look at him. If she did, she might never look away. Which was utterly absurd, and wholly perturbing. So the man was handsome with his dark look and piercing scar. And she could not allow her curiosity to be piqued by him.

Ever!

Mr. Peregrine gave a small chuckle, inclining his head. "Of course. I didn't mean to upturn your morning." He collected his purchase and, with a final tip of his head, strode out the door.

Her landlord, however, waited a fraction of a moment before following suit. She lifted her gaze. He stopped in the doorway and glanced over his shoulder, their eyes locking. "Remember what I said. Be careful who you trust. And call me Maxen, Calliope."

Then he vanished, leaving her to blink after him.

Calliope pressed her palm to her heart.

The sense of unease didn't leave with him but sprouted into a nagging feeling that her life was no longer as safe and predictable as she'd dreamed. She'd come to Brighton for peace, to escape the shadows of her past and start fresh. But there seemed to be beasts of a different nature lurking here.

Could she escape them, too?

MAXEN'S EYES NARROWED on the back of Deveraux Peregrine's head. The name scraped against his teeth every time he heard it. Pomp without merit. A man who had never built a damn thing in his life. Only took. And took. And took.

He stepped up to Peregrine so that they were out of sight of his tenant's shop. What had possessed him to make that last statement, he couldn't say. Only that hearing "Mr. Fury" from her lips made him sound like an old man.

"I shouldn't have to remind you to stay off my land," Maxen growled in annoyance.

Peregrine turned, that insufferable smirk already in place. "Brighton doesn't belong to you, Fury."

"Not to me alone, no."

"Ah." Peregrine's gaze swept over him. "Your brothers."

There was something about that look. The way he said *brothers*. He didn't like it. Didn't like the whisper of threat beneath it. What was this fool up to now?

"I admit," Peregrine continued, "your property expansion is impressive, but it's hardly *that* impressive."

"It's far greater than you can imagine."

Much greater.

Over the years, he and his brothers had built a tightly knit network in Brighton, their influence extending beyond the shadows and into every crevice of the town's economy. But he had no intention of sharing that detail with this arse.

Peregrine cocked his head. "I see you finally rented that shop of yours."

A flare of warning raced through Maxen's gut.

He'd known the moment he learned Dagger had leased the shop that trouble would follow. But he hadn't expected trouble to arrive so soon or in this particular form. Of course, this puffed-up nob had heard the local speculations—rumors that he never rented the place because the property concealed buried treasure or some long-lost fortune. Nothing could be further from the truth. Yet those misguided tales had a way of attracting exactly the wrong sort, and Peregrine was no exception.

"I have," Maxen replied, his voice cold, uninterested. "What about it? Don't tell me you were interested?"

"On the contrary," Peregrine said, his gaze flicking to the scent shop and back. "I merely wondered what finally made the place worth leasing. Quite the tenant you have there."

Maxen cursed in his heart. Men like Peregrine were vultures. So long as they could get what they wanted, little else mattered. "I don't care to decipher the nonsense rattling around in that goat head of yours, but she lives on my land. Under my roof. If you cause her any trouble, I'll make damn sure you regret ever learning to walk upright. Stay away from me and mine."

"How arrogant of you to presume that pretty little thing is yours. What if I take a fancy to her?"

Maxen's fists clenched.

The thought of Peregrine's hands anywhere near his new tenant stirred a bone-deep urge to throttle the man. Something primitive snarled inside him. It was madness. She was nothing to him. A tenant. A nuisance. A loose thread.

Yet Peregrine's words left a bitter taste in his mouth.

Only because she is living on my turf.

And in *that* space.

He didn't want any vermin sniffing around there.

"That's unfortunate for her. I mean it, Peregrine. Test me if you want to lose a limb."

"Honestly, Fury, why so sensitive? I accidentally burned down your brothel two years ago. Get over it."

"It was a tavern, not a brothel," Maxen bit out. "And it just *happened* to go up in flames the same night one of my warehouses was robbed. I've looked into your affairs. That wasn't the first time things mysteriously burned down around you." There was also still the matter of his current shipment.

"Nothing mysterious about it," Peregrine replied with a shrug. "I compensated you fully, didn't I?"

"I lost ten times what you paid me." Not to mention crates and crates of black tea and silks. "I don't tolerate loss, so I don't tolerate you." He nodded to the building on his right, and Dagger stepped from the shadows, his long black coat parting just enough to reveal the outline of daggers lining the inside. Then, he lifted his chin to one of the rooftops, and Reaper's silhouette moved into view, signature coin flipping between his fingers. Drake must have slipped off to tend other matters. "I'd clear out, if I were you. That is, if you still wish to keep all your limbs attached to your body."

Peregrine's smile faded, his gaze flicking between the brothers, jaw clenching. He lifted his hands in mock surrender, forcing a smile. "I'm off. No need to puff yourself up, Fury."

Maxen watched the blackguard stride away, whistling as though he hadn't a care in the world. Instinct warned him that this wasn't the end of it. No, Peregrine, as was evident by his damnable presence, was the type to reappear.

Dagger walked over. "You think he's going to be a problem?"

"Yes, though I'm not yet sure how big of one."

"The shipment."

Maxen nodded. "His appearance is too convenient. Find out when he arrived in town and whether it coincides with our crates being stolen. Also," he glanced back at The Whispering Wick, "see if there's any connection between him and my tenant."

God help them both if there were.

"You still suspect she's a spy?"

"She's hiding something." And he didn't like it. "Mysteries rarely bode well for us."

"Then it's unfortunate she's a woman. Their secrets and mysteries run deep."

"I don't care how bloody deep they run, so long as they don't interfere with my business." Maxen gritted his teeth and shot his brother a look. "Which is already a moot point, seeing as you rented her this particular space."

"Do you know how many properties we have? I thought you moved the barrels of gunpowder next door."

"That one connects to the tunnels," Maxen bit out.

Dagger gave a slight shrug. "It was dark, and I was half in my cups. I can barely get your tunnels straight when I'm sober."

Maxen curled his lip but said nothing. It didn't matter. The barrels were safely hidden, so the chances of her finding them were slim. However, their access to them would be blocked for the duration of her lease. Until then, all he had to do was steer clear of the sweet-smelling Calliope Turner yet keep an eye on her at the same time.

As easy as snatching sweets from a babe.

He would know.

They'd been snatched from him more times than he could count.

Chapter Four

The following afternoon

THE BELL ABOVE the inn door gave a prim jangle as Calliope stepped onto the street after posting her letter, relieved it was no longer burning a hole in her reticule. She'd half expected her landlord to leap from the shadows, seize her belongings, and discover the truth.

He hadn't, thank the sun and stars.

And posting news to Mr. Fitz had been easy enough.

However, something else blazed in her reticule like a cursed relic. Satin. Flat-soled. Impossibly incriminating.

The thought made her wince. She hadn't wanted to leave her shop with the slipper. Just the thought felt like peeling skin from bone. But she had no choice.

She would not—*could not*—live under the shadow of fear.

From Maxen Fury.

The landlord. The beast. The darkness personified. A thorn wedged most rudely in her otherwise perfect new beginning. A man whose shadow seemed to swallow the sunlight and block out her stars.

And *he* had her slipper.

It wasn't just that he'd found it. It was *how* he had looked at it—like a man unearthing a secret. Like he already knew it was hers. The man was suspicious. Too perceptive by half.

But no matter.

Today, she was clever. Careful. *Invisible.*

She would rid herself of the other half of that blasted pair of slippers and erase the evidence before the beast sniffed out the truth. Who knew what he would do in his quest to find the culprit of that night. Her imagination also wasn't of any help! Would he break in and rifle through her belongings? Something more nefarious?

Her shoulders crept up in revulsion.

Who's overly suspicious now, Calliope?

Well. She was.

And frankly, she considered it *prudent.*

Dark eyes swam in her mind.

Ah, stars.

Why did the man have to be so sinfully, wickedly, *uncomfortably* handsome?

It wasn't until after she'd closed the shop yesterday that she'd let herself *feel* the full impression he'd left behind. Not just the obvious things—danger, damnation, destruction—but something else. Something that seemed to linger right beneath her skin. The way her breath had wanted to catch each time he looked at her—not from fear, but, when she looked closer, from something far more foolish.

Recognition.

Not of him but of herself.

Of something inside her, bottled and waiting.

And the sound of his voice—it hadn't threatened. Well, it *had*—but the promise of his undertone had also stirred. Rough and calm, yet it had traced through her like a whisper of a warning. As though he were speaking not to her ears, but to something buried deep under layers of good sense. A part of her she hadn't known was paying attention. And that scar? She'd tried her very best to ignore her curiosity, but she couldn't help but wonder about its origin. How had he gotten injured? It must have hurt terribly, mustn't it?

Don't be a fool, Calliope.

He'd gotten that scar doing underhanded things! She'd be better off directing all her thoughts to Mr. Rollings and let him serve as a continuing reminder of what happened to those associated with her landlord and his cronies. What might happen to her if she lost vigilance. Look at how she had trembled after their two encounters! If her landlord had been an ordinary man in ordinary circumstances, she might have believed the flutters to be something perilously close to attraction.

Calliope would love to believe she had more sense than that. No, those flutters had been instinct. A warning. The body's natural response to a predator.

Most certainly *not* attraction.

In any case, what attraction could it be? Despite her rather sheltered upbringing, she was no prude. She loved books and stories and romantic tales. How many times had she dreamed a powerful hero had rescued her from Duvessa all those nightmar-ish years? But stars, Maxen Fury was no prince! A dark prince, perhaps. Certainly not one who saved ladies from draconian stepmothers.

A ridiculous notion, truly. One man with a deep voice and a brooding stare and suddenly some buried part of her thought it recognized him?

What nonsense.

The breeze teased a strand of hair loose from her bonnet as she searched for the perfect spot to dump her slipper. She had scouted a dark, narrow alley earlier. One where a clever girl might consign a slipper to ruin.

Ah. There.

Her heart gave a hard thump. Not with guilt. Also not with anticipation. She couldn't quite describe what she was feeling. It wasn't just one thing, but several things so fused she couldn't name the bundle of nerves gathering in the pit of her belly.

Let's not think about that right now.

A prickling sensation kissed the back of her neck. Again. It had been doing that since he left her shop.

She paused and turned.

Besides people going about their business, a child darting across the street, and a shaggy dog sniffing at a wheelbarrow, nothing else.

Still.

That *feeling*.

A flicker of unease clung to the prickles on her neck. An unmistakable itch. Calliope knew that feeling. She'd lived with it for years—on stairs that creaked wrong, in rooms where doors locked from the outside, hearing whispers in corridors. She had learned to trust the itch. To move before it became a snare. But that was in another life.

"See?" she muttered under her breath. "That man is already a disruption to your peace, and he's not even here."

How on earth was she going to get through the next six months? Leave that man behind and let someone else fall under his unwanted scrutiny. For now, it was time to rid herself of the curse in her reticule. Calliope stopped beside the alley and reached into her bag for the slipper, her fingers circling the object, but she couldn't move. Her fingers curled, loosened, then curled around the slipper again.

Blast it.

Why was it suddenly so hard to let go of a shoe? This wasn't about sentiment. She couldn't cling to that forever. It wasn't about . . . about *him*, either.

It was about erasing evidence.

So why did tossing the slipper away feel like casting off a piece of herself she hadn't yet finished mourning?

Because it is proof.

Proof she'd escaped her fate.

Calliope swallowed hard, thumb brushing the fabric.

Then, instead of plucking the slipper out and disregarding it as she ought, she withdrew her hand.

She couldn't do it.

Not yet. It hurt too much to do it in this very moment. Hurt in a way she couldn't explain. This small, seemingly insignificant footwear was proof of where she'd been. Of what she had been willing to risk. And yes, in the wrong hands, it could undo everything.

Calliope wasn't ready to erase that truth.

The road seemed to lengthen as she continued on her way. Her heart, on the other hand, had unburdened some. If she could survive Duvessa and her brood, she could survive anything.

The prickle on her neck flared once more.

Her steps softened, just as they had when she'd stolen moments of play outside, lowering her presence. Necessity had taught her well. Years of practice had made moving without drawing notice almost second nature. That didn't mean she enjoyed honed responses. No one should have to be good at shrinking smaller. But still, that odd sensation chased her as she made her way back home.

She glanced over her shoulder again.

Still nothing.

Urh, Calliope! Of course no one was watching. Of course she hadn't been followed. Her nerves were simply on edge from being upturned by that beast in black. Nothing more.

Her shoulders had just eased when a voice stopped her in her tracks.

"Miss Turner."

MAXEN DIDN'T BELIEVE in coincidences.

Coincidence was for the idle. The easily fooled. For those who believed the world unfolded in a slew of accidents and misunderstandings.

He knew better.

The world moved in intentions—some merciless as sharpened daggers, some soft as the finest spun silk. And this little tenant of his, weaving through the streets with purposeful steps, was a bloody atlas of intention.

Calliope Turner.

His gut had been right.

She was a bloody complication. A spark in a gunpowder barrel. Thankfully, he'd kept an eye on her even as the smarter half of him warned to stay away. He'd almost listened to that part. Almost. But when something snagged his attention like she did, there was no way to turn.

Deuced troublesome.

Trouble he didn't know what to do about.

If she was a spy, she was a bloody good one. Or the bloody worst. He honestly couldn't tell. On the one hand, she walked like someone used to being unnoticed—efficient, light-footed, vanishing between crowds and carts with impressive grace. For all that, not perfect. She checked over her shoulder too often. Noted the passersby too carefully. And most telling of all—she clutched her satchel like her life depended on the damn thing.

Perhaps it did.

What are you hiding, little tenant?

The tips of his fingers twitched.

He *wanted* to unearth every single secret she possessed. Wanted to unravel them all. And that . . . well that made her the most dangerous thing of all.

When she stopped beside the entrance of a narrow side street—an unremarkable slit between shops—he knew, beyond the shadow of a doubt, this was the climax of her little mission. Her visit to the posting inn hadn't rung any alarms. Since her solicitor had handled her lease, he'd expected her to inform him of their meeting. But this stop here, this was ripe with suspicion.

He eased closer, careful not to arouse any notice.

Her hand disappeared beneath the flap of the bag. Interesting. Was she about to discard something? He waited, tension coiling tight with each second her hand stayed hidden from his view, but she didn't withdraw anything.

Another heartbeat passed.

Another.

Then she pulled her hand from her bag and continued walking.

Maxen's eyes narrowed.

What the devil was she doing?

"So, is she the mouse from that night, *frère*?"

Maxen grimaced, turning to find Reaper leaning against a stack of crates, his expression unreadable beneath the brim of his hat. His brother had a way of appearing when least wanted. And his use of the French word for brother made Maxen grit his teeth even as it had the maddening habit of softening his annoyance. Christ. "Are you following me?"

"What are you doing following *her*?"

"Don't waste my time asking questions you already know the answers to."

"Dagger is worried."

"About what?" Maxen turned back to Calliope, and his face darkened when Peregrine appeared at her side.

A coincidence? He thought not.

His gut coiled tight when she smiled up at the arse.

"You're following this mouse like a dog at her heels," Reaper said, low but sharp. "He might have a point being worried."

Maxen's jaw tightened. His brother should get his eyesight examined. "Why? He's the one who leased my property to her."

"He says you have a look in your eye."

"What bloody look?" Maxen's gaze narrowed on Peregrine's catlike smile. "I have no look."

"At first, I had my doubts about our brother's worries. Now, witnessing it firsthand, not so much."

"Get out of my sight."

"I'm not *in* your sight, *frère*."

"You want to keep your teeth?" Maxen snapped. "Then leave."

"Ah, I can't do that now, can I? You have the look of a man who's found a loose thread and can't decide whether to pull it or set it on fire."

"It's still my thread." At least until her lease ran out.

Reaper clicked his tongue. "You should know better, *frère*. Threads like her don't unravel easy. They catch, twist, and turn into nooses."

Well, that was his damn problem, was it not? His jaw worked as Peregrine leaned closer to Calliope, uttering some nonsense that made her laugh. The sort of laugh that belonged to someone playing a part.

Maxen knew all about parts. He'd worn enough faces in his life to know when someone else wore one too.

Calliope Turning was acting.

Always acting.

She reached up then, brushing something from the man's lapel. Casual. Familiar. Nothing about that sat well with him. Nothing.

His fists clenched and unclenched. What in hell's name was going on between those two?

"Mm." Reaper stepped forward, boots crunching. "There it is again."

"What?" Maxen snarled.

"That thing Dagger picked up on."

Maxen tore his gaze from Calliope long enough to glare at his brother. "There is no thing. There is no look."

Reaper arched his brow. Then, as though bored of the subject entirely, he shoved his hands into his coat pockets. "Dagger wants you to pull back. Since he leased her the property, he'll take responsibility for the mouse."

A growl instantly erupted from his chest, and he turned away from his brother. "He can want all he likes. It's not happening."

"Think, *frère*. It's better for you to leave this one for us."

"*Careful*," Maxen warned. "I will not tolerate interference."

"Jesu," Reaper muttered. "Fine, but do yourself a kindness,

please. If you're going to follow her, try not to look like a man on the brink."

"I'm not on the brink."

"No," Reaper said. "You're in the bloody chasm."

"You have seconds to vanish."

Reaper chuckled, flipping his coin into the air and catching it on the back of his palm.

Then he was gone. Just like that. Maxen didn't even have to glance over his shoulder to confirm it—Reaper had been vanishing like that since he found him.

Still, his words held fast. Twisted.

He shook his head, refocused his attention.

However, Peregrine was gone.

As was she.

He cursed under his breath, low and vicious. When was the last time thoughts had distracted him to the point that he couldn't damn well notice that his prey had slipped from his sight? Never. Until now.

He strode to the place she'd stopped, not bothering with caution as he approached the place she'd stood only moments ago. No trace of her remained. Not her scent. Not a damn footprint. Just the memory of that damn smile she'd given Peregrine.

A trifling thing. Nothing of consequence.

Yet it pressed upon him all the same.

Perhaps his brothers had a point. Perhaps he did have a certain look about him. Perhaps he should step back and let them hunt for the owner of the slipper and pry into his tenant's affairs. But he couldn't look away from her anymore. Even if she wasn't the owner of the slipper, she was hiding something, and since she lived under his roof, *that* roof, he couldn't look away anyway.

And the devil take it, he had no desire to either.

Chapter Five

THE PRICKLES ALONG the nape of her neck had vanished for a while, only to burst across her skin again when she and Mr. Peregrine reached her shop. Fortunately, the man hadn't tarried and left right after escorting her over. As much as she questioned his motives after yesterday, it was hard to hold onto them when he acted like a proper gentleman.

Let's not think about that right now.

She placed her reticule on the counter, scratching Prince's head when he jotted over, before retrieving the two letters she'd received. One was from Mr. Fitz, who kept her abreast of her matters in London. The second was from Clemence, her former maid, keeping her informed of any developments in her old household.

She quickly skimmed over Clemence's one first.

Oh. So Duvessa was still raging day and night about her disappearance but had stopped sending footmen all over London in search of her. She now believed her stepdaughter had run off to Wales or Scotland.

Calliope's mood lifted.

This was exactly what she and Mr. Fitz had wanted. Now all she had to do was wait for her solicitor's response to her own enquires about her landlord, the lease, and what might have happened to Mr. Rollings.

The bell above the door jingled.

Her whole body jerked. Calliope braced for a shadowy figure in black, but instead, a young woman wearing soft green muslin stepped inside, her cheeks flushed and her lips curved in a bright, guileless smile.

"Good morning!" She glanced over the shelves in open delight. "It smells like heaven in here."

"Thank you," Calliope murmured. "Feel free to have a look around."

The girl nodded. "I walked by three times before deciding to come in. Your window display is charming. Are those . . . violet candles?"

"They are."

"Well, then I must have a bunch. I have a friend with the same name, so I must gift them to her for her birthday."

Calliope's mouth curved despite the tightness that formed at the word *friend*. It was one of her biggest dreams to meet a friend here in Brighton. "That seems like sound logic."

"I certainly like to pretend it is." The woman stepped toward the shelves, running her fingers along the bundled sets. "It's so lovely in here, unlike *some* places. Warm. You can instantly tell great care has gone into every element of the shop."

"I try," Calliope murmured, heat spreading across her cheeks. She took great pride in her candles and shop, and no one had ever complimented her like this.

"Have you been here long?" the woman asked.

Ah, this question again. "Only a few weeks." She hesitated, then added. "I'm Calliope. Calliope Turner."

"Holly Tremont. But please, just call me Holly." She grinned at Calliope. "Violet will be *so* jealous. Your shop already feels like it belongs here while hers still looks like a florist had a brawl with a haunted attic."

"Oh?" Calliope's interest spiked. "Your friend opened a shop here in Brighton?"

"Soon. It's a few streets over. The Bloom Room. It's a mess, but Violet is determined."

Calliope already liked her. And this girl, Holly, as well. There was something extremely magnetic about her. Easy in her own skin. A sharpness beneath the sweetness. "I'll have to stop by some time."

"We'd love that." Holly picked up a candle and sniffed. "And this one. It smells like tea and thunderstorms. Perfect."

"That's the black tea and oakmoss."

"Sold."

Calliope laughed. "You said 'we.' Are you helping her with the shop?"

"You could say so, though I'm exploring more than I'm helping." She reached for her coin purse before pausing. "Oh, before I forget, was that your friend who you spoke to earlier?"

Calliope stilled. "Pardon?"

"Tall, golden, smug as sin."

"Mr. Peregrine? He is not a friend, just a customer. Do you know him?"

She shook her head. "He looks familiar, but I can't place from where."

Ah.

Would she know about Maxen Fury, Calliope wondered? Honestly, after what had happened to Mr. Rollings, she ought to feel more fear. Even guilt for that matter. She'd run away and left the man behind, after all. Instead, all she could about was the way her landlord's gaze burned into her—ever so watchful, like she was a puzzle he was already halfway to solving. It made her feel . . . noticed. And infuriatingly alive.

Should she ask?

It couldn't hurt, could it?

"I wonder if we share the same landlord," Calliope tested.

"Landlord? I'm not sure," Holly said thoughtfully. "But I can find out. The shop is opening in a few days. I'll send over an invitation."

Well, it was worth a try. Calliope smiled. "Thank you."

Holly nodded. "If anyone troubles you, send them to The Bloom Room. Violet will wrap them a bouquet of nettles. My husband is also very good at discouraging nuisances."

"What about you?" Calliope asked with amusement.

"Oh, I'll just watch with glee."

Calliope laughed, wrapping the candles. "Useful to know."

"I find women make the best weapons." Holly's gaze sharpened just a touch. "Especially when the world expects us to be ornaments and follow their rules."

Calliope's smile faded a little. "I tend to avoid such worlds."

"Then you'll do just fine. I sense you have good instincts. How much do I owe you?"

"Your first bundle is free of charge." She couldn't bring herself to charge the woman. She wished to make more connections, and friendship, she believed, was best begun with kindness.

Holly's grin spread. "Then I shall return the sentiment when you come visit The Bloom Room."

Calliope inclined her head. Maybe her dream would come true sooner than she had imagined. "I look forward to the opening."

Holly tucked her package under her arm. "Then I shall see you again soon." Calliope laughed again when Holly waved enthusiastically before hurrying off.

Prince stretched out his legs, not a care in the world, and Calliope lowered onto the stool.

Maxen Fury.

She hadn't dared to say his name aloud. Not even to herself. Even his name had a dark-prince sense curling around each vowel. She didn't trust him. Not even a little. And yet, her pulse hadn't gotten the notice.

If she were clever—and she'd like to imagine she was—she would turn her attention elsewhere. To her dismay, the part of her, the very part that had learned to survive by making herself small, the very part that hated the way he made her feel *seen, exposed*—that part leaned in.

And stars, why didn't that feel absolutely petrifying?

MAXEN SAT AT a table in *Fury's*, a glass in his hand and a mood fouler than Brighton's shoreline fog. Behind the bar, Knight kept his post, his body half-lost to shadow, while Maxen replayed the afternoon in his mind. He'd followed Peregrine after he'd deposited Calliope at her shop only to be led on a merry route of pompousness. A hatmaker. A tailor. A stroll on the beach. It was as if the man knew he was being followed and had toyed with him.

He ground his teeth.

Annoying blackguard.

Dagger slumped into a chair at his table, hooked another one close and flung his boots up on it. "That woman—"

"You leased her the place behind my back," Maxen stopped him.

"I leased it to the bird, yes, but I didn't expect you to take such interest. Dangerous interest."

"And why is that?"

"She's a woman. A liability. We have enemies from all seven corners of Britain. If she turns out to be no threat, you risk placing her in danger."

Maxen turned his attention to his brandy. "Seven corners, you say."

"How ever many there are."

"She's certainly something," Reaper chimed as he sauntered over, plucking a bottle from behind the bar and popping the cork with his teeth. "At least when I'm not tailing our noble Prince of Brighton. Who knew you were such a brooder, *frère*? Oh, right, we all knew. But such focus. Such dedication."

Maxen tossed back half the liquor in his glass. "Why are you speaking?"

Reaper gave a mock gasp. "To deliver the heartfelt concerns of your loving brothers, obviously."

Maxen drained his glass.

Dagger leaned over, tapping against the bar with his finger. "You're distracted. We can't have you distracted."

"I'm alert."

"You're acting strange," Reaper pointed out.

"I am acting in the interest of our business."

Dagger crossed his arms. "You never get this involved with marks."

"She's my tenant, and you're bloody annoying."

Reaper chuckled. "We're always annoying."

True.

Dagger clapped him on the shoulder. "All we're saying is that you don't need to handle the matter of her."

"*I* need to figure her out." The moment those words left his mouth, he cursed. Did he really just bloody say that out loud? To his brothers? If they weren't annoying before, they'd certainly be now.

Reaper whistled. "Well, cock on a duck, would you listen to that? Our *frère* has needs. Seems old Dagger over there did you a favor."

Maxen glared at his brother and yanked the bottle from his hands, filling his glass. "You really don't value your teeth."

"I've long since grown immune to your threats, *frère*."

Dagger snorted.

Maxen sneered into his drink. With brothers like these, who needed enemies threatening to topple their empire?

"Do we need to reinforce our concerned brotherly concerns?" Reaper went on. "Because I've got a list." The arse held up his hand and counted off. "One: Max is acting weird. Two: He's not sleeping. Three: He's loitering outside her candle shop like a pitiful poet. Four: Dagger might have leased the property to a spy. Five: We might all die."

Bloody hell.

Knight grunted from his spot behind the bar.

"Then I die," Maxen muttered.

"Shite off," Dagger said with a scowl. "You don't die."

Reaper gave a long-suffering sigh. "You don't love me, do you, *frère?*"

"I'm in hell," Maxen bit out. Could his brothers get off his damn back? "Where are the others?"

Dagger shrugged, his lip still pulled up in annoyance. "Saint's here somewhere. Serpent is off enquiring about the shipment. Drake's upstairs resting for a fight."

Maxen gave a curt nod. "Anything with Rollings?"

Dagger gave a slight shake of his head. "What are we going to do with him?"

Reaper sent a toothy grin their way. "China."

"No." Not if Calliope was involved with the man. He had no proof beyond his suspicion, beyond the slipper. Perhaps the man could shed light on the matter. Plus, his threat level was minor. Only the supreme levels got sent off.

"Why the devil not?" Reaper demanded, his face darkening.

"I need to find out if my tenant is involved."

Reaper snorted. "That little thing? She looks harmless enough."

Dagger tipped his head, considering. "Did you learn something about the bird today?"

Maxen swallowed back a sip. "No."

He found himself the recipient of three flat stares.

"These things take time." Christ, now he did sound like a pitiful poet.

Knight scoffed. "Seems to me the girl is dangerous."

"She's not," Maxen denied.

"All women are dangerous," Knight countered.

Maxen wasn't in the mood for this.

Reaper snatched his bottle again and saluted, "To dangerous girls," before taking a long swig.

Well, he might as well just go ahead and say it. "I'm moving into the place beside her for the time being."

A long pause.

Dagger cursed. "I don't like this."

"Neither do I," Reaper growled.

Knight grunted.

"It's done." He knew they wouldn't like it. All of them stayed in the lodgings above the tavern. However, since he'd told her they were neighbors, he'd yet to stay there a night, which meant he hadn't slept. He rested poorly when too much lay beyond his sight, so he'd best switch over tonight.

Maxen's gaze stayed fixed on his drink. "Trail her, or me, if you must, but stay out of my way."

"The others aren't going to like this either," Dagger said.

"I'm a grown bloody man."

"Oh, good," Reaper sneered. "Just the response we were hoping for, grown man. Vague, ominous, and completely unhelpful."

Maxen's jaw ticked. "I can handle one woman." Such a tiny one at that, too.

"Well, don't mind if I take you up on the offer to trail you, *frère*. But don't worry, I'll be a shadow in the shadows." Reaper flashed a row of teeth. "Like a whisper in a nightmare."

Christ. "You've always been a nightmare."

"And proud of it," Reaper shot back.

A chair scraped at the far end of the tavern and Maxen glanced over. Saint emerged from whatever dark recess he'd been brooding in, big as a bloody Viking, sleeves rolled. He didn't speak. He rarely did. But his scowl was loud enough to match any ruckus.

Maxen arched his brow.

"You moving next door to that woman," Saint said darkly, voice rough as gravel and twice as hard, "is either the best idea you've ever had, or the worst."

Maxen nodded. "Likely both."

"That's comforting," Dagger muttered.

"Should we send for Serpent and Drake?" Knight asked, arms folded as he leaned his shoulder on the post behind the bar. His gaze was steady, dark, and unreadable.

"Won't matter," Maxen said coldly. "I've made my decision."

"Serpent could help, you know." Reaper chirped, half-pouring, half-slopping brandy into his mouth. "He could have the color of her drawers within the hour."

"No." His tone brooked no argument. "I don't want anyone acting on this but me."

Saint exhaled through his nose. "You sure this isn't personal?"

Maxen glanced at him, eyes hard as iron. "Everything's personal."

That earned silence.

Even Reaper—bottle midway to lips—paused.

Dagger was the first to break it, shaking his head. "So what then? We let you play landlord with a tenant we've *seen*, with our own damn eyes, interact with the very man who's been poking our operations?"

"She and Peregrine—"

Reaper snorted. "Are not associated?"

Maxen sent him a warning glance. "That is yet to be determined."

"Seemed pretty determined to me, *frère*."

Saint demanded, "Then why the hell aren't we handling her as we should?"

"Because I don't want to make the same mistake I made with my mother," Maxen snapped. He hadn't paid attention back then. Had missed key tells, and he'd paid a great price for it. No, this time, all his attention would be on his mark until he had all the answers he sought.

That silenced them again.

"Christ, *frère*," Reaper murmured, and for once, without a trace of sarcasm.

Dagger's boots hit the ground with a thud as he leaned forward. "So she matters, then."

"I didn't say that," Maxen bit out.

"You did." This from Knight.

"Don't talk shite." He only didn't want to overlook anything when it came to her. That was all. Vigilance was not attachment. Suspicion was not interest. And yet, what he would never admit to these cretins was that she mattered because he didn't want her to matter. Because he kept hearing her voice in his head when he was trying to forget it. Because when she looked at him, something old and rusted inside him moved.

"Well cock on a duck."

"Stop bloody saying that," Dagger snapped at Reaper.

Maxen's lips curled. "Agreed."

Knight gave a low sound of agreement, too.

"How long before you challenge us to a fistfight over the mouse?" Reaper asked. "I bet five-hundred quid it will happen in a week."

"Two," Knight said.

"Never," Saint offered.

Damn them all to perdition.

"Whether you like it or not," Dagger said, "we need Drake to do an in-depth inquiry into her. He's got contacts in London."

"Why London?" Knight asked.

"That's where her solicitor is stationed," Dagger informed them.

Maxen didn't disagree.

"I don't need to tell you all the things that can go wrong," Dagger added. "Too many threads, too many unknown variables."

Maxen tightened his fingers around his glass. "I need a word with Rollings."

The man might have information about her they needed.

A gust of wind howled against the windows, and Reaper shivered. "I bloody hate the wind. It's days like these I miss a good old lit fire."

Maxen's growl split the room. "Don't you bloody dare."

Reaper groaned. "I'm only complaining about the cold, *frère*. Serpent's not even listening."

"Doesn't matter. No fire. Ever."

Chapter Six

CALLIOPE GLANCED UP when the door opened and three women spilled into her shop. She smiled when she spotted the girl she'd met last time. Holly. The day had passed rather uneventfully so far, though that, to her, was indeed the most perfect day. Her dreams of last night, however . . .

She dared to dwell on those! They were too . . . too confusing. Too full of heat. Too much of *him*.

But none of that now.

"Welcome," she murmured to the women.

"Calliope! I brought my friends to introduce to you and your shop." Holly was already crossing the threshold with familiar ease, her eyes sparkling with mischief. She gestured to each of the other women. "This is Pippa Avery, the Countess of Chatteris, and Violet Sharpe, the owner of The Bloom Room I mentioned."

A countess?

Instant wariness filled her whole body. Duvessa was a countess.

That doesn't mean anything.

"I told you not to introduce me as a countess!" The Countess of Chatteris turned to Holly, exasperated. "You are forever scolding me when I introduce you as the Marchioness of Warton!"

A marchioness, too?

Calliope's throat constricted.

What were the chances they *knew* Duvessa?

"I forgot, all right?" Holly sent a sheepish look toward Calliope. "Forgive us. It's not that we mean to hide our designations, we'd simply rather not be defined by them. More so outside of London."

Calliope understood and managed a small nod, but her discomfort did not quite settle. She had spent the better part of three months avoiding anyone titled only to find herself in the company of two titled women at once. Of course, she couldn't choose her customers. The fashionable still visited Brighton. Simply not her stepmother.

She would have to reconcile herself to it, sooner or later. Denial, after all, was a temporary shelter at best.

The women wandered farther inside, chatting amongst themselves. The countess paused to examine a display of honey balm, while Holly pulled Miss Sharpe toward the shelf near the window where Calliope kept her wilder blends.

Miss Sharpe sniffed at a bundle of candles, her expression bright with interest. "It smells like something I once dreamed of. Is that absurd?"

Calliope found her voice. "Not at all." This whole shop, all her candles, after all, was the result of a dream.

"I adore this," Miss Sharpe said, running her fingers over the elegant glass label. "I'm just about to open a flower shop not far from here, and I'm considering creating scent pairings to complement my bouquets. Would you ever consider collaborating?"

Surprised, Calliope eyes flew wide. Collaborate? A wave of warmth unfurled in the deepest part of her. "I might," she said carefully, cautious to commit too fast. She couldn't quite relax, but her lingering discomfort softened a little bit. "It all depends on the flowers."

"Fabulous! Then we shall talk once I've settled in."

Calliope didn't mean to stare, but something about Miss Sharpe's sincerity, the dreaminess in her voice as she spoke, stirred something in her that reminded her of *that* dream, which had stirred a host of other things!

What a lost cause you are, Calliope!

"You're not from Brighton originally, are you?" Miss Sharpe asked, her tone curious but not prying. "Your accent is polished. London?"

The growing warmth waned slightly. Her accent? One could tell with these sorts of things? "I'm not from Brighton, no, but I've decided to settle here." For now. Where she might end up after her lease of six months only time could tell.

She could feel Holly's gaze shift toward her and pretended she didn't notice. The fewer questions, the better. The fact that she hadn't confirmed or denied or answered where she hailed from was probably telling in itself.

Dreams . . . they were strange, elusive things, all the more when they were finally in reach. As though they shifted the moment you believed them secure. Like her dream of opening this shop and living peacefully hidden away from Duvessa.

And the dream she'd had of a certain landlord last night. But then, she hadn't *just* dreamed of Maxen Fury, had she?

She'd dreamed of *touch*.

Of fingers trailing over her collarbone. Of dark eyes watching her from the shadows, daring her to run. Of *greed*, not for coin or power—but for her. His hands, his mouth, his *voice*. It wasn't the sort of dream a sensible woman allowed to linger past dawn. And certainly not one she let bloom while surrounded by marchionesses and countesses!

But even now, the memory pressed deep against her skin.

For the love of wax . . .

If she was going to dream about a man, why him? Why not someone safe, distant, and utterly uninvolved with landlords and missing merchants and an unfortunate urge to *see* him again? Because Maxen Fury—no matter how dangerous, no matter how maddening—had cracked something in her the moment he'd stepped into her shop. She'd *felt* it, damn him. As if the air had changed texture. As if her body recognized something before her mind could put words to it. Still couldn't put words to it.

She didn't need that kind of peril in her life.

Not again.

This little shop, wherever it may be located, here or in Wales or anywhere else, was her sanctuary because it was first carved in her heart. Every candle she molded was a small declaration: *I am here. I have survived. You cannot find me. You cannot strip me of this life.*

"Well, no matter," Holly piped up. "It doesn't matter where you are from, only where you go from here."

"Exactly!" The countess grinned.

"Agreed," Miss Sharpe said softly, as if sensing Calliope's sudden storm. "And I do hope you'll consider the idea of working together. But you must feel no pressure to do so. I know what it's like to build something new from the bones of a former life."

A lump rose in Calliope's throat. These weren't empty niceties. Miss Sharpe meant every word. Holly and the countess nodded enthusiastically. "Thank you."

The women beamed at her and were soon debating whether mint made for a better morning or evening scent.

Calliope watched them, her fingers curling slightly at her sides. For all her moments of cynicism, for all the shadows she'd left behind, she still wanted connection.

Still wanted to *trust*.

But this was also what petrified her. If her dreams were any indication . . . her instincts couldn't be trusted. Not when they'd already wrapped themselves around Maxen Fury like roots seeking life in barren earth. Which was precisely why she needed to cut them out before they grew any deeper. For if they took root in him, she feared they'd be the death of her.

MAXEN STEPPED INTO their dungeon, his gaze falling on Rollings, dirty, bedraggled, and tied to a chair in the center of the room. There was nothing spectacular about the man. Nor anything diabolical. But then, those were the kind that a man had to be most cautious of.

They were the kind most prone to betray.

Many overlooked them. Many dismissed them. And those men? The men like Rollings? They listened. They observed. They made calculated moves.

And he'd slipped past Maxen's notice.

Another failure.

Drake, who'd finally showed face again, stepped up beside him. Silent.

Rollings lifted his head sluggishly. His right eye was swollen shut, and a trail of blood had dripped off the side of his face and spread along the edge of his collar. Maxen didn't speak immediately, simply crossed the room to a table with water and two cups.

"I didn't betray you," Rollings croaked.

Maxen poured a measure of water into a cup, the whisper of leather stretching across his hands with the movements, placed it on the table, then leaned against it, arms crossed.

The older man swallowed, eyes flicking toward the cup before back at Maxen, and expressed again, "I did not betray you."

"No? Then you simply lost the shipping ledger that would expose our routes, and several of our warehouses, by accident?"

The man's eyes flew wide. "How did you—"

"Reliable sources, Rollings. Much more reliable than you. Why didn't you inform us of the missing ledger?"

"I . . . I was . . . I—"

"You were afraid. I can understand. It's not a tolerable excuse, however."

"I—I'm sorry, Mr. Fury. I didn't know how to tell you. I planned to, I really did, I just . . . I told you everything else."

"You didn't tell us about Calliope Turner and her little candle shop, The Whispering Wick."

The man's eyes rounded even more.

So, he did know her. The confirmation brought him nothing but coldness.

Drake cursed.

"She has nothing to do with this," Rollings hurried to say. "You must believe me!"

"And what exactly is *this*?"

"I am her supplier. I brought her products from France."

Is that so? "On my ship?"

"It's not much. Barely takes up any space."

So bloody dishonest. Using his route, his ship, to bring over products for others. Do it for one, do it for many.

"She doesn't know anything about what I do other than supply her with her oils."

"Methinks the man doth protest too much," Drake said darkly.

"It's true! Our initial arrangement came through another party!"

Maxen arched a brow. "Oh? And who is that party? Who *else* did you do these secret shipments for?"

The man's mouth clamped shut.

Heh.

Maxen pushed off the table. "Let me explain something, Rollings. The last man who lied to me left this room breathing, just not walking. And he doesn't live on this godforsaken island anymore."

Rollings paled.

"And you're about to tell me," Maxen added, voice like ice, "or you're about to face a monster you've only heard whispers about."

Beads of sweat gathered on the man's brow. "An acquaintance of mine approached me in regard to the oils and introduced me to Miss Turner. But—but, he is of no consequence. And I only shipped for one other client, but I do not know his identity."

"Not good enough."

"That client . . . he worked through another man. Hair shaved. Brute looking. He gave me the request and payment, and that was that."

That could be hundreds of men.

"And what was this request?"

"I—I only had to send a letter over to France. That was all."

Maxen's blood turned to ice. "So, not only do you lose an important ledger and not inform us, but you also did side jobs on our time, using our ships." Maxen pressed the heel of his palm against the bridge his nose before looking at the man again. "Who is the man who introduced you to Calliope Turner?"

The man came up short, spluttering. "I-I-I—"

"Do you want to walk out here," Maxen snapped, "or crawl?"

"Fitz," the man rasped. "John Fitz."

"The solicitor Dagger brokered the rental deal through," Drake spoke up.

Maxen nodded and jutted a chin to the water. His brother stepped up to free one of the Rollings arms, handing him the cup. Rollings gulped the contents down in one go.

"And how do you know John Fitz?" Drake asked.

Rollings inhaled a sharp breath. "Known him for years. Met through a mutual acquaintance."

"So many acquaintances," Maxen murmured. "Who is the mutual one?"

"Passed away last year."

Maxen sneered. "And how does Calliope Turner know John Fitz?" What woman had a solicitor in London? Not his kind. Not unless she belonged to a world he despised.

"You'll have to ask Fitz that."

Maxen sneered. "Or Miss Turner, correct?"

The man pursed his lips.

Maxen's fists clenched, and he stalked a slow circle around the chair. "If I discover you are lying . . ."

"I'm not! I vow I'm not!"

Drake made a sound like a half-scoff, half-snort.

Maxen stopped behind Rollings, fingers flexing. "What else?" he asked. "What else do you know about her?"

"N-nothing," Rollings stammered. "Nothing, I swear."

"Are you sure?" Maxen watched the man's spine from behind.

"I'm sure, I swear!"

The man wasn't lying. Even so, it wasn't enough. Not when Maxen could still see her green eyes narrowing on him like a ruffled little mouse ready to scatter if he made one wrong move. The deliberate way she chose to answer questions, not to flinch, not to give anything away. Not when he kept recalling how she looked at him like she was the one observing him and not the other way around.

"She doesn't belong in this world," Rollings said in a rush, as though reading Maxen's mind. "Too decent. Too . . ."

"Too what?" Maxen asked in a low voice.

"Good."

Maxen's jaw ticked. That was what bothered him too. Not what she did. But what she didn't.

"I warned her," the man babbled on. "I warned her about you—"

Maxen stiffened.

"—warned her about the beasts that rule Brighton. But," he hastily added. "I didn't give your names. Only warned her to be careful."

Fury exploded. Maxen wanted to throttle the damn man.

"Maxen," Drake warned. "Don't."

Damnation! The only reason he managed to restrain every urge to beat Rollings into the floor was due to that last part. He hadn't given their names.

"So she's just an ordinary woman?" Drake asked.

"Yes," Rollings said, nodding fiercely. "Ordinary."

How bloody laughable. Calliope Turner ordinary? There was nothing *ordinary* about her. "When you've met Miss Turner," he balled and unballed his fists, "what did you talk about?"

"She thanked me for the delivery. Paid in full. Politely asked after my journey."

Drake crossed his arms, but Maxen paid him no mind. He didn't need to look at his brother to know both brows were raised.

"That's all?" he pressed.

"It's always the same." Rollings hesitated. "She's only ever asked once if I miss home when I travel a lot, that's all. Nothing more."

That was all?

Perhaps to a man like Rollings it didn't mean anything, but to Maxen? That simple question slithered into a knot in his gut, like a snake. She missed something too. Or someone. Or some time before she'd landed here in Brighton.

He rubbed a hand over his jaw. "If she is everything you claim she is, then you pushed her into the middle of a bloody storm without her knowing it."

Rollings shuddered.

Good.

"Pray she's as ordinary as you say, because if she's not . . . this storm won't spare her."

He turned and strode for the stairs, Drake falling into step behind him.

Chapter Seven

TWO DAYS AND nights passed in a flash. Three if one counted this night.

Nary a sight of her landlord.

However, the sense of his presence never left. It brooded in the corners of her shop like unfinished business waiting to be begun again. It brought her no ease.

Not in her skin.

Not in her bones.

Every time the bell above the shop chimed, her breath caught—just slightly, very slightly—before she could command it otherwise. Her body knew before her mind had the chance to remind it that they were *safe*, that he was *gone*, that Maxen Fury had no reason to return.

Because still she felt him.

Mostly in her dreams. It seemed they had decided that the beast was the object for their entertainment, and her torture. She hadn't had another like *that*, thank stars, but sleep had become a slippery, restless thing.

All because of that man.

Both a promise and a warning.

She was coming to find that was the most dangerous of combinations. Which led her to the most curious question. If Maxen

Fury could be molded into a candle, what scent would he carry?

Spiced rum, perhaps? With a hint of charred tobacco? Topped with a hint of black leather.

Mmm.

No, Calliope! Absolutely not.

She was *done* with people who wielded too much power.

Done with danger.

Done with anyone who looked at her like she was a threat that needed handling or a pawn to be controlled. Or, God forbid, a man looking at her like she was a secret worth uncovering.

Lord.

He was just such a man.

In fact, he was all of the aforementioned.

And if she didn't nip her curiosity in the bud, she might start looking for him in every shadow.

Too late, Calliope.

No. Not too late. Rather, just in time.

She sighed, blinking up to the ceiling. Easier said than done. Already her mind catalogued her vials of scented oil. They didn't bottle the scent of black leather, so how to mirror it?

A deep, low growl rumbled through the room.

Calliope jerked upright. Prince stood at the foot of the bed, his eyes fixed on the bedroom door. "Prince?" But the hound didn't so much as flick an ear at her voice. He growled again, this time deeper, sounding harsh in the quiet night.

She cocked her head to listen.

Calliope heard nothing at first. Nothing after several beats. Then . . .

A muffled thud.

Her eyes shot wide and she scrambled from her bed to drop to her knees, placing her ear on the ground, listening carefully. Had that come from her place? Downstairs?

Another muffled sound.

For stars' sake! There was someone in her shop!

What on earth did she do? She couldn't think past the pulse

thundering in her ears. She lifted her head slowly, barely daring to breathe. Prince's growl remained low, protectively stationed between her and whatever danger prowled below.

Her gaze flew to the window.

Was it too high to jump from? No. She couldn't jump with Prince. Nor without. The door? Dare she sneak out back? But if she stepped onto the stairwell, she might alert the intruder.

No. No. No.

Could it be Duvessa? Her men? Had they found her? Had she been recognized in town? Followed? Had something happened to Mr. Fitz? Had he betrayed her? Had one of the servants?

She had taken every precaution. She had been *careful*. And Mr. Fitz was the last person on earth who'd betray her.

Do you know for certain?

No. There was no one on this earth she could trust with so much certainty. Not beyond any shadow of doubt. She had abandoned her old name, hadn't contacted anyone from London but Clemence, and even Clemence wrote in riddles. And Mr. Fitz.

Just hang on a little longer.

Years of dealing with Duvessa and those nasty daughters of hers had taught her to keep calm. That calmness meant safety. Meant survival. And so she obeyed the instinct drilled deep into her bones.

Only, it didn't work.

Calliope! This is not a closet! Or the attic! This is life or death!

Right.

She crouched beside the bed, one hand clutching the leg of the frame, the other pressed to her chest. Her heart beat against her palm like it wanted to flee without her.

She squeezed her eyes shut.

She wasn't meant for this kind of fear. She wasn't strong like the women she admired in the novels she read. Or the women who so confidently entered her shop. Calliope's way had always been to endure. To wait until the storm passed.

But what if this storm didn't? What if this storm was the very end?

Of her.

Prince.

By blazes, *no*. She refused to let this be her end! However, her body wouldn't move. Not even the hand clutching her heart shifted an inch.

Her gaze caught on something beside Prince.

One of the boots she'd tossed aside after she'd settled in for the night.

The image of her slipper popped into her head, and the memory of *him* holding her slipper, casually sliding it into his coat like it belonged there. The memory gave her a reckless sort of courage. She forced her limbs to obey and rose on unsteady legs, crossing space and collected the boot. Not the best of weapons, but she could slam it against the wall that separated her from her neighbor, from him, and hope he heard.

Prince's growl changed, softer now. Lower.

Not a good sign.

A noise exploded from below. Glass shattering? She stumbled backward, her legs striking the bed frame. What on earth was happening down there? Weren't intruders stealthier?

Hide. You know how to hide.

Her skin crawled with the thought, the memories it drew to the surface.

Not that way. Not anymore.

She hurried over to the door, plastering herself against the wall beside it, clutching the boot tightly.

And waited.

Prince padded to her side silently, his body pressed close. "Good boy," she murmured, patting his head.

Footsteps creaked.

So the intruder intended to intrude upstairs as well. She had hoped . . . never mind. She glanced at Prince. Two against one.

The sound came again. Patient. Steady. Closer.

Calliope pressed her back harder against the wall, clutching the boot like a lifeline. Her entire body was ice and fire—numb, but burning. She had never before fought.

Hide. Be silent. Wait to be spared. Not defend.

But this was her shop. *Hers.* And Prince . . .What would happen to him if something happened to her? Nothing! Because she refused to allow anything to happen to her.

No more hiding.

No more freezing.

No more letting the storm swallow her whole.

By blazes—*no.*

She had come too far to allow her sense of peace to be stolen in such a manner. Fear had always taught her how to endure, how to wait out the storm, how to make herself small until it passed, but this was *her* shop. Her life. And Prince's. Whatever waited on the other side of that door, she would not greet it hiding in the shadows or frozen in place. She drew in a careful breath and held fast to it, bracing herself.

The latch clicked, and the door creaked open, and Calliope saw a shadow fall across the floorboards of her chamber.

A heavy step.

A dark coat.

A booted leg.

Without thinking, she let out a wild cry and *swung* the boot with all the force she had, slamming it directly into the man. To her utter shock, and surprise, he crumpled with a pained grunt, folding to his knees with a groan so raw she flinched.

She stared at him, wide-eyed, panting, heart in her throat.

Why did he look so . . .?

Furious eyes met her.

"Maxen?"

PAIN BOOMED THROUGH every part of Maxen's body.

A gut-splitting, soul-leaving, *what-the-devil-just-happened* kind of pain. It exploded from his groin and spread like fire through his stomach, his spine, his very teeth. He couldn't breathe. Couldn't think. Could barely *see*.

Just stars, burning, blinking stars.

And her.

"What the bloody—?" he choked out, cupping the site of impact. Sweet Christ. Every instinct screamed for him to topple, curl, and protect. He swallowed the string of curses working their way up his throat and forced himself to focus, jaw locked hard enough to crack his damn teeth.

A boot dropped to the floor before him.

Ah. So he'd been assaulted with a *boot*.

Calliope bloody Turner.

She stood staring at him bright-eyed, her breath ragged, her cheeks flushed with either terror or fury—or both. Her dog growled behind her like a guard summoned straight from Hades. But he did not attack him.

He ought to be grateful for small mercies.

Maxen squinted up at her. "Good aim, love."

She blinked at him as if dazed, then hurriedly said, "I'm sorry. I didn't mean to hit something vital. That is, I did, but I didn't aim for *that*. I just hit."

"If I stand, will your dog attack?"

"Uh, no." She glanced to the hound. "Prince." The dog instantly settled. She patted his head. "Good boy."

Maxen slowly rose to his feet. Well, mostly. The nauseating throb still pounded at him. "Thank you."

"You're the one with explaining to do, Mr. Landlord. Is it customary to break into tenants' shops? Should I call for the authorities?"

Authorities? Maxen couldn't hold back a laugh. "I am the authorities."

Her eyes rolled heavenward. God help him, what a sight. He almost reached out to snatch a strand of her hair, which tumbled over her shoulders to her waist, drawing his attention to her near-transparent nightgown.

He should have thought this over.

"You believe my words arrogance."

"Not even *you* can deny they sound like arrogance."

"They remain fact."

She studied him, and he stiffened against the damnable urge to puff himself up like a peacock. The sensation of her attention crept along his spine, setting his nerves on edge and leaving him acutely conscious of the invading sense that she was deciding something about him.

"Well, well, well," a drawl came from behind them, "this must be the first time in my life I've heard you laugh, *frère*."

Maxen cursed, shifting to block his brother's view, tossing over his shoulder, "I told you to stay downstairs."

Reaper, blade dangling from one hand, his coin dancing over the knuckles of the other, appeared with the relaxed menace of a man who enjoyed chaos just a little too damn much.

"*Reaper.*"

"What? I couldn't resist following." His brother's focus shifted, trying to see around him to Calliope. "Sounded like you were dying there. Thought I'd missed something good. Now I know I did."

Bloody hell.

"What about the man downstairs?"

"The bald one Rollings outed?" Reaper shrugged "Tied up like a sack of potatoes. Couldn't put up much of a fight."

"Rollings?" Calliope exclaimed. "He is alive?"

Maxen's attention snapped back to her, meeting her delighted, but astonished gaze. He scowled. "Why would you think he wasn't alive?"

"Oh." Her lips parted and closed before she said, "I, uh, purchased oil from him but he never delivered my last order. I thought something might've . . . happened to him."

Plausible.

Matched Rollings tale.

However, why would she presume something had happened to Rollings if she didn't know a speck of his profession? Perhaps bore witness to something she shouldn't have? "I see."

"So this is the little mouse," Reaper piped up from the back. "Our wily spy."

"Stand down, Reaper," Maxen warned.

"I can't even get a glance?" his brother lamented. "How disappointing."

"Enough," Maxen snapped.

"A *spy?*" came Calliope's shocked exclamation. "You believe me to be a *spy?*"

Maxen sighed.

"Oh dear," Reaper murmured. "I was not supposed to say that, was I?" At Maxen's glare, he stepped back. "No need for violence, *frère*, I'll leave the little mouse to you."

"Who is that and why is he calling me little mouse?" Calliope demanded. "I am not a mouse!"

A drink would be good right about now. "Handle the bald one," Maxen instructed his brother.

"Done."

Only when Reaper disappeared, did he say to the bristling woman before him, "Don't listen to him. He belongs in Bedlam."

Her gaze cut through him. "I have so many questions, but first, who broke into my shop?"

"Why don't you tell me, Calliope?" He stared.

And she stared right back.

So small. So furious. So utterly unwilling to back down. Whatever this woman was caught in, and he had no doubt she was caught in something, had bled into his world. And that made her his. Now, more than ever, he couldn't let her out of his sight. Not until he understood exactly who she was and what she might drag here with her.

"How would I know that?" Her incredulous look almost made him smile. "I was upstairs. Ready for sleep. Until someone disturbed my peace!"

"I am merely asking, love."

"*Don't* call me love." She smoothed some wayward locks back. "It's disconcerting."

It felt rather natural for him. "It's just a question." *Love.*

"It's never just a question with you, is it? Well, I don't know who that bald man is, and I'm *not* a spy." Her gaze broke away, then charged back again. "I heard glass break. What happened?"

Another thorn in his arse. "An unfortunate scuffle." He didn't add that the broken glass had come from throwing the man across the room and into the door.

She scrunched her brow. "Then should I find another accommodation."

"That would be best." He cursed the words rolling off his tongue but didn't swallow them back. "You'll come with me."

A stunned expression crossed her face. "What do you mean with you?"

Yes, you fool, what did you mean by that? "You'll stay with me next door. It's not safe here."

She stared at him like he'd grown a second head. Perhaps he had.

"You can't be serious."

Maxen folded his arms, ignoring the slow throb still pulsing through his balls. "I'm always serious."

The woman didn't move. Didn't respond. Simply watched him with that guarded, assessing look he was beginning to become familiar with.

"If you're trying to intuit whether this is a trap," he said softly, "it's not. You're not nearly a threat enough to warrant one."

That earned him a snort. "How reassuring."

Maxen didn't smile, but it was close. "Pack a bag, Calliope. You're staying with me."

Chapter Eight

CALLIOPE STILL DIDN'T know what had happened.

One moment she was blinking up at Maxen Fury, still half-winded by the aftermath of swinging a boot at his—well, his everything—and the next she was following him to his lodgings.

His cold, dark, *barren* lodgings.

Prince sniffed here and there before giving her a look that said: *This is where you brought us?*

Well, she wasn't thrilled either.

She tightened her cloak around her. Was this place even lived in? The quarters looked like they hadn't been touched in over a decade. Even the shop below wasn't a shop. The space was filled with boxes and barrels containing only God knew what.

What had she agreed to?

She wasn't even sure how the words *all right, fine* had made it past her lips. Had she perhaps fallen unconscious for a second? That would explain her lapse! The lasting trace of shock of the break-in, the cold fear, the other man calling her a mouse, a *spy*, and Maxen suddenly—absurdly—blocking his view of her. Maxen calling her *love*.

She refused to dwell on that endearment.

Refused to!

But she could stare in fascination as he struck flint to steel and coaxed a flame to life on a solitary candle that sat on a lone table with a lone chair, the sudden glow carving his features in sharpness.

Her gaze lifted to the scar on his lips, stark and vicious in the flickering light. How would it feel to trace a finger along the edges? She quickly glanced away, cheeks threatening to heat, her gaze falling on the black leather gloves covering his hands instead.

"Do you not find those uncomfortable?" she asked before she could think better of it, nodding faintly toward his hands.

"I don't take them off."

"Ever?"

"Not in company."

It was on the tip of her tongue to ask why, but she swallowed the question back. What did he keep hidden from the world? Heaven help her, he made her want to peel them back finger by finger. Conflictingly, some part of her almost preferred the barrier. The gloves had become part of him—dark, forbidden, and somehow unspeakably alluring.

She rubbed her temples. "I think this was a mistake."

"I couldn't agree more," he agreed, leaning against the doorframe, arms folded, gaze on her.

"Weren't you the one who invited me over?" If his command could even be called an invitation. "Then I should just return to *my* living quarters."

"I couldn't disagree more."

She crossed her arms, mirroring him. "You just agreed it's a mistake."

"I've made worse choices."

Hah! She didn't doubt *that*. "I should still go back," she insisted. "To my own space. My own bed."

"And sleep with the door to your shop in splinters?"

"I'll barricade it."

"You'll still be alone."

She opened her mouth, then promptly pursed her lips. Yes. She'd be alone. Which, she finally grasped, was why she had agreed to come with her landlord in the first place. She hadn't wanted to spend the night questioning every sound the night welcomed. "Just so you know, I *can* take care of myself."

"Of course," he said softly. "But tonight, you don't have to."

She pointed toward the small chamber beyond, where an open door showed that a single bed waited. "Where am I to sleep?"

He straightened from his lazy lean and stepped inside. "Bring the light."

She hesitated, then lifted the candlestick and followed him in, the soft glow throwing their shadows across the walls. She swallowed. How could two shadows on the wall look so . . . *intimate?*

"I'll sleep on the floor."

Naturally, she didn't argue. The situation was awkward enough without drawing more attention to the fact that she was alone with a man. Calliope ought to even have felt a slight pinch of wariness. Maybe even fear. But those things were curiously absent. And well, the man looked like no floor could bring him down. Like he'd slept in alleys and battlefields all his life. She shouldn't admire that. She absolutely did.

Have you forgotten he's a ruffian?

Of course not, but it was hard to remember when he looked like a dark knight existing only to protect her! Besides, hadn't they mentioned Mr. Rollings earlier? The very alive Mr. Rollings? That counted for something, right?

"The sheets are clean."

Oh! Lord. Had she been staring at the bed too long? "Thank you," she mumbled, placing the candle on a small table and making haste in slipping between the covers, shrugging off her boots as she did so and tugging the blanket up to her chin before glancing over at him.

The man moved like a storm barely held at bay, meticulously shrugging off his coat, tossing the garment over the back of a chair before pulling a quilt from the closet and spreading it right beside her bed. They might as well have shared the coverlet. They were so close. Too close. Closer than she'd ever been to any man at night.

Stars. His presence was all consuming even when he wasn't with her. Like this? The man was impossible to ignore. Impossible not to feel. He wrapped himself around the room. Around her. How was she meant to fall asleep with him so near? He was everywhere. No matter how tightly she closed her eyes, she wouldn't be able to shut him out.

He blew out the candle before lowering himself onto this rough pallet, stretching out on the floor, and Prince promptly trotted over and curled against his side.

Traitor.

"Do you honestly believe I'm a spy?" she asked to distract herself.

The answer came instantly. "No."

She blinked into the dark. "No? I should be relieved, so why do I feel oddly offended?"

A low chuckle. "You don't hide well."

Impossible! She was the best at hiding! "I do too," she whispered. "You just . . . see too much." From what she could gather, at least.

A beat of silence followed, then the low creak of floorboards beneath his weight. "You noticed that."

"How could I not?"

Two heartbeats passed. "It's how I stay alive. Keep my brothers alive."

Her scalp prickled. What kind of life required noticing *everything* just to survive? But was she really one to ask? Hadn't she been the same in that household? Letting her guard down meant she could be separated from Prince, locked in some small space, or even trapped and beaten.

"Is that how you noticed someone broke into the shop?" She'd wondered about that.

"Mmm."

What? No details? Such a Maxen Fury thing to do. She would accept the lack of information, but only for tonight. Tomorrow, she wanted answers. "Well, for what it's worth, I'm sorry. I didn't mean to bring trouble to your doorstep."

"You didn't." Another slight pause. "Trouble was already there."

Her brows furrowed. "What does that mean?"

"It means . . ." He exhaled, a sound that somehow managed to brush against her skin even though it was nowhere close. "Trouble doesn't always knock. Sometimes it sneaks in through the back and waits for you to step through the door."

She didn't know if he meant him or herself.

Knowing the man, likely both.

She rolled to her side, her front facing the direction of his voice. Though the room was cloaked in darkness, she could make out the shape of him lying on the floor. One arm behind his head. The other stretched toward the edge of her bed—but not touching.

Just . . . close.

He shifted, and her skin prickled.

This wasn't a man who gave away pieces of himself freely. But she couldn't help the absurd sense that maybe—just maybe—he'd handed her a corner of something about him tonight. A little scrap of the true man. The man hiding beneath all that black. Beneath those black leather gloves.

She tugged the covers up just a little higher.

"Maxen?" she murmured, her voice barely above a breath.

"Hm."

"Thank you for tonight."

He didn't answer for a moment, then simply said, "Always."

She almost laughed. Everything about this situation was ridiculous. Uncomfortable. Dangerous, even. And yet, here she lay. Not exactly a bed of her own making, but one she'd willingly entered.

Trouble had clearly found her. And at this moment, it was

lying just an arm's breadth away.

I'm never going to fall asleep.

MAXEN OPENED THE door and scowled at Drake, who had disturbed them at the arse crack of dawn. "Do you know what time it is?" he asked in a low voice, blocking the entrance with his body.

"I do. Do you?"

The hour must be later than he thought. He stretched out his arms, joints cracking. His back ached somewhat, but at least his balls didn't anymore. "What are you doing here? Did something happen?"

"You slept with a woman."

"False. And even if I did, is that bloody newsworthy?"

"You brought a woman home." Drake's brows rose. "That's a Fury first. And of all of us, unlike you the most."

"Get lost."

Drake pushed past him anyway. "But she's here, in *your* bed-chamber."

Maxen dragged a hand down his face and closed the door behind him with more force than necessary but less than he wanted. "She's in the bed. I was on the floor."

"How very proper of you." Drake gaze tracked the room, landing on the door of his chamber. "I'd be impressed if I believed for one damned second you slept."

He hadn't.

He'd lain on the floor all night, muscles tense, listening to the various states of her breathing. The subtle shifts of her body.

But not the damn point.

He wasn't sure what unsettled him more—the fact that she'd taken up so much space in his thoughts . . . or how *right* it had felt to have her here. Which in itself was so bloody damn wrong. She was soft. Light. He was . . .

Not.

Drake leaned against the windowpane, arms folded. "I've never known you to offer protection to anyone outside of blood."

"It's my duty as a landlord," Maxen defended flatly.

"Right. Your duties as a landlord."

"She's an innocent."

"Yet to be proven."

Maxen's jaw ticked. "She's not a spy. Might even be in danger."

"I didn't say she was or that she wasn't."

Christ. It was too early for this. "Are you telling me you didn't just imply both?"

"I *noticed*." Drake's eyes narrowed. "You've been watching her like you were waiting for her to disappear."

Had he? He couldn't deny it. Ever since he met her that first day he'd been riveted to a degree. It was irrational. Infuriating. Unacceptable.

She was a stranger.

A complication.

A potential threat.

And yet. Bloody yet. All it had taken was a whispered *thank you* for a silent vow to burn Brighton down if anyone harmed her. Period.

"She's not your problem," Maxen clarified.

"She's yours, which makes her mine."

"She's not *yours*," the snap of a growl came before he could stop himself.

Drake gave a low whistle.

Before Drake could further mock him, the unmistakable creak of a bed frame had them freeze.

Maxen's spine snapped straight. "Leave," he commanded his brother.

Drake grinned. "Now why would I do that when I'm just about to meet the woman who made you laugh last night?"

Damn Reaper's hide.

"Drake—"

A door opened.

And there she was. Tousled and with sleep-heavy eyes, she blinked. And God . . . during the night he could forcibly overlook her nightwear. But in the light of day? A string of curses tore across his mind. Everything was just *more*. Her golden hair, tumbled in loose waves over her shoulders, seemed to glow, as if lit from within. The swell of her breasts was near blinding. Even her bare feet felt too intimate to witness.

His eyes, however, latched onto the coat she wore.

His coat.

Which swallowed her small frame.

Drake let out another low whistle. "Well, good morning, Miss Turner."

Maxen wanted to snatch her from his brother's sight.

Prince padded over to stop beside her. "You are?" she asked.

His brother stepped up and, with an audacious smile, offered his hand. "How rude of me. Drake Fury at your service."

Her eyes flicked between them before placing her hand in Drake's, and Maxen nearly grabbed his brother by the collar and tossed him out.

She pulled back her hand. "You were the man that settled my lease with Mr. Fitz?"

"That would be my other brother, Dagger."

"I see. Are you here about what happened last night? Where is the man you caught?"

Maxen looked to his brother. He hadn't had a chance to ask.

Drake's humor vanished. "He still hasn't spoken a damn word."

"Then he's trained," Maxen suggested.

"Trained?" Calliope asked, brows pinching.

What the devil was wrong with Drake, choosing *now* of all times?

"In interrogation," Drake clarified, voice clipped. "Which means he's a professional. The only question is whether he was after you, Miss Turner, or after us. Do you have any enemies who would wish to harm you?"

She stilled, visibly paling.

"No," she said slowly. Too slowly.

Drake cocked his head to the side. "Lying never goes over well with us, Miss Turner."

"Drake," Maxen warned.

But Calliope didn't flinch at his brother's tone. Instead, she squared her shoulders and lifted her chin. "Everyone has an enemy or two, but that man, whoever sent him, is not mine."

"Do you know that for certain?" Maxen asked her. Rather be sure than careless.

She reached down to pat Prince's head, as if the action brought her comfort. "No enemy of mine would send a lone ruffian to break into my shop."

Maxen's gaze sharpened. "A *lone* one? They'd send more, then?"

She hesitated, just a blink, but he caught the falter.

"That is . . . I misspoke. Whatever enemy I may have, they are no one you have to worry about."

Wrong.

He also didn't miss the *they* of that sentence.

His brother arched a brow. "If you believe that, you don't know us all that well."

"Drake," Maxen warned again, quieter this time, but with no less authority. He glared at his brother. *Get your brute hide gone.*

"I'll leave," Drake acquiesced. "Hopefully Saint will have found some answers for us by the time I return."

"Let me know if there's anything."

Drake nodded, turning to Calliope. "A pleasure to meet you, Miss Turner. Until next time."

She offered a small smile, but her eyes remained guarded.

When the door clicked shut behind Drake, Maxen dragged a hand through his hair.

"He's your brother."

"He is."

"That's quite a scar he has," she murmured, her gaze dropping to his.

Yes, well, they were all scarred one way or another.

She didn't press. Instead, she asked, "What about the man from last night? Also your brother?"

Maxen gave a curt not. "The least favorite one."

Her smile lifted somewhat. "I see."

"Who are your enemies?" Maxen asked her. That was his biggest concern at the moment. They were unknown variables.

She shook her head. "Like I said, no one you need to worry about."

"If it affects me or mine, I worry about it, Calliope."

"Well, please don't waste time for my sake. My troubles won't affect you or yours."

Maxen wasn't so sure about that, but he let the matter go. For now. She looked tired. Wary. And if he had to wager, not from lack of sleep, but from the kind of exhaustion that ran much deeper. The kind that rose from the ashes of pain. It was no use pressing her in this state. Best focus on the answers the bald intruder could provide.

Maxen's hand twitched at his side. He wanted to reach for her, to catch one of those tendrils of hair between his fingers.

He clenched his fist behind his back instead. His attention snagged on the way his coat dwarfed her again, an image he did not want lodged in his mind but suspected would never leave him.

Distance. He needed distance.

He just didn't think he could bear it.

Chapter Nine

CALLIOPE STARED AT the mess of her shop. She'd been ushered next door so fast, she hadn't gotten a proper look last night, but now, in the cold clarity of morning, she stood in the threshold, disheartened at the destruction.

The damage, she supposed, could have been worse.

Already, men were sweeping splinters and shards into neat piles. A new door stood propped against the wall, ready to be hung. Another man—broad-shouldered, sleeves rolled—was fitting fresh hinges into the frame.

Maxen Fury worked fast.

The response was rather impressive. Her landlord also hadn't left her side once. No wonder he'd insisted on breakfast first. The man had everything under the thumb of his hand. Food had been delivered, workers had been enlisted, and Prince had been fed and taken for a morning walk.

"Oh, dear me!" a feminine voice exclaimed. "What on earth happened here?"

Calliope turned just as Holly the marchioness and Violet Sharpe entered her battered shop, their eyes wide and expressions caught somewhere between horror and curiosity.

"Are you all right?" Holly asked, stepping carefully over a stray shard of glass.

Miss Sharpe's concerned gaze found her, too.

"I'm fine," she assured them. "Honestly. It looks worse than it is."

"You were robbed?" Miss Sharpe whispered, aghast.

"Marauded, more like," Calliope said. "Late last night."

Holly's brows snapped together. "Did you catch the blackguard?"

"That's . . . still being figured out." She dared not say anything else, lest she provoke more questions from them she couldn't answer. She still hadn't gotten the whole story of how Maxen had come to spot and catch the intruder.

"How dreadful," Miss Sharpe murmured. "And terrifying. Was anything taken?"

"Not that I've noticed." Calliope shifted, hating to spin the truth. "But I haven't done a full inventory yet."

"And you were here when it happened?" Miss Sharpe asked, eyes darting round.

Calliope nodded. "Upstairs."

"This is rather troublesome," Holly said. "You must have been stricken with fear."

"I had Prince." She pointed at the dog, lying on his pillow, overlording the workings. "And my landlord fortunately came across the scene and dealt with it."

"This is indeed troubling," Miss Sharpe agreed. "I hope this isn't a new trend in Brighton."

Oh, right. She had her own store. Calliope wished she could set her mind at ease, but at the moment, she couldn't do anything that wouldn't reveal more than she dared. "I hope so too, Miss Sharpe."

"Please, call me Violet, and you must not have slept a wink last night," Miss Sharpe, Violet said. "You are more than welcome to . . ." she trailed off as her gaze landed on something behind Calliope. She glanced over her shoulder.

Or rather someone.

Maxen.

All black and brooding, leaning against a shelf, arms and ankles crossed, staring at them.

Stars, did the man have to look so intimidating?

And ruthlessly handsome?

"Who is *that*?" Holly asked, the intrigue in her voice almost making Calliope laugh.

"That is my landlord."

Holly fanned her face. "That doesn't look like any landlord I've ever seen."

Calliope arched a brow. "Your husband must be one, no?" He was a marquess, after all. He must own properties, have tenants.

Holly cast her A Look. "Yes, but he doesn't count. He also doesn't lurk in corners like a gothic novel hero waiting to pounce." She gave a thoughtful pause. "Oh, no wait, he does do that, but he still doesn't count."

Calliope did laugh at that. "Ah, well, *my* landlord is merely . . . tall." And all the other things.

"An understatement," Holly supplied.

"He's also glowering," Violet murmured.

"Another understatement."

"That's merely how he looks." And Calliope found it hard to believe, given Maxen's identity, Violet wasn't leasing from him. "You've never met your landlord?"

Violet shook her head. "My lease was brokered through the man of affairs of the owner."

Heh. Probably the same Fury "man of affairs" who brokered hers. Or another Fury. Then again, perhaps the almighty Furys did not own all the land.

"Is he always dressed like that?" Holly asked. "Like he's in mourning? *Is* he in mourning?"

Calliope paused. She never thought of that. "I don't know, honestly."

"Holly," Violet chastised. "He's standing right there."

"I know," the woman said sweetly. "He's been standing there like a statue for *some* time without uttering a word." She smiled at

Calliope, her voice dropping to a whisper. "And his gaze follows you like a shadow."

Really? "I'm not moving."

"But it would if you moved."

Calliope shook her head, chuckling. "Ladies, may I remind you that my shop was broken into?"

Maxen, for his part, said absolutely nothing even though he must have heard most of their conversation, if not all. But she did feel his amusement, if that were at all possible from the man, in his silence.

"My shop is set to open in the next few days. Should I postpone?" Violet asked.

"No!" Holly said vehemently. "We should not let something like this stop you."

Calliope nodded. "Just be a bit more vigilant."

Violet reached out and squeezed her hand. "You don't have to go through this alone, you know. If you need anything at all, supplies, extra hands, cake, you can always come to me."

Something soft blossomed inside her.

"Oh!" Holly perked up. "And I've just received a fresh delivery of lemon tarts. You simply must come by for tea this afternoon. It will do wonders for your nerves."

"I appreciate that, truly," Calliope said, though she wasn't quite sure she'd feel at ease anywhere just yet. Her shop was meant to be her sanctuary, and it had been violated. And she wouldn't be at ease until they discovered why. "But I shall pass this time."

"You're certain you don't need any help?" Violet asked. "Anything at all?"

She shook her head. Nothing they could provide. In fact, she'd rather not take the chance of placing them in any danger.

Their attention flicked past her shoulder again.

Calliope turned, and locked eyes with a hot stare. Maxen uncrossed his arms and pushed off the shelf, moving toward her like something carved from shadow. The workers all straightened the moment he did, and the hammering paused mid-stroke.

She wondered if she could ever command such attention one day. That would be quite marvelous.

A man stepped up to Maxen, jolting her back to the present. "I have the additional lock you ordered, sir."

Calliope glanced at Maxen, who offered, "You can never be too careful."

"Oh," she murmured. "Thank you."

His gaze held hers for a moment even more breathtaking than any other before. "No one's getting in again," he said gruffly.

Lord, my heart.

He turned to leave without another word, striding through the mess and out the door.

What on earth . . .? Where was he going?

Violet let out a sigh. "Well, that was something."

"What was?" Calliope asked, trying to ignore how her pulse quickened.

"That," Violet said, eyes still fixed on the door. "The way he looked at you. Like you are a treasure of unfathomable value."

"Nonsense." Had he?

"Your landlord is quite protective," Holly pointed out, still fanning her face.

Calliope didn't know what to say to that. Perhaps. Perhaps not. If they knew the full truth, they might see matters in another light. The word *spy* had been circled, for Saints' sake! She turned back to the chaos of her shop, suddenly very aware of how much had changed in the span of a single night.

"Come," Violet said gently. "Let's help you sweep up a bit. We have a bit of time on our hands."

Holly grinned. "I love a good sweeping."

Was this woman really a marchioness?

Calliope let out a soft laugh despite herself. Nothing about this was right. But perhaps with a mop, some friends, and a terrifyingly attentive landlord—she just might be.

MAXEN NEEDED AIR.

Lots of air.

He pressed his spine to the brick wall opposite the shop, the cool stone biting through his coat—useless against the heat simmering beneath his skin. He hadn't meant to listen to the women. But damned if their teasing hadn't hit a nerve. Two nerves. Perhaps three. The moment one had called him a gothic novel hero, he'd felt like a deuced villain. Lurking in corners, watching a woman he had no business watching.

But this wasn't just *watching*, was it?

It was wanting.

He scrubbed a hand over his jaw, ignoring the bite of stubble.

She twisted something inside him already knotted. She had merely looked at the mess in pain and he wanted nothing more than to rip the blackguard responsible apart and teach him the true cost of fear. The kind that persisted long after the blood was cleaned away.

He balled his fists, the leather that covered his hands pulling tight. He hadn't felt this out of control since . . . Christ, since his mother's death.

A shadow moved at the edge of his vision.

Saint.

Silent as ever.

"You've got news?" Maxen asked without turning.

His brother nodded.

Maxen straightened, instincts bracing. "Where are Drake and Reaper?" They were the usual barnacles on his arse.

"Caves."

Maxen frowned. That was not a casual errand. "Why?"

"Went looking for Serpent."

Maxen stiffened, a sense of dread prickling along his scalp. "He hasn't accounted for himself?"

"No."

Coldness settled in his blood. Serpent never failed to send word. Never. Something had gone very wrong.

Saint's expression gave nothing away, but the rigid line of his shoulders told Maxen he was just as unsettled.

"What's the news then?" Maxen asked, forcing his attention back to the matter at hand. "Our captive?"

Saint shook his head. "Laughing. Like a damn lunatic."

Christ. That was worse than silence. "Maybe I should be the next to visit."

"He's either mad or smart. Either way, he's not talking."

"You think he's playing for time?"

Saint shrugged. "But that's not all."

Maxen waited.

"Rollings."

The name landed like a thunderclap. Him again? "I thought we were done with him. We let him go with a warning."

"Knight trailed him to the post office and," he reached into his coat and withdrew a letter, seal already cracked, "intercepted this. It's addressed to John Fitz."

Calliope's solicitor.

Maxen unfolded the thing and cursed. Then cursed again. Only one line scrawled there.

She's been exposed.

"Damn it." Damn it all to hell.

"Does this mean she's trouble?" Saint asked.

Devil take it and devil if he knew. "Could be many things." Exposed to danger. Exposed to them. "Where is Rollings now?"

"In the wind." Saint glanced toward the shop. "Might be connected to last night."

Maxen grunted. "I don't believe in coincidences." But. "She claims this was not because of her."

Saint didn't argue, but his silence said enough. If last night's invasion wasn't because of her, it could only be because of them, and that meant Calliope had been targeted because . . . she was his tenant? Had someone gotten the wrong idea? It couldn't be because of the gunpowder. No one except the brothers knew about that. The rumored treasure? The culprit of last night was no treasure hunter.

"Targeting her makes no sense," Maxen muttered. "She's not anything to us." The lie tasted bitter the moment it left his mouth.

His brother shrugged. "Doesn't mean they don't think she is with the way you've been acting."

Maxen froze. "She's not part of this world."

Saint didn't spare him. "She's in it now."

The words settled like a ton of bricks.

Calliope Turner had walked into their territory, their turf, with secrets, a dog, and no knowledge of who she'd rented from. He wanted the situation to stay that way until her lease was up. Until she was gone. He didn't want her in this world.

But his enemies clearly didn't care what he wanted.

"Do you have eyes on Peregrine?"

"Dagger."

Maxen raked a hand through his hair. "Get word to Knight. Tell him to find Rollings but not engage. If Serpent is missing, we've got a bigger problem."

Saint nodded.

"And Saint?"

His brother paused, looked at him.

"Keep out of trouble."

Saint's eyes flicked back to the shop. "That may no longer be possible."

Maxen bit down on his jaw. "Be careful anyway."

Saint gave a single nod. "She's something different, isn't she?"

Maxen shot him a hard look.

"You've been watching her."

Why was every damn brother of his saying that? "I watch everything in Brighton."

"She's not Brighton."

"Don't make me beat your arse." Maxen turned his gaze toward the shop, toward the faint silhouette of Calliope moving inside, conversing with the women. The dog was stationed near the door now, ears twitching like he sensed the gathering storm outside. "Do you know those women?" Maxen asked.

Saint looked over. "No."

"I believe one of them has a shop nearby. One of ours?" Little here was not theirs, but it was possible.

"I could find out."

"Get Dagger on it when he returns. This whole lease debacle is his fault, and if this is another slip, I'm going to throttle him."

"Done."

"We need to locate Serpent," he said. "That takes priority."

Saint nodded once. "I'll head to the caves."

"No. Let Drake and Reaper handle that for now. Someone needs to man the tavern. Whoever is behind this might want us scattered. But send a runner to dig up everything they can on John Fitz. Quietly. If someone knows Calliope's background, it should be him."

"If there are traps . . ."

Maxen met his brother's gaze. "Then we'll be the ones to spring them."

Saint gave a rare smile—sharp and humorless. "Very well."

He turned to go, but Maxen called after him. "If Rollings or Peregrine so much as twitches wrong, I want to know."

Saint tipped his cap then vanished down the street.

Maxen turned the paper over in his hand before crumbling it in his fist.

Exposed . . .

In their world, that single sentence might get a person killed. Damn Rollings. He'd tried hard to convince them she had no part in his shady dealings. Then, who, exactly was John Fitz? More than a solicitor? More to Calliope? He'd seen enough cryptic messages in his life to know this one wasn't a bluff. Rollings wanted Fitz to act. And act fast.

So Calliope could run?

So she could hide?

If he were a better man, he'd allow it. He was not.

He smoothed the letter and folded it again, sliding damning missive into his inner pocket. His hands were steady, though every muscle in his body quivered with the urge to strike first and ask questions never.

She might be his enemy yet.

God help them both if that were the case. But then, better men had fallen to less.

Chapter Ten

CALLIOPE FACED A rather disturbing dilemma.

Two, if she counted the door she stood before.

Fury's. The word loomed above her in bold, slashing strokes, as though the very paint had been laid down with a snarl. Stars, it was only a door, only a building, and yet the word alone had been enough to stir up dilemma one—the Maxen-shaped one.

The mess in her shop had been cleared, floors scrubbed clean, and the new door practically glowed in its newness. But that wasn't the dilemma. The dilemma wasn't even rational. It was that . . .

Urhg.

She had no reason to stay next door.

No excuse to stick to Maxen Fury's side. Which meant, of course, she would be alone tonight. Upstairs. In the dark. In the same place she'd been when a stranger had broken in. Since using his bed again was out of the question, she told herself she would be fine. The intruder had been caught. There were new locks now, reinforced windows, *and* she still had Prince.

But there was one thought she hadn't dared let herself think until now.

What if the person behind the intruder *was* Duvessa?

The moment she allowed the question to surface, the possibility latched on. Cold. Relentless. Petrifying. She hadn't run all this way only for her past to follow. Quite frankly, if she were being absolutely honest with herself, she didn't believe she'd gained enough of a foothold, enough confidence, to stand her ground against her stepmother.

Which in itself was rather disappointing.

And then had come the summons. Delivered by a boy no older than twelve, a folded note with no signature.

Miss Turner, please meet me at Fury's at seven o'clock.

The request still made her skin crawl.

So ominous.

And *Fury's?*

This establishment must belong to Maxen or one of his brothers. However, this missive could not be from any of them. No, Maxen and his brood weren't the type to send over notes. They didn't summon. They collected. There was only one man who might send such a thing, and who also had a similar scrawl.

Mr. Rollings.

Fie. What was she to do? Her heart told her not to go. Her brain shouted the same. After all, nothing good had come of the last time she'd followed such a request. However . . .

She wanted answers.

Which was why Calliope had once again ventured out dressed as a lad—the same garments she'd worn the night she'd fled the scene of Mr. Rollings's . . . misfortune. Not smart. Not safe. But not entirely reckless either. After all, it was early evening, and it was public. People were inside. Light from candles glowed from the windows. She harbored no illusions that she passed for a boy, but the clothing was serviceable, unencumbered. It allowed her to move quickly, to melt into the edges of the street rather than announce herself as a woman strolling around in the dark.

She squared her shoulders, pushed open the door, and stepped inside.

The smell pressed against her first. Not of drink or smoke, but of absence—like her father's study after he passed away, when his presence could no longer be found, yet the scent of him still faintly clung to his chair. The memory of herself curled in that very chair flashed in her mind.

How odd that it should resurface here.

Her gaze swept the room.

The tavern was all but empty—except for four men. One behind the bar, drying a glass with a rag, his sleeves rolled up to his elbows. A second had dragged a chair close to the counter and sprawled there as if the spot belonged to him, legs stretched out and crossed at his ankles. A third slouched in a far corner, his coat open, daggers visible along the inside cut. The fourth man across from him . . .

All had grim faces. Unsmiling. Watchful.

And all their focus turned to her the moment she entered.

A chill seized her.

Every single instinct demanded she turn and run. Who was she to deny that warning? Calliope spun toward the door. This was a mistake. A huge, colossal, dreadful mistake—

"Well, good day, little mouse."

The voice curled around her nerves like a snare of thorns.

She froze. *Mouse?*

Slowly, Calliope turned. Was this the man from last night? Maxen's man? The one who carelessly used the word *spy?*

He grinned at her from ear to ear, pushing to his feet from his spot at the table, a coin moving over his knuckles. "What brings you to our humble lair this time of night?"

Her gaze couldn't help but jump between that smile, the scar that slashed his brow, and the wicked flash in his eyes. Now that she took in him, his companions, the place itself, the tavern bore the unmistakable feel of a *lair*. The space reminded Calliope of a bit of the attic where she spent much of her time as a girl. Although that place was used to lock her away at times, that cramped room had become a refuge of sorts, even when the door locked shut.

"I am meeting someone."

His smile turned wolfish. *"Here?"*

Her mouth dried. *Where are you. Mr. Rollings?* "Yes, here."

The man arched a brow. "Is that so? Who would you be meeting, then, little mouse?"

She lifted her chin, challenging, "Is that any of your business, sir?"

"Of course. This is not just any tavern where people can meet."

Right. This was a lair. "Is this tavern open to business?"

"Open, yes, to people who have business with us. Do you have business with us, little mouse?"

"I am *not* a mouse." And she didn't have business with anyone present. But Mr. Rollings might? But why lure her here? Unless he wanted her to walk into this situation . . . which would be beyond disturbing. Stars, she should feel fear, concern, downright panic, but instead, all she felt was that same crackle beneath her skin she'd felt while slipping out of her old house without being caught.

No. This was most certainly not the work of Duvessa. But that begged the question. Who?

Her gaze flicked between the men staring at her.

Unmoving.

Expressionless.

Like gargoyles carved from stone. Well, except for Mr. Grin over here.

"See something interesting?" Mr. Grin asked.

"Friends of yours?" she countered, gaze drifted over the other men present again.

A chuckle. "Something like that."

On second glance, they all did look similar. Familiar.

All dressed in black.

All with dark hair.

All with eyes like ink—deep and shadowed and far too knowing.

Like they could be—

Furys.

Her breath locked.

They had to be. The resemblance was so uncanny she didn't know why she didn't notice the similarities from the start. They each resembled him in one form or another. There was a reflection of Maxen in each man.

Fury's.

Indeed.

A family tavern.

She swept the place with a renewed understanding. Cold. No fire crackled to heat up the room. No other people from about town. No liveliness here. Maxen's quarters came to mind.

Another lair, she supposed.

And while nothing about this place felt safe, nothing about their presence felt threatening either.

"You're Maxen's brothers."

He laughed. "That we are, little mouse."

"Did you send me a note to meet here?" she asked the man.

"Little mouse, I never send notes." He cocked his head. "With or without a note, you shouldn't come alone to a place like this."

Calliope jutted out her chin defiantly. "I can handle myself." She could run really, really fast.

"Is that so?" He raked his gaze over her too knowingly.

"I'm sure whoever asked to meet here has their reasons. However, I hate to intrude on your lair—"

"You're not."

Hah. "So I'll be on my way."

"But you just got here." His voice dropped to a purr.

Calliope's hand twitched near her side. She'd once again forgotten to add her pistol to her outfit. "That doesn't mean I can't leave."

The man's smile turned into a smirk, and he shared a look with the man at the bar. "Did you really get a note to meet you here or were you just curious?"

"I'm *not* a spy."

"Interesting that this is the first thing your pretty little head jumps to."

Urgh! What an annoying man. "You accused me of that last night, too."

He tipped his head thoughtfully. "Did I?"

She narrowed her eyes, crossing her arms. "And I'm not in the habit of wandering into strange places out of curiosity."

"Well, from where I stand, you are either fiercely brave or wildly foolish."

"I assure you, I am both."

At that, one of the other men—one still seated lazily—let out a dry chuckle. Well, just a short one, but the sound scraped down her nerves like a match struck too close to her skin. How diabolical!

"That you may just be," the man behind the bar said flatly.

"You said you didn't send a note," Calliope pointed out to man before her. "What about one of them?"

"They didn't either," came the matter-of-fact response. "No one in their right mind would ask you to meet them here."

Not even Mr. Rollings?

But she couldn't ask that, and that in itself made her pause. Mr. Rollings would never ask her to meet here, would he? He'd have come to her, or given how his interaction with her landlord had transpired, meet her somewhere else. Given their relationship, despite that one request to meet outside, she didn't think he would purposefully place her under the attention from these men.

She knew it for certain then.

This was the doing of someone else. But why her? She'd done nothing wrong. She only had one enemy—family. This must have something to do with Maxen. But what, and how, she couldn't begin to imagine.

Something was most decidedly afoot.

A thought struck her.

He didn't know she was here.

And for the first time since stepping through that door, Calliope felt something entirely different curl through her belly.

Anticipation.

The man was a criminal, yes. Yet ever since she'd learned Mr. Rollings had survived, and that Maxen had caught the intruder, she no longer saw him as the villain who prowled the shadows. Perhaps he was sullen, brooding, impossible, but he did not seem bad. Wicked men did not trouble themselves with the safety of others, did they? Sleep on the floor for them? Make their heart flutter for them?

Hah, Calliope. That's just you!

She let out a little cough and gave the man before her, her best arched brow. "I suppose they are not in their right mind, then. That being said, are you going to offer me something to drink or not?"

MAXEN STALKED UP to Fury's in a rare mood. The kind between fluster and foul. The worst kind. He'd only felt this way once before, nineteen years ago, the day his mother had perished.

Christ.

Don't think about that. That . . .

He cursed.

Calliope was not his mother.

However, he had left for only a few hours to take care of some business, and when he'd returned, her shop had been closed. Very well. But he had knocked. And knocked. And finally, slipped his key into the lock to go and hunt her down. Moral? No. But he wasn't in the moral business. He hadn't entered her lodgings upstairs, though, unlike last time. Something her innocent head hadn't thought to question.

He had knocked.

But no Calliope.

Prince, yes, sniffing at the door, but no owner. Damn it. The clock would be striking seven in the evening. Where would she have gone? He pushed through their tavern door with a scowl. Reaper had a network of little urchins all around Brighton. They'd find her in an hour. But how the hell had she slipped away without *him* being notified?

"Reaper, I need you to—" Maxen stopped dead in his tracks.

There she was.

Calliope Turner.

Standing at the bar.

In *his* damn tavern.

At the center of his world.

She turned as if she'd *felt* him before she heard him, her eyes widening the smallest fraction.

But dear Christ.

Breeches hugged her shapely legs like she'd been born for them. His gaze skipped to the grey cap that failed to hide her hair, several curls spilling free, refusing to be tamed. But it was the ale she'd taken a sip from, leaving her lips glistening, that struck low, hard, and straight at his cock.

Not even her boot had clobbered this hard.

And every one of his brothers present had their eyes on her. Not one of them seemed to have attempted to stop whatever she was up to here. No, they had served her ale.

Did he even bloody exist?

And Calliope? She looked pleased. No. More than that.

She looked *comfortable*.

"What," he bit out, stepping forward, "in God's name are you doing here? And what in God's name are you wearing?"

She grinned up at him. "Maxen."

The sound of his name on her lips, those *glistening* lips, stoked more heat in his loins. He resisted the urge to shift uncomfortably. Damn it. She had no right to look unbothered while he had no patience for this burn in his body. He stalked over to her. "I asked you a question."

"I'm here on a matter of business."

"In *that*?" He gestured to her ensemble.

She glanced down at said ensemble before lifting her far too innocent gaze back to him. "It's my business guise."

It was meant to drive him insane. "Damn reckless." He shrugged out of his coat and draped it over her shoulders. "And it's cold."

Reaper snorted.

Maxen shot him a warning look. "People don't do business here except with us."

She nodded, taking a slow sip of ale, and damn if he couldn't help but follow way she tipped her glass, the way her throat worked as she swallowed, the way her tongue darted out to chase the last drop.

He must have lost his reason entirely.

"So your brother told me," she murmured as she lowered the mug.

"We asked her, too," Reaper said. "But so far, we haven't been able to get a serious answer from her."

"I went to your shop," Maxen said. "You were gone."

She cocked her head, and the smallest smile curved her lips. "Would you believe me if I said I was summoned here?"

Summoned? No. "Were you?"

"I received a request to meet here. I thought it might be," she paused for a breath before saying, "Mr. Rollings. I believe you may be acquainted with him."

Rollings? Impossible. But still, "You came here thinking Rollings would be waiting?" He could throttle her for her recklessness.

Reaper chuckled. "How rare to see you in such a state of agitation, *frère*."

Maxen kept his attention locked on Calliope, continuing to ignore that arse he called a brother. "Who delivered the note?"

"A boy. I didn't recognize him."

That could be one in hundreds. "What did he look like?"

"Twelve, maybe younger. Brown hair. Cap too big for his head. A face full of freckles."

That narrowed it down to exactly still one in hundreds. Maxen's jaw ticked. He turned to Reaper. "Any of yours assigned to keep an eye on her?"

Reaper shook his head. "Didn't think she'd need eyes with you casting a long shadows and darkening doorways playing landlord, practically haunting the place."

Calliope choked on her ale.

"She does now," Maxen bit out, a flush spreading to the tips of his ears, cursing his brother to perdition.

Calliope's brows lifted, placing her glass on the bar. "What's going on? I'm right here, you know."

"Exactly," Maxen growled. "*Here.* Dressed like that. In the one place no outsider has any business being, let alone unarmed."

"I'm not unarmed." She crossed her arms. "I brought my wits."

"She brought her wits," Reaper echoed, laughing into his drink. "I'm starting to like her more than you, *frère.*"

"This isn't amusing," Maxen snarled. At least the others had the foresight to keep their mouths shut.

Reaper flicked a coin over his knuckles. "Didn't say it was."

Maxen looked to Dagger. Honestly, he just needed to catch a breath from the sight of Calliope wrapped in his coat. "Any news on Serpent yet? Where is Drake?"

His brother's face hardened. "No word. Serpent seems to be missing. We were just about to discuss our next course of action when she arrived. Drake should circle back any moment."

"Someone went missing?" Calliope exclaimed, aghast.

"Our brother," Reaper said darkly. "And someone will pay dearly if he doesn't show face soon."

"*Oh.*"

"This is no longer a trivial matter. We need to tighten the ship." He glanced at Calliope. "That means you, too."

"Me? What exactly does tightening the ship mean?"

"It means," Reaper spoke first. "Welcome aboard the Fury ship. You are moving in."

"What?" If her eyes had been wide before, they were practically full moons now. "Why me?"

"You might have become a target to get to us." As much as he loathed admitting the truth, he refused to deny the severity of the note she'd received.

Someone was playing with them.

"What us?" Knight muttered from behind the bar. *"You."*

She shook her head. "A target? That's absurd. Isn't it?"

He wished that were the case. "Whoever sent that note wanted you in here. Standing among us. They probably wanted to confirm how we would receive you." His voice dropped. "To question what you are to us."

Dagger grunted. "That's not the worst theory."

Saint, Knight, and Reaper, for once, remained silent.

Calliope's brows furrowed. "Oh? And what am I to you?"

"That's irrelevant. Someone is baiting us, and you stepped willingly into their trap."

"I didn't know it was a trap," she snapped. "I thought I was finally getting answers."

His gaze sharpened, hunting for any tell. "To what exactly?"

She clamped her mouth shut.

"What answers, Calliope?"

Her chin lifted a fraction. "And why should I tell you?"

"Because I'm asking nicely."

"This is *nicely?*" She scoffed, so did half his brothers, but she still said, "About you, if you must know. After I learned we share an acquaintance, I thought I'd ask if the opportunity arose."

That was nothing he didn't know. Nothing Rollings hadn't told them. Nothing suspicious on the surface. Beneath, suspicious as hell. Why else would she be curious about him if she didn't suspect their business?

Was she the woman of that night with Rollings or not? He

had yet to broaden his search for the owner of the slipper beyond her, his gut still pointing to this little tenant enjoying a pint in *his* tavern.

"You could have just asked me."

One brow ticked upward. "I doubt you'd tell me all I want to know."

"Sharp as a blade, this one," Reaper drawled. "And what do you want to know?"

She bit her lip, glanced at each of his brothers before meeting his gaze again. "Whether you all are the beasts of Brighton."

Bloody Rollings.

"Beasts?" Reaper chuckled. "Could we consider ourselves beasts?"

Saint grunted.

"So, Maxen, I ask again, what *am* I to you? Because I assure you, I don't find the answer to that irrelevant at all."

Maxen opened his mouth, closed it. Her words blazed with damn danger. Because the truth wasn't safe. Not for her. Not for him. And not in this world where blood covered his hands and death was just a question of time.

So he didn't answer.

Couldn't.

She'd just asked the one question he'd been shoving into the dark where it couldn't touch him for a long, long time.

Chapter Eleven

W HAT DID YOU *expect him to answer, Calliope?*
Anything. But instead, he stood across from her like a storm just barely contained, jaw locked, shoulders tight, staring at her, eyes dark and fathomless, as though she'd asked him to lay bare every scar he'd ever hidden. His silence struck like a rebuke.

She hadn't even meant to press.

At first, the question had just slipped out. Foolish. Brazen. Dangerous. A question that, once spoken, begged to be answered. Even the fact that she might have been used for something nefarious fell short beside the answer.

She wished she could look away. Pretend the answer didn't matter.

But she knew better.

The answer mattered a great deal.

Stars, even if he told her she was his *tenant*, that would be something. That was all she needed. Anything but that she was trouble. A hindrance. A nuisance. And perhaps she was foolish to give sentiment to the question, but she couldn't help herself. Foolish, she knew. Irrational, she understood. Yet, done, nonetheless. His lack of response, however, was telling enough.

Urgh. She wished the topic had never surfaced. She hated how the silence wedged itself in her head. His lack of answer struck her with a shocking truth.

Maxen wasn't just a landlord.

He wasn't just a beast who ruled this town.

He wasn't just danger itself.

He was where she felt most secure. The one place her fears seemed to hush. He ruled shadows, yes, but with him, she wasn't afraid of the dark.

And she . . .

She ruled nothing. Only a tiny shop. She fled. She hid. She could never measure up to this man. Never stand equal to him. Even now, with her carefully planned, peaceful life in shambles, she was being hidden away here in the "ship." She would laugh at the irony if she didn't want to scream at the injustice.

Calliope changed the subject before she was tempted to swing another boot at him. "And what if I don't wish to stay here?"

Maxen said nothing. Didn't move. Didn't so much as blink at her.

The whole room seemed to take on a new hush.

Right, then. She simply didn't have a choice. How long had her freedom lasted? Three months? Just a bit more?

"My hound . . ."

"I'll have Reaper retrieve him and your belongings."

Reaper groaned. "Why me? You know how I feel about dogs. They scare me."

"Because you have the biggest mouth," Maxen snapped.

Calliope slipped his coat from her shoulders and set it over the chair. "I'll go with your brother."

"No." Final.

"Yes," she challenged back. "I don't want anyone rifling through my drawers." Stars. Her slipper! She'd almost completely forgotten about the thing! She might have been brave enough to reveal her connection with Mr. Rollings, but not that she was the woman who'd lost the slipper. They had already suspected her to be a spy at one point. What would they suspect next if they discovered the truth?

Hah! Finding the slipper would serve him right, though!

"Then I'll accompany you," Maxen announced.

"No need. I'd rather your brother accompany me." She arched a brow. "Unless you have a problem with not supervising."

The eyes that bore into her flashed before he gave a curt nod.

She stepped past him—close enough that her shoulder brushed his—and forced herself to keep walking. The nerves along her scalp prickled. How could it hurt to breathe so much? She didn't even look to see if his brother, Reaper, followed. But she could feel all their eyes on her. They burned like a hot poker, making her want to escape all the more.

Her hand reached for the doorknob.

"Calliope."

Her name, a clipped command.

She stopped but didn't turn around.

His voice came again, quieter now. Rougher. "Don't take too long packing."

Oh, I won't.

She strode from the cursed place.

Seconds later, Reaper joined at her side, his broodiness palpable. Well, hers should be, too. She'd certainly learned a valuable lesson tonight—ignore requests to meet at suspect places. One would have thought she'd have learned this lesson the first time. Tonight, however, had been an excellent reminder. She could not afford to lose focus on her dream. Only disappointing things happened when she did.

"You're trouble," the brother at her side suddenly said.

She glanced at him.

"You're careless, too curious by half, and seem incapable of leaving things well enough alone. A bad combination in our world."

Calliope averted her gaze. So, in the end, she was all the things she hadn't wanted to be. Trouble. A hindrance. A nuisance.

Was this her curse?

Maxen hadn't outright called her a burden—nor had his brothers, for that matter—but Calliope could read between the lines. Read between faces, pursed lips, stiff posture, and all that lay unsaid.

"Just who are you lot?" she muttered. Weren't they the ones who were supposed to be trouble, hindrances, and nuisances? How was *she* once again the one to be made to feel this way?

"You said it yourself. We are the beasts of Brighton."

"I heard that from someone else. I want to hear it from you."

"That, little mouse, you're safer not knowing."

"Am I?" She wasn't so sure about that anymore.

"Trust me, you are."

Trust him? Heh! She trusted that he would obey his brother, but not much else. The only person she might ever rely upon, in the end, was herself. She alone was responsible for her life. Her happiness. Her future.

Calliope made a decision then.

She had not fled one cage merely to be thrust into another. Stars, no. She had come here to vanish, to live her small dream of freedom, not to be ensnared afresh. Given no choice in the matter.

You're already ensnared, Calliope . . .

No, she refused to believe that.

They entered the shop in silence. Delay was not an option. Without a word, she led him up the stairs. Her living quarters were dark except for the natural light of the moon spilling through the windows. Prince trotted over to greet her excitedly when they entered, and she patted his head to appease him, her gaze shifting to her bedroom.

Thank stars she had slipped her pistol beneath her pillow.

She headed directly for the bed.

"Like my brother said," he called after her, footsteps soon following to the doorway of her chamber, "gather your belongings quickly so we can return."

Prince trotted over curiously as she gripped the pistol in both hands. What did she do now? Ah, this was so much harder than how she imagined in her mind! Drawing in a deep breath, she remained with her back to him and nodded at the chair by the window. "There."

He didn't question her, merely strode over. "What's here?"

Calliope turned and leveled the pistol straight at his chest.

He glanced over his shoulder and froze, turning slowly back to face her, and for the first time since they'd met, he looked utterly, dangerously solemn. All the good nature left his gaze, leaving only ice-cold instinct. *There* was the beast. The change confirmed she'd made the right decision.

"I'm afraid I have other plans tonight."

THE MOMENT THE door shut behind Reaper, Maxen had set after them, only to be stopped by Dagger's low drawl.

"I wouldn't."

He froze mid-stride and turned to glare at his brother. "Why the devil not?"

Dagger lounged back, idly swirling his glass. "Just give the woman some space. Nothing will happen to her with Reaper there."

Space? What did damn space have to do with anything? "She won't even know I'm following."

"But *he* will."

Damn it.

Maxen clenched his fists, directing his glare at his coat she'd left behind. Dagger was right. If he followed now, Reaper would never let him hear the end of his mockery, which meant she would hear of his lapse, too—and accuse him of all manner of things far from the truth. And that was how far he'd fallen into this wretched unsettlement.

"You should've just answered her," Knight said.

"And said *what*, exactly?" Maxen growled. "What the devil is there to say?"

"Anything but *nothing*," Saint said quietly. "Even I know that."

His jaw locked so tight his teeth ached. He needed to move. Needed to do something. Anything. Waiting never suited him. Not in situations where his whole body commanded him to act. Especially now that Saint's words wrapped around him like damn stinging nettles.

Anything but nothing.

He simply hadn't known how to speak the answer to that question.

Who was she to him?

She was his tenant. His responsibility. His puzzle. His—confound it. There was the knot. Right bloody there. The reason she'd chosen his brother over him to go with her. And now she was out there, dressed in those intoxicating trousers, defenseless, *mostly*, and clever enough to run circles around Reaper if she wanted to. And she might want to.

Unease burrowed in his gut.

He grabbed his coat from the chair and shrugged it on.

"Maxen," Dagger warned again. "Don't do something you'll regret."

He scowled. "I'm not following her."

"Since when do we lie to each other?"

He cast his brother a dark look. "I'm not bloody lying."

Dagger arched a brow, shoving to his feet. "Where are you going, then?"

"Rooftop."

"So you *are* following her."

Maxen gave his brother a grim smile. "No. I'm watching for her. There's a damn difference."

"I'll join you," Knight spoke up.

Saint and Dagger nodded their agreement.

Fine. He had barnacles.

Maxen didn't wait. He stalked toward the back, shouldered through the door, and cut left into the narrow corridor. Past the storeroom, through another door, and up the iron stairs. He took them two at a time, impatient. He'd climbed them a thousand times, usually with a clear head and a single purpose. Tonight, his thoughts were scattered, circling one name that refused to let him go.

The space widened as he emerged onto Fury's rooftop. The night lay unnaturally quiet, broken only by the distant wash of the waves along the shoreline. He strode over to the ledge, the Lanes unfurling beneath him like a sleeping beast.

Beast . . .

Much like him, no?

Maxen crouched on the edge, watching for movement, the cold slowly creeping into his bones. He could make out the rooflines along her street, but the street itself lay hidden from view.

He shouldn't have let her go. Had made an error shrugging off her question as irrelevant the first time. She clearly believed otherwise. If only he could read her mind to know what answer she wanted from him. He grunted. If only life were sweet dreams and clear blue skies.

Bloody fanciful.

Dagger crouched beside him. "I'm worried about Serpent," his brother admitted. "And you, for that matter, but Serpent takes precedence since his whole person is missing. You're just missing your head."

Knight and Saint echoed their agreement.

Maxen's face darkened. "We'll find him."

Dagger gave a curt nod. "I know. I'm just worried he won't be alive when we do."

Maxen didn't say anything to that. Whoever was behind these little schemes was toying with them, not killing them. At least not yet. However, they had resorted to using Calliope.

That was unacceptable.

Everything was going to hell at once. That was the main reason he'd decided to lock things down and tighten the ship. Another was that his mind always kept circling back to *her*, a growing weakness, and he wanted to, *needed to*, keep her close.

"She's not what we expected," Knight said from his other side.

"She's something," Maxen muttered. "More than I can make sense of."

Saint hunched down in the corner farthest from them. "I'm happy for you."

"What the bloody hell does that mean?" Maxen snapped.

"He means you trail," Dagger pointed out. "You hover. You watch. You had her sleep at one of your dens. In your bed. When have we ever let women into our private rooms?"

"I had no other choice." Should he have left her to her own devices? Out of the question. Beyond imagining. In no realm of possibility.

"There is always another choice," Knight said.

Maxen clenched his hands a few times. Fine. He did do all those things. Did his brothers have to be on his arse about it? "Have we learned anything about John Fitz?"

Dagger shook his head. "Drake has sent inquiries to London."

Still too many unknowns.

He hated unknowns.

"I shouldn't have let her go alone," Maxen muttered, jaw clenching. Reaper's "Why me?" came to haunt him in that moment. Yes, why did he have to send that arse? *He* should have taken responsibility for her belongings. She was, after all, his responsibility. Sending another man felt efficient in theory. In practice, the whole thing tasted like abdication.

"She's not alone," Dagger said.

No, she wasn't.

But that didn't bring him any damn comfort.

Not when the woman who had turned him inside out had disappeared from his view. Not when so many rows of buildings blocked his view, and not when all he could do was wait. His eyes narrowed into the distance.

"Something's not right." Maxen rose to his feet. He knew it as surely as he knew the sky above him was black.

"Are you certain?" Dagger asked.

"Yes."

Knight glanced over. "She's a woman. She's angry. That might be what's not right."

No, this was something else. Something in the air.

His gut was hollowing in warning.

Maxen spun on his heel and strode to the door. They needed to go. Now.

Chapter Twelve

CALLIOPE TIGHTENED HER grip on the pistol.

Her hands were steady. Her heart was not.

"You had that pistol on you the entire time?" Reaper asked, the faintest edge of admiration in his voice, his mask of carefree ruffian having once again slipped into place. Rather admirable, if one stopped to think about the nerve involved.

Calliope was beginning to understand.

They all wore masks. Each and every one of them. Even Maxen.

Even her.

"Perhaps I did, perhaps I didn't," she answered vaguely. They probably kept their weapons in much more sophisticated places than beneath a pillow. They probably didn't forget them when they left home either.

His lips quirked. "Cunning wench. Why didn't you pull your pistol out earlier when I approached you?"

"You mean when you goaded me? I was outnumbered. I choose my battles more wisely than that." True enough. She tipped her chin to the chair. "Sit."

He gave a low chuckle, but the humor didn't reach his eyes. He also didn't argue. He moved, slowly, never taking his eyes off her, as he settled into the chair.

"What are you going to do next, little mouse?"

She edged to her bed, pistol steady, bending to pull out a travel case and shoving it open. A neat coil of rope rested inside, bought for laundry and odd jobs. Who would have thought she'd use it to tie up a man? Hopefully there was enough.

She tossed the rope to him.

"Tie yourself to the chair. You understand?"

He caught the bindings easily, eyeing her the entire time. "I do. You plan to run away, then?"

"I plan to leave," she corrected. "Which is not the same thing."

"And you think my brother won't hunt you down the moment he realizes you're gone?"

"Why would he hunt me down?" She was doing him a favor by removing herself from whatever nightmare was circling them.

"You have much to learn about men, little mouse," Reaper said looping the rope around his chest and the chair as she wanted.

"I know enough."

"Do you? I rather doubt that. But you do seem to possess the sort of fire that burns holes through cold men."

Was he mocking her? "You all like to believe you're so very cold. But you're ruled by loyalty, are you not? By blood. Seems all very hot to me. And that's why you won't try to stop me from leaving."

His gaze sharpened. "I fail to see your reasoning."

"It's better for your brother if I disappear," Calliope said calmly, stepping up to the man, considering how to bind him from here. He observed her like a hawk but stayed seated. Stayed loosely bound. "Don't move. I'm going to secure you now, and I don't want to use my pistol on you. However, one word from me, and Prince sinks his teeth in a region you'd very much like to keep intact."

The air around him froze.

Well, look at that. See? She was a fast learner.

His expression didn't change, but his gaze flicked toward Prince sticking close to her feet, staring at him, ears twitching as if he understood every word. Calliope didn't give him time to reconsider. She moved quickly, efficiently, knotting the rope tight around his chest and the arms of the chair, then looping the binding around the legs twice more for good measure. A good purchase, if she had to say so herself.

She stepped back, breath slightly unsteady.

She was doing this, then.

Leaving.

Leaving everything behind.

Mr. Fitz would help her retrieve her belongings and send them along to where she next decided to settle.

"Look at you, little mouse. You've a talent with rope. Where did you learn such a *skill*?"

She didn't know if he was being dry or serious, but she smiled sweetly. "I guess you'll have plenty of time to wonder."

"The time will be less than you think."

Calliope backed toward the wardrobe where she quickly retrieved her valise. The contents weren't much—a change of clothes, a purse with coins, and some books. The exact bag she'd prepared for fleeing her old house. She had hoped she would never have need for this one, but as long as Duvessa was in search of her, she had to be prepared.

Thank stars she was.

Her gaze locked on one lone shoe.

Ah.

The slipper that started it all. Should she take the shoe with her? She hadn't been able to part with it before, but today she found she could. Let him find the thing. She would not see him— or any of them—again.

"Little mouse, you really think you're going to get far?"

Calliope sighed and turned to Maxen's brother and tucked the pistol in her valise. "Far enough."

"Alone?"

"Don't sound so skeptical. I have Prince."

"You are still alone."

"And what of being alone?" she asked. "I was alone here for three months before I met the likes of you."

"You still met the likes of me, didn't you?" He flashed her a grin. "But now you've no idea what you're stepping into."

"Perhaps, but I know what I'm stepping out of." She hated how her voice wavered slightly. "I will *never* be trapped again."

The beast's brows furrowed, drawing her gaze to his scar.

"You think we mean to cage you," he said without humor, cocking his head, studying her.

Calliope shrugged. "Trap. Cage. Tighten the ship. It's all the same."

"You're wrong about that. It's not all the same."

Perhaps she was wrong. But, "Let us agree to disagree on this score."

He simply gazed at her.

She clutched her valise tightly and crossed to the door, every step shadowed by those dark eyes of his. At the threshold, she paused. "Tell your brother whatever you want." She hesitated, but still added, "And that I'm sorry I was troublesome."

He gave a low chuckle. "Do not fool yourself into believing that running would make our world better. Running never makes anything better. Trust me, I know."

She shook her head. "I'm *leaving* while I still have a say in the matter, still have a chance."

He didn't respond, for a moment, she simply stood there, valise in hand, heart in confusion. She had not thought withdrawing from Brighton would feel quite like this. Both an ache and a release. Almost like her moment of departure was about to tear something vital apart.

Regret filled her.

Which was foolish, was it not? But it was also proof she had something to walk away from. So unlike her old home. That, at least, was something.

She cast one last glance at Reaper.

"I don't belong in your 'ship.'" Calliope said softly. "Goodbye, Mr. Fury."

She motioned for Prince, and the hound followed her out, the door closing between them with a final snap. She forced her steps forward, down the narrow passage, through the back exit, and into the dark that always seemed to wait for her—the dark she hated, and knew too well.

MAXEN SHOVED THE door to Calliope's shop open with such force the frame's hinges rattled.

"Calliope!"

No bloody answer.

He'd been right, and the silence only fed his urgency. He surged into motion, boots thundering up the stairs two at a time, heart pounding like war drums in his chest. He didn't pause. Didn't breathe. Didn't think.

He couldn't.

If he did, he'd remember the way she'd looked at him before walking out of Fury's. An expression he hadn't pieced together until he sprinted to her shop at full speed. Her look had been different from any other she'd given him before. One of finality. How the hell hadn't he recognized the glance? With each second that passed, the shape of her reaction became more and more clear.

He reached her living quarters in seconds and burst through, and finding no trace of her, strode straight for her chamber, ready to drag her back to Fury's, to demand why the devil she'd thought she could run from—

Maxen stopped.

Dead.

Reaper sat tied to a chair, arms and legs bound with a length of rope that, at first glance, looked haphazard as hell, yet was also far too competent for a mere shop owner.

"Ah, *frère*, you're finally here. I expected you sooner."

Maxen took in the room with a swift glance, cataloguing every detail in seconds. The wardrobe gaped wide. A pillow lay by the bed for her hound. A travel case—open, empty. And beneath it all, the faintest trace of sweetness.

She was gone.

Her hound was gone.

His growl was lower than usual. Menacing. "Where is she?"

Reaper sneered. "Left about five minutes ago."

Maxen's vision narrowed.

Not rage. First, disbelief. That she'd left. That she'd bound his brother to a chair, walked out, and not looked back. The thought hit him harder than any blow. He'd let her go. He'd let her leave with his brother. Hadn't stopped her. He'd stood there like a blasted fool. And for what? Because he hadn't wanted to let the bloody words past his tongue?

"Saint. Knight," Maxen barked over his shoulder.

"On it," Knight returned, already moving.

Reaper called after them, "She might have left through the back door."

Maxen crossed the room in two strides and grabbed his brother by his jacket. "You *let* her go?"

"Maxen," Dagger cautioned.

"Did I?" Reaper cocked his head mockingly. "Hard to stop a woman when she's got a pistol trained on you. Even harder when she threatens to set the dog on your—well, future bloodline."

"You think this is damn funny?" Maxen growled. "You could have disarmed her in a second."

Reaper raised his brows. "Her I could disarm, sure. The teeth of her hound, not so much. *Frère*. She is not our hostage."

Maxen let go of his brother, clenching and unclenching his leather covered fists until they hurt.

"Did she say anything?"

"Let me *think* . . ."

"*Reaper.*"

"Ah, I remember," the arse drawled. "Something about never wanting to be trapped again, having been alone all her life, alone in Brighton for three months, and sorry for being troublesome."

"She said a lot," Dagger muttered.

"Why the devil did she apologize for being troublesome?"

Reaper gave a half-hearted shrug. "Your mouse was leaving no matter what."

"This is what happens when you ignore a woman's questions," Dagger pitched in with a drawl.

"I bloody get it," Maxen snapped at his brothers. "Move on."

"Also," Reaper said. "Your little mouse said something about leaving while she still had a chance. Still had a choice."

Damnation.

Maxen's gaze caught on the wardrobe. Brows furrowing, he stalked over, bending over to carefully lift a very familiar slipper. The companion to the one he still had in his possession.

It was her all along.

Reaper cleared his throat pointedly, the chair scraping forward. "Will someone untie me, please?"

"No."

"Why the devil not?" Reaper demanded.

Dagger chuckled. "Isn't it shameful that you haven't been able to free yourself in the minutes between her leaving and our arrival?"

"How about I tie you up and you try escaping this travesty of looping?"

Dagger scoffed. "I'm not an idiot like you, you clout. Maxen? What do you want to do?"

Maxen clutched the slipper in his hand.

"You're not going after her, *frère*?" Reaper asked.

No.

Yes.

Not yet.

He needed to catch his faculties first.

Perhaps this outcome was better. Better for her. Better for him. Better for them all. Not because she was troublesome. Trouble, yes, but those were two different things. He'd rather keep that trouble where he could see it than have any unforeseen danger slip beyond his sight. The latter was far more troublesome.

Dagger shifted near the door. "You're not exactly the sit-back-and-let-it-be type, brother. I need to know what you're planning to do."

"She made her choice." He only still wrestled with his, torn between hunting her down or letting her escape him.

"She made a choice without understanding the scope of that choice," Dagger pointed out.

"Agreed," Reaper muttered, straining against the bindings. "You didn't give her a reason to stay."

Maxen's jaw flexed, his thumb stroking over the slipper. "And if I do? I drag her deeper into this world. Into danger. Into us. Into me?"

Dagger pushed off the doorframe. "She's already in our world, brother."

"He's just stubbornly refusing to acknowledge the truth, like stubbornly refusing to untie me."

"Reaper is right. You don't have to acknowledge the fact aloud, but don't lie to yourself. We don't lie."

Bloody hell. Since when was denial lying?

However, somewhere between their first and last meeting, he'd grown used to the idea of Calliope Turner in his life. Not as a mere tenant.

But as something else.

Something vital.

Indispensable.

Somewhere between her stubborn questions and that damned look of finality, she had settled herself beneath his skin. Maxen clamped down on his jaw. He should have answered her.

God help him, he should have answered her. The next time he saw her, he would. He rarely ever made the same mistake twice.

He slid the slipper into the inner pocket of his coat, sending a cold *do not ask* look when Dagger raised his brows. A better man would let her go. A better man wouldn't be selfish. But he not a better man.

He was a beast.

"Let's hunt."

Chapter Thirteen

CALLIOPE HURRIED THROUGH the Lanes of Brighton, Prince loping faithfully at her side, cold biting at her cheeks. Wind rose, whipping at the cloak she'd snatched up in her flight. She was only glad she'd left it draped forgotten over a box of candles in the first place. Her heart galloped like a runaway horse, her gaze darting from shadow to shadow. She didn't even know where she was going, where she could go. An inn, certainly, but one far enough away from the shop she'd pulled together with her own hands. Away from the life she'd tried to carve. Away from Maxen Fury and the madness she'd stumbled into.

She and Prince rounded a corner near the edge of the market district when a carriage pulled up beside them. The man from inside waved for her to stop. Calliope slowed instinctively, clutching her valise tighter. This was not her landlord or any of his brood.

The door creaked open.

"Miss Turner?" A voice, smooth and startled, carried down the street. "What a surprise."

Of all the men she could've run into tonight . . . "Oh, Mr. Peregrine."

His features shifted from curiosity to something almost like concern. "Are you all right?"

"I'm . . ." How to answer that?

"Are you in trouble? I can help if you are."

Prince growled. Calliope placed a hand on his head, reassuring him.

"I don't mean to pry," he glanced up and down the street, then back at her, "but it's not safe to walk about on your own, even with your hound and dressed like that. Let me offer you a ride."

Calliope really wanted to take him up on the offer. It was cold, night, and she wasn't certain how long her hostage would stay tied. "I'd hate to be trouble . . ."

"Nonsense." He stepped out and held the door wide open for her. "Where are you heading?"

Calliope hesitated. "I need to find lodgings for the night."

"Ah. You're in luck. I know an excellent place, and best of all, they take hounds as well."

Relieved, Calliope nodded. Honestly, if she didn't have a pistol tucked in her valise, she would never have agreed. The weapon, along with Prince, gave her just enough ease to accept his offer. "Then I shall rely on you just this once."

"Of course."

Prince hopped in first, and Calliope followed. The moment the wheels began to roll, she let herself exhale. Mr. Peregrine, who had settled across from her, rested a gloved hand casually on his knee. She couldn't help noticing the blunt difference in his soft, brown leather gloves and Maxen's dark, black ones. But then, these men were day and night, were they not? Even Mr. Peregrine's eyes were a soft brown and his hair fair.

Did all the men here dress to match their features?

How peculiar.

"You look pale," he said after a moment. "Are you sure there isn't anything amiss?"

He must know there was, or she wouldn't be looking for lodging this time of night. "I'm truly fine. There's no need to worry about me."

A soft sigh escaped him. "If you need help, Miss Turner, whatever it may be, I am at your disposal."

Trust me, Mr. Peregrine, you do not want me to ask for help. She would only prove troublesome yet again. "Well, thank you. I shall keep that in mind."

He inclined his head. "I heard an intruder broke into your shop."

Could she even be taken aback at this point? "Word travels fast."

"Indeed, though I'm not surprised. That shop has a rather interesting story."

"*Oh?*" Her brows lifted in spite of herself. *Hopeless, Calliope!*

He nodded. "Rumors of buried treasure."

Heh? Given the owner, such rumors shouldn't come as any form of shock, she supposed. However, "Treasure in a shop in the middle of Brighton?"

"You don't believe in pirates, treasures, smugglers, and loot?"

Well . . .

Dark eyes flashed in her mind.

Yes. She did. "It's not that I don't believe, but I've found keeping to my own business a much more prudent venture."

He chuckled. "Prudent you say."

Calliope arched a brow. "Are you not prudent, Mr. Peregrine?"

A low laugh this time. "I don't believe I possess even an ounce of prudence."

Calliope found herself returning his grin. "I don't suppose you do."

He leaned forward slightly, extending a hand toward Prince, who sniffed it with mild interest before accepting a brief pat. "I adore dogs, but my work doesn't allow me to keep any."

"That's a pity. Dogs are the best companions."

He agreed with a slight nod. "I travel too much."

"I see. That must be tiring." And disruptive, surely. Just look at her and Prince now. Displaced and unsettled. At the same time, she still recalled her thrill on the road between London and Brighton. She supposed there were advantages and disadvantages to both staying still and being on the move.

He studied her. "I can't tell whether you enjoy it or not—traveling?"

She rested a hand over Prince's body. "I haven't had much chance to travel in the past, though I doubt I'll do so in the future either."

"And here I believed all women liked to travel."

"I like home." Though she didn't have one. Hadn't had one since her father passed away. Urgh. The word alone was enough for her heart to sink into the soles of her feet.

"Seems to me," he said softly, "you've yet to find one."

She met Mr. Peregrine's gaze. "You do not mince words, do you? Is that a Brighton thing?"

He shrugged. "Perhaps it's simply a man thing."

She scoffed. "Certainly not a *gentle*man thing."

"Oh, Miss Turner,"—he flashed his teeth—"I am no gentleman."

Were it not for his amusement, she might have been alarmed. "I seem to have a knack for attracting rogues."

She had believed Brighton would be her home. The shop. Her candles. Prince. Morning walks on the beach, though she'd yet to do that. The only significant thing she'd ever accomplished in her life had been escaping her old house. Nothing had gone to plan after that. Was that the grand sum of her life's accomplishment? Just that one thing? Would she have to live her life always escaping one circumstance after the other?

But when she thought of home, truly thought of the meaning, the *feeling*, what flashed before her wasn't the shop at all.

He filled the space.

Maxen Fury.

The way he'd wrapped his coat around her. The way he'd stood still as a rock when she'd asked him what she was to him. The way his eyes had burned, even when his lips hadn't moved.

The throb in her chest was sharp. Immediate. Unwelcome.

"Miss Turner?"

"Oh, my apologies," she said quickly. Her face must be giving away her state of mind more clearly than before.

"Thinking about ruffians?"

A quick laugh burst free. "Something like that."

He didn't press. Just leaned back and glanced out the window, murmuring, "I've never had a home. Not a proper one."

Calliope studied his slanted face. "I'm sorry."

"No need to be. My circumstances . . . Well, let's just say, I never met my father. And my mother refused to admit she even gave birth to a son. I was passed from family member to family member. Different estates, different counties. Until my uncle took me in on a more permanent footing."

"That must have been difficult."

He shrugged, meeting her gaze. "It made me the man I am today."

"A ruffian?" she teased.

He grinned. "Exactly so."

The carriage slowed.

"Ah, we seem to be arriving. I'll make arrangements with the innkeeper. You'll have complete discretion, no questions, until you decide what you want to do."

"That's unnecessary, Mr. Peregrine."

"On the contrary, I find purpose in helping you with this small matter."

What a peculiar man. "Are you staying at the inn as well?"

He winked at her. "I own this inn."

Calliope's jaw slackened, but before she had time to respond, the carriage came to a halt and Mr. Peregrine jumped out and offered his hand.

Prince hopped out first.

Calliope hesitated. What if she was making a mistake? They were certainly not in Maxen's territory anymore . . . She had no idea what she was doing. No idea if she'd made the right choice.

All she knew was that she hadn't expected her heart to pinch like this. All for a man whose world was chaos. A man she'd walked away from. A man she hadn't stopped thinking about for a single breath.

She placed her palm in his and stepped out from the carriage.

MAXEN TORE THROUGH the streets of Brighton, his boots striking the ground with the fury of a man barely holding himself together. And he was barely holding himself together. By a thread thinner than the last miserable wisp of a man hair on a balding man.

She was gone.

Gone.

And he hadn't the faintest bloody notion where.

He hadn't felt this unmoored—this utterly *lost*—since he'd stood on the scorched earth of his youth, broken, beaten, and furious, with nothing but the name of his father on his tongue and a fire in his chest that refused to die. That fire had led him to *them.*

To his brothers.

One by one, he'd found them. Hunted them down. Claimed them. The duke thought them weak. And alone, they were, but together, they would always be stronger. Stronger than any opposition. At first, it had only been a mission. A purpose. But then, as he collected his brothers, came the first shared drink. The first fight. The first laugh. And suddenly, *they* were his. His bloody, scarred, ill-tempered *brothers.*

His world.

His *family.*

The similarity was bloody hard to deny, so he wouldn't deny it any longer.

She was *his.*

"This is driving me insane," he bit out, glancing at Drake,

who'd finally showed his face, jogging up beside him. They'd split up to cover more ground, but now they'd completed the circle. People had never vanished this fast from his turf. Not without a damn witness in sight. Someone had to have seen something.

"We've gone over this area twice," his brother said. "Nothing."

"The boys?"

Drake shook his head. "Not even a whiff of the little bird's shadow."

Maxen growled low in his throat. The wind lashed at his face as they stalked down another winding lane. Brighton's darkened corners had never felt so vast. So empty. So bloody useless. "She couldn't have vanished like this. She's not trained for it."

"She's clever," Drake replied. "We both know that."

That word again. He wanted to curse that blasted word. Calliope Turner was clever. Clever enough to know to choose his brother, to get him tied up, to even elude Maxen that very first night. Nothing had ever driven him this damn crazy before.

He stopped abruptly and braced a palm against the nearest stone wall. "Bloody hell."

"You're not used to this," Drake said evenly.

"What?" Maxen pushed from the wall with a scowl. Feeling crazy?

"Losing people."

He shot him a glare, but Drake didn't flinch. His brother never did.

"I've lost plenty," Maxen said.

"Not a woman."

He couldn't hold his brother's gaze and snapped it away. Lost a woman. No, he hadn't. His mother didn't count. She was his mother. Calliope was just . . . his. And now she'd vanished, and he was left clutching her blasted slipper like some lovesick fool.

"Keep your trap shut and keep moving."

"I'm not the one who stopped."

His brother had more nerve than anyone alive. They

searched the rest of the Lanes with no result. Prince would've been easy to track if anyone had spotted them, but they had no such luck.

Maxen paused as they arrived on East Street. "She couldn't have come this far on foot without someone noticing."

"You think she found a carriage?" Drake asked, gaze sweeping the street.

"Either she's cleverer than we gave her credit for, or she has more luck than Prinny himself."

"Which way do you think she went? North for the coaches, or south for the Steine?"

Either way, the direction would be a guess. "How much time has passed?" Maxen asked.

"Few hours."

They spotted Knight approaching, damp locks falling over his brow, lips pressed in a hard line.

"Anything?" Maxen asked, gaze fixed on his brother. Tension knotted his shoulders so tight he had to roll them once to loosen the stiffness.

Knight shook his head. "Not a trace of her or the dog."

"You searched the inns?" Drake asked.

Knight nodded.

Maxen's hands curled into fists, pulling apart every damn possibility. What route she might've taken. Who she might trust. No clear answer besides John Fitz came up, which meant she might be heading toward London. His, gut, however, told her that wouldn't be her destination.

"She has to be bloody somewhere," Drake muttered, perplexed. "She couldn't have gone far on foot."

"She's already where she wants to be," Maxen bit out. What other explanation could there be?

Knight looked up sharply. "Someone slipped our notice?"

Maxen bit down on his jaw. "It seems that way."

"Who the hell would she trust?" Drake questioned. "Rollings?"

Maybe. The women from her shop came to mind, but he quickly dismissed that idea. She wouldn't wish to put anyone in possible danger. But there was another name that sat like acid in the back of his mind. He'd spotted them together on more than one occasion. But it couldn't be. Could it? "No, not possible," he muttered.

Drake arched a brow and muttered, "Everything is damn possible at this point. Just look at us scrambling like headless fowl."

Saint rounded the corner ahead and slowed when he spotted them. He walked over, the breeze tugging at his hair, his expression grim.

Maxen tensed, his gut already answering before his mouth did. "You found her?"

"She was on foot," Saint confirmed solemnly, "but not for long."

Maxen clenched his fists. "You saw her with your own eyes? You're sure?"

Saint nodded. "Caught sight of her and her hound near the edge of the market district."

"Not alone," Knight guessed.

Saint shook his head. "No, not alone."

Maxen had a feeling he was not going to like the answer. "Who?" Maxen demanded.

Saint met his gaze, expression turning even graver. "Peregrine."

The name landed like a stone in Maxen's gut. Peregrine. Again. A vulture who never seemed to respect boundaries and delighted in testing his. For a fleeting moment, Maxen imagined his hands closing around the man's throat and squeezing the life from his eyes. He gave a vicious curse, forcing the image from his head.

Too damn tempting.

"That miscreant?" Drake asked sharply. "What the devil is he playing at this time?"

Saint nodded. "He stopped his carriage. She got in."

Maxen's lungs turned to damn ash. The image of throttling Peregrine flashed again.

Drake swore under his breath.

"Then she *is* a spy?" Knight tested. "For him."

"No," Maxen ground out. "I refuse to believe that."

"She willingly went with him," Saint pointed out.

There could be many reasons for that. One of which being that she simply didn't see Peregrine as a threat. Neither did the hound. But then, the hound hadn't seen *him* as a threat either.

"Where is she now?" Maxen asked.

"I followed them to Talon's."

"Talon's? I haven't heard of the place before." And that was never a good bloody thing.

"A new inn on the outskirts," Saint clarified.

Bloody Peregrine. Talon's? He scoffed. About as subtle as their tavern's name. He also noted that the blackguard perhaps thought he had taken her out of their territory. He would soon learn a valuable lesson: All that touched Brighton, touched him.

Maxen was already moving.

Saint caught his arm. "There might be more beneath the surface here."

He met his brother's gaze. "I know." People who ran usually had something to run from. She was either fleeing from him or something, someone, else.

Saint slowly let go of his arm. "So long as you know."

"Even if my judgment is clouded, it's not bloody lost."

His brother nodded, stepping back. "Good, then."

Drake stepped up to his side. "What do you want to do now?"

Maxen's lips curved. "Now we go retrieve our missing lamb."

"Christ," Drake muttered. "Don't let her hear you say that."

$$\text{❧}$$

Chapter Fourteen

CALLIOPE PERCHED ON the edge of the narrow bed by the window, Prince sprawled at her feet. Her gaze drifted over her room but fastened on nothing in particular. The air smelled faintly floral—rosewater, perhaps—but beneath another scent, something odd. Musty. It made her wrinkle her nose every time she caught it.

She still couldn't believe she'd fled like that.

I really left.

The valise at her feet was gaping open from her last attempt to take stock of her belongings, though she never touched them, even though she'd reached for them about a hundred times. It was just that her hands needed something to do. Anything other than fidgeting with the hem of her sleeve or brushing over the spot on her breast where her heart had once been neatly contained. Now that place throbbed wildly.

Prince let out a dissatisfied whine.

"I know," she said softly. "You're still judging me, aren't you?"

He didn't so much as blink at her.

And truly, who could blame him? Her grand plan had been to leave, no—escape, had sounded clever. Daring. Necessary. Except she'd overlooked one rather glaring flaw: she had no blazing idea where to go next.

Brighton was no longer safe for her dream.

London had never been safe.

And everywhere else on the map of England felt more like exile than anything else. She hadn't packed hope. She hadn't packed direction. She hadn't packed a dream long in the making.

Not exactly a plan.

She sighed and dropped her head into her hands and allowed herself exactly three heartbeats of despair. On the fourth, she straightened. *I've lived through worse.* This hurdle, she could survive. She just needed to think. To plot a course of action. That was what she'd always done. Quiet survival, clever pivots, always finding a way.

Except . . .

This time it wasn't Duvessa who held her captive in all but name. This time the person was Maxen Fury. His web. Protection, as he would call it, by tightening the ship. The man who'd looked at her as if she were both the problem and the answer. The man who hadn't said a word when it mattered most. The man who—

Urgh.

Stop it, Calliope!

So he hadn't said anything. They were from different worlds. She couldn't expect anything from him. She couldn't place any hope there. Her heart had been pummeled by expectations too many times before. She couldn't allow her wits to scatter like this. This wasn't heartbreak. Maxen hadn't broken her heart. This was merely disappointment. Sharp, yes. Searing, somewhat. And entirely her own fault.

She'd let herself imagine a life here.

Allowed herself to believe she could carve out a wedge of light beneath the shadow of a beast.

"You fool," she whispered. She didn't know if she meant him or herself. On the bright side of things, at least she had a place to stay for the night. She could worry about the rest tomorrow. Mr.

Peregrine had been kind. *Too* kind. He had even settled her account. Of course, she would have taken care of her account herself, but her pistol had been right atop her coin purse!

How embarrassing.

But what had he said before? No one would question her presence. Which, she belatedly realized, was precisely why she didn't fully trust his promise. Years in Duvessa's net had taught her that kindness always came with a cost. And if caught in such a trap again, she feared she'd not be able to bear the cost.

She rose and stepped up to the window, pushing the sash open despite the frigid breeze. Her fingers tightened on the frame, knuckles white. Gripping the frame might very well be the only thing keeping her from leaping right out.

And what? Run back to him?

Heh. A fool she could be called no longer. There wasn't a word that existed yet for her!

Calliope spotted a cat darting from below a tree and vanishing into the shadows.

Lucky creature.

She wished she could move freely without fearing what waited in the dark. Of course, she didn't want to vanish. At least not into the shadows. She just didn't want to be found.

Not by Duvessa, anyway.

Or *him*.

Had he found his brother yet? All sorts of suspicions must be gathering in his head. Spy sorts of suspicions. A shiver raced through her, though whether the slight chill came from the wind or the memory of Maxen Fury's voice growling her name, she couldn't say.

He hadn't growled.

Hah. Tell her memory that! Every part of her still burned with the sound. That roughness. The promise of chaos and ruin. The hope she hadn't wanted but had somehow gathered to herself anyway.

Stars, she was a fool.

Calliope inhaled a deep, fortifying breath. Just like she'd had to do the first few nights after escaping the old house. She'd have to find another opportunity to send Mr. Fitz a letter. Perhaps Wales would be the best option for now?

Maybe.

"I have not loved the world, nor the world me," she whispered aloud, suddenly recalling a passage from Byron's *Childe Harold's Pilgrimage.* She had never taken a liking to reading, but sometimes a book helped her sleep. This one sentence, however, had stayed with her from the moment she'd read the words.

But she had no need for the whole world. Just a small piece of earth she could tend. One she could love. Love well. And one that might, in time, love her in return.

She sank back onto the bed and drew the coverlet over her, the thought of changing out of her breeches into something more comfortable flickering briefly before exhaustion smothered the idea. Unfortunately, the blanket was far too thin to serve as a shield. Prince bounded up and collapsed against her, his canine sigh shuddering through the mattress.

"Just one night," she murmured, stroking his soft ears. "One night to catch our breaths." Just a little longer.

But the quiet didn't soothe this time.

She closed her eyes anyway.

MAXEN PUSHED THE door open to Calliope's chamber and slipped inside. He spotted the lump on the bed instantly. Two lumps, to be exact. One of them lifted its head to look at him, and he stilled. The hound stared for a full second before dropping his head back down.

Good boy.

He closed the door behind him and crossed the room soundlessly. She did not stir, not even when a gust of wind set the curtains billowing. At the foot of the bed he paused, unmoving, staring.

Contemplating.

Her face was half-buried in the pillow, hair tumbling loose about her. Her lashes lay dark against her cheeks, and for once her mouth held no stubborn curve—only a soft, parted bow that did something to the flow of blood to his heart. Even the proud line of her nose seemed gentled in sleep. She looked more innocent. Softer. As though the world had never sought to carve its due from her.

A heaviness pressed against his chest, too dangerous to name aloud. He had no right to be here. He should leave. Walk out. Pretend he hadn't come this far, hadn't threatened to burn this damn inn to the ground, hadn't crossed this line.

His feet refused to move.

What now, you clever simpleton?

Her eyelids twitched and her brow slightly furrowed.

Was she having a nightmare?

Bad dreams were probably the only foe he could not fight. His gaze dropped to her valise. He hadn't known what he'd find. Somehow, her and her hound sleeping so utterly defenselessly had not crossed his mind.

His hand brushed over her slipper in his pocket.

She was not someone they had to worry about.

But she was the woman from that night. One mystery solved, a dozen more crowding in. He wasn't ready to wake her. Wasn't ready to face her eyes when they opened. Still, there were things he had to say. Words he hadn't managed when they counted. Words that didn't come easily to men like him. Orders, silence, fists? Yes, *that* was his language. Not one he could speak with her, however.

He carefully drew a chair closer and lowered himself into the seat. And waited. Yet the longer he sat, the harder it became to keep still. He leaned forward, elbows braced against his knees, and let his gaze settle on her face. Close enough now to see the pale freckles on her face. Close enough to hear the even breath she drew. Too close.

His hand rose before he could stop it, tracing a finger over her cheek. He froze. What in God's name was he doing? He drew his hand back, fingers curling into a fist, then reached out again.

Just once.

His fingertip skimmed over her cheekbone.

So soft.

He couldn't exactly feel her skin through his gloves, but imagination had no mercy. He almost removed a glove just to confirm what he already knew to be true. But there, he drew the line.

He never removed his gloves.

Not in front of people.

Not even his brothers.

How many times had he done this? Sat in the dark beside the bed of one of his brothers—watching over them as they slept off wounds or too much whisky. Too many. Knight, after he'd taken a blade for a message gone wrong. Dagger, when he'd nearly drowned himself in a bottle after he lost a friend to an unknown death. Even Saint, whose silence could bleed into something far more dangerous when left without a compass. Maxen had always kept watch. If he didn't, who would?

But this was different.

She wasn't his brother.

She wasn't his family.

And yet she had lodged in his veins like gunpowder, a spark away from ruin. Impossible to dig out.

He leaned back, the chair creaking beneath him, and pressed the heels of his palms to his eyes. His heart hadn't settled since he'd found Reaper tied up and her gone. Fury was his name, the name he had chosen, but he hadn't known fury like that. And not the raging kind. Or yes, perhaps raging. But not raging in anger. Raging in all the ways but that.

She didn't belong in his ship?

This wasn't a matter of belonging anymore. This was a matter of survival. Protection. Hunt the threat. Though, when she woke up, he might very well find himself staring at the black eye of her pistol.

Christ, he didn't know how to string sentences together that weren't either commands, warnings, blunt facts, or sarcasm. Commands wouldn't work, and sarcasm was out of the question. What was left to him was blunt facts and warnings. State a blunt fact, then follow up with a warning?

His gaze shifted to her face when she moved in her sleep, brow furrowing. He balled his hands into fists before he attempted to smooth the furrow for her.

Just who are you, Miss Turner?

"I've maimed men for less than what you made me feel," he muttered softly.

She stirred again, her lashes fluttering.

Maxen froze, then his mouth twisted, bitter with self-loathing. Maybe she'd wake. Maybe she'd sleep through the night. Maybe she'd send him away. Maybe she'd hear the words he hadn't even figured out how to say. There simply was no control where she was concerned. She dismantled everything.

But he would wait.

For once in his bloody, brutal life, he chose not to deny himself.

"You can't leave Brighton, Miss Turner. Not before I peel away each and every one of your secrets."

Chapter Fifteen

CALLIOPE WOKE WITH the creeping sense that she wasn't alone. Not in the comforting sense of Prince curled at her side, but something . . . *else*. She opened her eyes to the morning light spilling through the curtains. However, the room held a dark, intruding, provocative scent that hadn't been there before. She shifted and grimaced, the coarse fabric of men's attire chafing in places no sensible garment should.

She nearly bolted upright when her gaze landed on a man.

A man.

A large man.

Right there. Beside her bed. Slumped in the chair like he had every right to be there, arms crossed, legs stretched out, head tilted just so.

Her breath caught somewhere between her lungs and heart.

Maxen was asleep. Or appeared to be. But even in this state, he looked like a predator only at rest. Honestly, the man resembled a sleeping beast out of a nightmare, or—ahem—a dream she should never admit to having. Heh. His face was all harsh angles and deep shadows in the soft light, his jaw rough with stubble and brows slightly drawn. He looked almost . . . tired. No. He looked *worn*.

And Prince?

She levered up onto her elbows and found him still curled at her side. Traitorous hound. "You're supposed to bark at intruders," she muttered softly. "Or growl." Certainly alert her.

She glanced back at Maxen, only to jerk.

His dark gaze pinned her in place. Sharp. Alert. As though he'd merely rested his eyes but never truly slept.

"How long have you been there?" she croaked. Wrong question, Calliope!

"Long enough," he said, his voice a low rasp that dragged across her nerves. And there it was again. A frisson of tension. That thing sparking between them with peril and promise and a heartbeat of its own.

She found the sensation both intolerable and craved it desperately like breath.

The charge robbed her tongue of sense, since instead of scolding the man for entering her room like a thief, she asked, "How in heaven's name did you find me?" Down to her room, no less!

Not the barest muscle stirred. "Did you truly believe I couldn't?"

"Well . . ." Honestly. "Brighton is rather large."

"Not large enough."

"It's the wanting to find me at all that I cannot quite grasp. You shouldn't be here."

He pushed to his feet, stretching in a slow, unhurried way that made her stomach flip. "I should be exactly where you are."

How could such a rough statement sound so sweet? "Because you find me suspicious and I drew a pistol on your brother and tied him up?"

The corner of his lips twitched. "Merely a day in the life of a Fury."

She slowly sat up straighter. "How reassuring."

"The fact I'm more concerned about is that you fled."

"I prefer to think of it as a graceful withdrawal." Fled was completely accurate! "Didn't your brother tell you? I don't want to be a nuisance."

"You're not." His expression didn't change, but his voice dropped. "You're not a nuisance. You're not troublesome."

Her heart fluttered, foolish thing. "You have your brothers. Your work. Your underworld empire or whatever your world is. You don't need me—"

"Stop."

She clamped her mouth shut.

He shoved a hand through his hair and slumped into the chair. "When I was sixteen, I tracked my brother Drake to a brothel outside Seven Dials. He was only a year younger, drunk off his arse, didn't even know I existed. But I dragged him out. Cleaned him up. Fed him."

Her lips parted, her throat too tight for words. Stars, this was his past. He was offering her a piece of his past . . .

"They were scattered. Bastards from different mothers. Different towns. I had no obligation to any of them, but I found them. One by one. Took them in. Even when they questioned my motives. Even when my face was as bare as a babe's."

Maxen as a boy. She would have loved to see him then.

His jaw flexed. "They acted like brats most of the time, but they were never a nuisance. Not when they fought, not when they got in trouble, not when they blew up half of Brighton with one bloody tavern brawl. My only fear has always been that I'd never live up to what they deserved."

Her chest squeezed, sharp and sudden. This fierce, fearsome man, afraid only of not being enough. The imbalance felt so utterly wrong.

"My point," he said, voice thick, "is that once I decide someone is mine to protect, they're mine, and I will not fail them."

So . . . he considered her his to protect? Reasonably, that should have alarmed her, but his claim did the exact opposite. "You count me among them? Yours to protect?"

"Yes."

"Why?" she challenged.

"You are my tenant."

Just his tenant? "That doesn't mean I'm yours to protect."

"That's not how this works, Calliope."

Her name. Not the first time spoken from his lips, but this time, she felt the change in her bones. Dark and deep and permanent.

He was right.

That *wasn't* how matters worked. Protection—true protection—always came at a price. Either the kind spoken plainly in coin or the kind extracted later in favors. Safety was nothing but a loan. And yet the main Beast of Brighton sat beside her bed, declaring her under his protection as if it were a simple fact. Immutable. Irrevocable.

A whisper of panic rose in her chest.

Because if she believed him—if she let herself lean even an inch toward the idea that someone like him could mean those words—what then? What would happen the next time she stumbled? When she failed to be agreeable, useful, obedient? What if he looked at her one day and saw a burden instead of someone worth protecting? She'd spent most of her life trying not to need anyone too much. Attempting to remain insignificant enough to stay safe, clever enough to survive, invisible enough to slip between the cracks.

And yet what other choices were at her disposal?

She *wanted* to believe him.

But what would the cost be if she did? What would the cost be if she didn't?

She was *tired*. Tired of belonging nowhere. Tired of imagining futures she never dared to reach for. Tired of fearing her longing. The infuriating hound hadn't even alerted her of his intrusion. Prince seemed as though he had chosen, too.

She lifted her gaze to Maxen's again. He hadn't moved. Hadn't pushed. Hadn't demanded. He'd simply stated and stayed.

Well then, let the tide carry her where it would. He might not be offering certainty, but his assurance was sincere. And perhaps—just perhaps—that was worth any peril.

"What if trouble follows me?" she had to ask. "What then? What if that trouble threatens you and your brothers?"

His gaze didn't falter. "I'll handle whatever comes."

"Without knowing what may come?"

"I don't need to know."

She didn't know what to say to that. To tell the truth, while she was grateful he didn't press her, she didn't trust his lack of curiosity. Who wouldn't want to know? They may be men with darkness and power here in Brighton, but would that beat an earl? A countess? Their titled friends? Hopefully, Duvessa would never discover her whereabouts. But hope was a thinner shield than her coverlet. "I find that hard to believe."

The corners of his lips twitched again. "Wanting to know and needing to know are two separate things. I don't need to know. For now."

Well, she could always flee again when he needed to know and she didn't wish to tell. "Do you expect me to leave my shop unattended while the ship is tightened?"

He arched a brow. "So that's what prompted this? My word choice?"

She would never admit to such a thing. "I would have had to move in a few months anyway," she muttered.

A light scoff. "We can discuss the extension of your lease another day."

Her ears pricked. Now that was of great interest indeed. Except—he would still be her criminal landlord. Heh. Well, if that allowed her to live her dream, certain allowances might be made. Plus, she loved her shop.

"Are you a good man, Maxen?" The question escaped before she could bite the words back.

His gaze never wavered. "Whatever I am, I'm not good."

Calliope didn't entirely believe that. He seemed good enough. Better than her stepmother, for sure. However, she dared not delve deeper than that for the moment. "Well, I appreciate the honesty."

"We don't lie about who we are," he offered plainly. "Even so, we don't kill, my brothers and I, if that is something you're worried about."

"Well," she muttered, almost on a laugh. "I suppose one must draw the line somewhere."

He grunted. "I thought it best to be clear."

She searched his face. "You make it sound so simple. To be clear."

"It is simple."

She wasn't so sure about that. To be clear often times invited trouble, especially, she imagined, for a man such as himself. Regardless, probably foolishly, her heart warmed. "What do you need from me?"

He leaned forward, forearms braced hard against his knees, eyes lit with a dangerous glow. "Stay safe."

Her lips parted. Stars, what was she meant to say to that? She could tell he meant those two words full-heartedly. "I shall try my best?"

He smiled.

The first smile he had ever given her. Calliope had never been dazzled by a smile before. But his? The tilt caught at the scar on his lip, turning the flaw into something devastating. She hadn't the faintest idea where to look—his lips, his eyes—the whole of him suddenly, ruinously changed.

"Good."

She eased her feet off the mattress, the blanket slipping after them. "Did you bribe the manager of the inn to enter my chamber?

He stood, moving toward the window, tugging the curtain back an inch to glance at the street. "Something to that effect."

Should she even ask?

Let's not.

"Peregrine brought you here."

She hadn't expected that. "You even know this?" Brighton truly wasn't as big as she thought. "He only happened upon me and offered help."

"He's dangerous."

Had she imagined it, or had his hand tightened on the curtain before he let it fall? "You're all dangerous."

"Not to you." He turned to her. "You are who I protect."

How was that not supposed to terrify and melt her at the same time?

MAXEN STEPPED OUT into the morning and lit a cigar, sucking deep, the pull raking his throat, sharp and unforgiving. He blew out slowly, smoke curling into crooked forms before dissolving. Unlike some ghosts. The blackguards who clung on.

Bloody hell.

He'd never told that story before. About finding Drake half-dead with drink, about dragging his brothers home one by one, claiming them as his. Not even to his brothers, who were the story.

He dragged in another breath, puffed out a billow of smoke.

She'd probably already crowned him a "good man" despite his words to the contrary. He rolled the cigar between his fingers. Some truths were his alone.

"Well, cock on a duck, you only ever light one when you're worried. Are you worried, *frère*?"

The voice came from the shadows beside the building. Familiar. Dry. A little too amused.

Maxen didn't turn. "I'm not worried."

Reaper stepped forward, arms folded over his chest, his coin conspicuously absent. "Then why are you smoking?"

"Habit."

"Liar."

Maxen sneered and tapped ash to the side. "I have things to think about."

"You mean worry about." Reaper nodded back to the inn.

"She kick you out?"

"No."

"She coming back?"

Maxen nodded. She and the hound were having a quick breakfast. He didn't have any hunger in him to join them. Peregrine had yet to show his face. He'd have *him* for breakfast, if he could. The vulture must have already heard they'd taken root in his establishment. The man was annoyingly well-informed.

Reaper leaned against the wall beside him. "Knight says you tore nearly half of Brighton apart looking for her."

"An exaggeration."

"Drake said you nearly took of the head of the manager."

"He was in the way." And he had given him options. Tell him Calliope's room, or he'd go through them all. The man had chosen wisely.

Reaper snorted. "I can't decide if she's the best thing to happen to you or the worst."

"You and me both."

They stood in silence for a minute. The area was quiet. The sun hadn't fully risen, and the town still slumbered beneath a mantle of mist. This was the sort of sight she might have paused to admire. For him, his body and mind remained braced, unmoved by the view. Only one view moved him.

Reaper suddenly chuckled. "You're less of an arse."

He turned, one brow arched. "Less of an arse?"

"You used to bark orders like gunfire. Now you bark less and growl more. Though now that I think about it, that might make you more of an arse."

Maxen took another draw from his cigar. "Keeping score is bad for your health."

"Says the man with a book of scores."

Maxen scowled. "They are called account books, you lack-wit."

"Moving on," Reaper said. "Now that little mouse has gotten under your skin, what are you going to do about her there?

Propose marriage?"

"Don't be bloody ridiculous."

"*Is* that ridiculous?"

"Yes." In fact, his whole body broke out in shivers at the mere word. Men like him didn't marry. What could he even offer a wife? Nothing a woman might want. A woman such as Calliope might want. Security. Constancy. *Light.*

Reaper gave a low whistle. "Savagely honest."

"I am what I am."

"And what's that?" Reaper asked drily. "A man?"

"A monster."

"Christ, *frère*. Even if you think like that, you shouldn't say it out loud."

Maxen disagreed. Simply thinking wasn't enough with Calliope. A man could think his thoughts away with the speed of another single thought. He could begin thinking of all sorts of things he shouldn't be thinking about. "There's no difference."

"Of course there is, *frère*. If she hears you, she might change her mind about what she imagines you could be, not what you are."

"What books have you been reading?" He flicked the cigar into the dirt, crushing the ember with his boot. "Save the sage advice for yourself."

Reaper tilted his head, grin crooked. "So what's the plan then? Install her at Fury's and then lock the door when she's not looking?"

Maxen cut him a sharp look.

Reaper shrugged. "What? You've got that look about you."

A muscle jumped in Maxen's jaw. "You're an imbecile."

"True." Reaper pushed off the wall, hands sliding into his pockets. "But you're the imbecile who went and caught *things*. Don't glare at me, *frère*. Those *things* are written all over your face. Well," he waved a hand at Maxen's scowl, "as much as anything *can* be written on that slab of granite."

Maxen's fingers itched to throttle his brother. Lock her up?

Absurd. He'd never do that to anyone. Enemies aside. Even so, he hadn't the faintest idea what to do with Calliope. She'd already twisted him into a shape he scarcely recognized.

Reaper clapped a hand on his shoulder. "You should think about what that plan is, *frère*. Before someone else decides for you."

"Keep talking and you'll find your teeth decorating the ground."

"See?" Reaper leaned closer. "That's the growl I was talking about. A bit of bark, more growling."

Maxen stared at him, unimpressed.

Both men turned as Drake approached on the back of a horse, dismounted, and walked over, a grim set to his jaw.

"What's wrong?" Maxen asked.

"I just received word one of the warehouses in Shoreham's been torched." Drake got to the point.

Maxen stiffened. "Shoreham?"

Drake nodded, rubbing the back of his neck. "Yes. The western outskirts. One of our oldest storage houses. Took out half the stock before the locals could put out the blaze. I've ordered my men to move what survived."

Reaper cursed. "Anyone hurt?"

"No bodies that I know of."

Maxen's mind raced. Calculating. Weighing. Could this be related to the shipment debacle? Or Rollings? Peregrine? Damn it. Both of whom, it couldn't be overlooked, shared a connection with Calliope Turner.

"Any witnesses?" There better be bloody witnesses.

Drake shook his head. "This was clean. Fast. No accident."

Christ. "A message for us, then?" What else could it bloody be?

"Exactly what I was thinking," Drake muttered.

Reaper crossed his arms again. "You think this has ties to your little mouse?"

"No way to know, but the timing's too damned convenient."

They had been out searching for Calliope last night. Distracted. Even so, Shoreham was miles away, and their mystery enemy could not have known how the night would play out.

Unless the blackguard was watching.

Drake glanced up at the inn's second-story window. "If someone's setting fires, they're not going to stop at one warehouse."

Maxen nodded. "Let Knight have his men double the guard at the warehouses in Lewes and Eastbourne. No one moves without us knowing it."

Drake gave a curt nod. "Already got a runner on that. We should have a final report on the final damage in a day or so."

"Good."

"You've got that look again," Reaper said, a coin appearing between his knuckles. "The one that means somebody's about to wake up without fingers."

Maxen didn't bother denying it.

"Ah, well," Reaper added with a thin smile. "Been too quiet lately. This will liven things up."

"Has Serpent reported yet?"

Silence.

So, no.

Maxen's teeth ground together. Whoever thought to touch what was his—his brothers, his business, or Calliope Turner—they'd just made the gravest mistake of their life. He'd carve a path straight to his enemy if that's what it took, dig the rat out by its tail and hang it for every soul in Brighton to see. There'd be no mistaking the lesson. Brighton belonged to the Furys. Every warehouse, every street, every property in their name and beyond. And Calliope . . . God help the blackguard who thought to use her against him.

Chapter Sixteen

CALLIOPE NEVER THOUGHT she'd set foot in the tavern again, yet here she was, still a bit dazed. How could she not be?

You are who I protect.

An intoxicating declaration. The last time she'd felt such a rush was when she'd found Prince as a pup. Only back then, she had been the protector. She hadn't declared her promise so loftily, though. But then, she wasn't Maxen Fury. She had come to an irrevocable conclusion, or rather finally, fully accepted the one already there.

She didn't want to leave.

Not her shop.

Not Brighton.

And not—ahem—well, just *not*.

So here she was.

Prince padded beside her, his presence reassuring. The fact that he calmly accepted this den of beasts without a growl or howl alone felt like a kind of sign. Dogs growled at people they didn't trust. People who threatened their territory. Bad people. As though they could sense the intentions behind the person.

Prince hadn't once growled at Maxen. And if the hound could sense something in Maxen Fury worth trusting . . . maybe she could, too. Granted, not everything. But enough.

Hah.

What would the big, bad beast think if he learned he wasn't so big and bad and beastly after all?

"Where are all your brothers?" she asked as Maxen led her to a door leading to the personal rooms.

"Out on business," came his simple reply.

"Is one of them still missing?" Calliope asked, recalling this matter.

The front door slammed open before he could respond. Calliope jumped, her heart leaping violently. Her hand brushed her trousers, as if to reassure herself she was still disguised, still someone who might pass unnoticed. Maxen moved at once, pivoting with feral quickness, shoving her behind him. The sudden menace in his body—the sheer readiness of his actions—sent her pulse racing for all the wrong reasons.

Two figures stood in the doorway.

One bore a jagged scar slashing down the side of his face; the other sagged against him, badly beaten. Stars, blood was dripping from his head to his ripped shirt.

Calliope grabbed the back of Maxen's coat.

"Found him," the scarred one said.

"What the bloody hell happened?" Maxen demanded.

"Run into a bit of trouble," the bloodied one said hoarsely.

Calliope blinked, her mind scrambling. This must be the missing brother. Yet she didn't recognize either man.

The pair staggered to the bar, the scarred man hauling his brother over, keeping him upright by sheer force. Maxen surged forward to meet them, and with her hand still holding onto his coat, she was yanked along before she could even blink! She released him at once, heat pricking her cheeks.

He stopped short, turning back. "Calliope?"

She waved him off. "It's nothing, go help your brother."

He hesitated, torn, his hand flexing as though he might reach for her, but he turned to meet his brothers.

"How bad is he, Drake?"

"Don't know," the one with the scar said. "We need to get him to his bed."

"I'm bloody fine."

"Serpent," Maxen said low. A warning.

What a strange name.

The one called Serpent looked at her. He didn't so much as blink. Didn't smile. Didn't ask who she was. He just stared.

Calliope shivered.

"Found him in a heap two streets over," Drake ground out. "Pair of cutthroats dogging his heels. Devil's own luck I chanced upon him when I did, or he'd be finished."

Serpent grunted.

Maxen turned to her. "Upstairs. Now."

"What happened?" Calliope asked, voice rising.

"We'll talk later."

"Maxen—"

"Go." He paused. "Please."

She hesitated, but one look at Serpent's blood-covered body and Drake's unreadable stare and she made a decision. "No. Whatever it is, I can help."

Maxen turned slowly, dark eyes flaring with more warning. "Calliope—"

"I am not made of porcelain." She crossed her arms. "I've seen blood." Duvessa had often beat the servant girls in a fit of rage, and Calliope had always helped patch them up. "I've seen blood, tended wounds, stitched flesh. Do not mistake me for something breakable."

Serpent groaned, swaying slightly. "Let the chit help if she's so eager," he muttered. "Or I might bleed out just to spite you."

Maxen gave her a long look before giving a single, curt nod. He joined his brothers, slipping beneath Serpent's other arm to take the weight across his shoulder. Together they half-hauled, half-carried him forward. "Upstairs. Second door on the left."

She nodded, already moving. "Come on, Prince," she called, though the hound was already shadowing her steps, nose twitching at the scent of blood. She led the way to the designated room and held the door open for them. The men helped lower their brother carefully to the bed.

Serpent let out a raw groan when his body hit the mattress.

"Where does it hurt?" Maxen asked.

"Every-bloody-where."

Calliope stepped up to the bed while Drake retreated to lean against the doorframe, arms crossed, jaw clenched.

"We need to clean and wrap the wound," she said, concerned.

"I'll go get what you need," Drake said, then disappeared.

"Who did this?" Maxen asked softly.

Calliope almost flinched. She'd never heard his voice that soft before.

"Don't know," Serpent muttered through clenched teeth. "Got jumped. Escaped."

Drake returned, and Calliope launched into action. She took the water from him and filled a basin. He handed her a cloth, and she soaked it thoroughly before she knelt by the man and started wiping the blood from his face.

Maxen dropped to his knees beside her and reached for the bloodstained shirt, but Serpent stopped him. "Don't."

"Serpent."

"Just see to my head. I need that more than anything else. I'll do the rest myself."

Was that an attempt at humor? It utterly failed!

Maxen withdrew his hand with a curse.

Within minutes, she had cleaned the worst of the blood from his face. As he showed no tolerance for their tending elsewhere, she didn't venture further.

Her gaze flicked to Drake. "Your lip is cut."

"I've had worse."

Maxen stood and crossed to him, reaching up to grip his brother's chin before Drake could stop him.

"It won't scar," he said firmly.

Calliope's gaze dropped to the scar splitting Maxen's lip. Had his injury come about the same way—just another day in the life of a Fury? She couldn't look away.

Drake pushed his hand aside. "It's nothing. More concerning is that the men who trailed our brother dearest had the same shaved heads as the one who broke into your Miss Turner's shop."

Shocked, Calliope shot to her feet. "What does this have to do with me?"

"It seems," Drake said. "That whoever is behind these assaults has taken an interest in my brother's interest in you."

Well, that sounded ominous.

Serpent hissed as he drew himself upright. "We're being provoked. Someone's testing our reach. Seeing how far we'll go. How far they can go."

Stars, this truly was the stuff of criminals!

Maxen scowled. "Power. They want to topple ours and seize their own."

"Did Peregrine say anything to you last night when he escorted you to the inn?" Maxen asked her.

Peregrine? Did they suspect him? "No. Does he have something to do with this?"

"Uncertain," Maxen said.

Calliope let out a slow breath. This all had been rather unexpected. "I think I shall retire to my room if you could point the way." Better to grant them space. Serpent's other wound would need tending, and she doubted he would allow it in her presence.

Maxen nodded, escorting her from the room. "Thank you."

She glanced up at him. "You're welcome."

Behind them, Serpent groaned again. "If you're going to start kissing, *warn me first.*"

Maxen scowled at his brother before leading her and Prince away. And for the first time since she'd set foot in Brighton, Calliope didn't feel like she was running anymore.

How long would it last?

ONCE MAXEN HAD seen Calliope and her hound to her room, he stalked back down the corridor toward his brother's chamber.

He wanted to kiss her.

That inappropriate thought landed like an even more inappropriate brand in his skull. The impression simply wouldn't be removed. He had never wanted to kiss anyone the way he wanted to kiss her. The way she'd helped clean his brother's face without flinching, how could he damn well not?

He sneered at himself. Him. Wanting to kiss a woman because she'd scrubbed gore from his brother's face? No doubt he was losing what little sense he had left. Most men were attracted to the flirtatious shenanigans of women. Him? He was apparently aroused by competence and the stench of iron. Charming.

His lip curled higher.

A kiss. As if he could be trusted with something so simple. He'd ruin her. And still—curse and damn it all—he wanted. He wanted until want clawed at him like starvation. Was it lunacy to want to stick to her side? Undoubtedly. Fortunately, his brother's state took precedence, sparing him a test he was bound to fail. When he returned, Serpent was half-dozing while Drake worked over him, binding a cut that slashed across a chest already ruined by old burns.

"You can go," Drake said without breaking focus. "I'll stay with him."

Maxen hesitated.

"Get some rest," his brother insisted. "You probably didn't get any sleep last night."

Whether he'd be able to do so now remained to be seen. "I'll be in my room if you need me." He gave Serpent one last glance, jaw tight, before he turned away. The door shut softly at his back, and he made his way toward his chamber—just beside hers.

No sleep for him.

A soft voice drifted from her room as he passed. He didn't mean to stop. And he certainly didn't mean to lean closer. But he did.

"I know he means well," her muffled voice carried through the door, soft but clear enough for him to catch.

Maxen froze.

"But stars, Prince," she went on, her tone turning wry, "the man could scare a storm off the sea just by frowning."

Maxen's brows drew together. Was that how she saw him?

Then came a soft chuckle. "I don't think he means to look like that. I think he just . . ." Her voiced dipped and he couldn't catch the last. He leaned in, and caught again, "But then he . . ." another dip, "and suddenly he doesn't seem quite so terrifying."

What? What did he do, exactly, to seem less terrifying?

"He still looks like he eats danger for breakfast," she added.

Now that was just bloody absurd.

A throat cleared behind him. Loudly.

Maxen snapped upright, head whipping to the side.

Reaper stood a few feet away, arms crossed, broth brows raised.

"I wasn't spying," Maxen muttered instantly in a hushed voice, caught off guard.

"I know," Reaper drawled.

Maxen nodded, stepping away from her door. "Good, then."

"You were eavesdropping."

Damnation. He glared at his brother. "She was talking. I thought she might need something."

Reaper grinned. "Did she ask through the door?"

Maxen turned away, annoyed at getting caught doing something so foolish.

Reaper followed. "You're turning all red."

"I'm not."

"Oh, you are."

Maxen swore under his breath. "Go look in on Serpent and Drake."

Reaper snorted but mercifully didn't argue.

Maxen ducked into his room, resisting the absurd urge to slam the door behind him like some ill-tempered brat. He let his back rest against the wood, then pressed a hand to his chest.

Ah, yes. He drew the slipper from his pocket. What to do about this?

Talon's had seemed the perfect place to confront her, but he hadn't been able to convince himself to bring the matter up. Crossing to the small chest on his desk, he flipped the lid open. Inside lay a lone dagger—their family blade, each brother had one—a faded ribbon that had belonged to his mother, and the mate to the shoe in his hand. He set the slipper beside its match.

So she thought he looked terrifying.

He stripped off his coat and tossed it to the chair. A man didn't survive the gutters by appearing approachable. Fear was useful. Fear kept knives from slipping into his back, kept enemies second-guessing. Terrifying had kept him alive. Terrifying had kept his brothers alive. But that word from her lips?

Maxen dragged a hand down his face. Perhaps it was absurd being bothered by what she thought of him, when half the town already quaked at his name. Restless, he left his room again and made his way downstairs. He'd go mad if he stayed in his room, next to hers, hunting for any and every sound from that side of the wall.

Knight looked up from his spot behind the bar. "Drink?"

Maxen nodded.

His brother poured him a glass of bourbon and pushed it over.

Reaper sidled over. "Your face is still red, by the by."

"Say another word and I'll relocate your jaw."

Knight raised a brow at them.

Dagger pushed through the entrance. "We've got a problem."

Maxen tipped the content of his glass down his throat in one go. Could a man not get a minute of peace? "What kind?"

"Warehouse in Newhaven. Another fire."

Maxen stilled. "Ours?"

Dagger nodded.

Damn it.

Knight set out more glasses and filled them.

"Anyone hurt?" Reaper asked grimly.

"Not badly," Dagger said, snatching up a glass and draining the contents. "Seems to have happened the same time as the Ashford fire."

Maxen wanted to kill someone. "And the goods?"

"Gone."

Knight and Reaper cursed.

"I've had enough of this damn shite," Maxen growled. "We've been betrayed."

Dagger's face turned dark. "Are we riding out?"

Maxen nodded. "Bring Saint. Knight and Reaper stay here. Drake's with Serpent. We need to keep this ship tight."

If someone was starting a war, they'd chosen the wrong bloody empire. And if they touched one hair on the woman upstairs . . .

Well.

They'd see just how terrifying he could be.

✿ ❧ ✿

Chapter Seventeen

CALLIOPE PUSHED OPEN the tavern door, returning from a quick stroll for Prince to do his business.

She had half-expected to be stopped.

Yet when she'd ventured downstairs a quarter of an hour ago, no one had barred her way. In fact, the place had been empty.

Now, two heads turned as one.

Reaper had pulled two stools up to the bar and sat on one as he lounged against the counter, one elbow propped on the surface, his boots sprawled across the second stool. His coin flicked between his fingers. Knight stood behind the bar, shirt sleeves rolled up to his elbows, expression unreadable.

Still no Maxen.

Calliope hesitated in the doorway, suddenly unsure. The last time she'd seen this man she hadn't been at her best. He wouldn't want revenge, would he?

Reaper offered a grin. "Well, look who didn't run for the hills. Please alert us next time you leave our den. For safety purposes."

Knight said nothing. Just watched her, eyes flicking briefly to the hound at her side.

"No one was here."

"A shout will do."

Calliope rolled her eyes. "Am I safe to enter?" she asked,

voice dry. "Or will I be threatened, tied up, or interrogated?"

His grin widened. "That depends. Are you planning to tie any more of us up?"

"I make no promises."

The man chuckled. Reaper motioned lazily to a table. "Hungry? Knight's cooked up his famous stew."

She ventured over, and Knight moved toward the back without a word.

"Sit. You're not a prisoner here, little mouse."

"I wish you'd stop calling me that," she muttered, but complied, Prince settling at her feet.

"Why? Do women not like sweet nicknames?"

Calliope arched a brow at the man. Was that a serious question? Her gaze flicked over his scar, the man as a whole. It probably was. "Yes, nothing flatters a woman more than being compared to a rodent."

He laughed.

Knight returned with a bowl and cutlery and set the dish before her, tossing a meaty bone at Prince. "Hot. Don't burn your tongue."

"Thank you," Calliope murmured.

Reaper chuckled. "That's as hot as *he* gets."

She wasn't complaining. Dipping the spoon into the thick broth, she took a cautious bite. Taste exploded in her mouth. "Stars, that's good." She looked over to Reaper. "Where's your brother?"

The man studied her. "Which one?"

Her look turned flat. "You know which one."

"Oh. Him. He's *busy*."

"With what?" she asked curiously.

Knight spoke from the bar. "Protecting what's his."

Well, then!

She returned her attention to her stew and tried not to think about where their brother was and whether he was safe.

"So, little mouse," Reaper sidled up to her, sliding into the chair next to her, studying her. "I completely forgot to ask. What did you do to make my brother laugh?"

"He laughed?" Knight asked, one brow arching.

"Yes, the big beast laughed. I heard him with my own ears."

"I don't believe you."

"He. Laughed. I'm going to win the bet."

Calliope glanced between the brothers. "You're wagering against your brother?"

Reaper winked at her. "Always."

"He actually laughed?" Knight pressed. "Did you see it?"

"No."

"Then it didn't happen."

Reaper scoffed. "You were there, little mouse. He laughed, didn't he?"

Calliope thought for a moment. Had he laughed? Could it be considered a laugh? A light chuckle perhaps. Needless to say, she wasn't going to enter this conversation, this bet, whatever it was. "I can't recall."

Knight snorted.

So did Reaper, his eyes narrowing on her. "Well, you're no fun, *petite souris.*"

"Don't think calling me mouse in French will endear you to me."

He scowled, then smoothed out the lines and smiled again. "Come, little mouse. Just what did you do to make my brother laugh in a way I've never heard from him?"

Knight took a sip of something, watching her.

Calliope set her spoon down with a sigh. He wasn't going to let this go. And the one with the *stare* was even worse. "I hit him in the nether regions with a boot."

Knight spit out the contents in his mouth all over the bar counter, coughing.

Reaper's mouth dropped open.

Well, they asked.

"You did what?" Reaper asked astonished. "And you haven't

been shipped off?"

"Should I have been?" she challenged.

Both men fell silent.

"Do you not own a gown?" a low voice growled from the doorway.

Maxen.

Calliope glanced over at him, her heart fluttering at the sight of him removing his cap and tossing it at Knight before striding over to her table. Once again, she had the odd sense that the man was a storm cloud straining to split open. However, she no longer saw that as danger. Rather, just the man.

She grinned. "Why yes, I do. Several."

He yanked Reaper from the chair beside her and took his spot. "Smart mouth."

"I only have one spare set of clothes with me," she clarified, her scalp prickling at his closeness. "Besides, it's good to maintain a form of disguise, isn't it?"

"You are a woman dressed in men's clothing. There is no disguise happening here. You look like a damn temptation that will lure every blackguard out of their hole."

"No need to grumble about it," Calliope muttered. Inside, her heart thrashed against her breast. A temptation? How? Why? "What if I put on a cap?"

"Calliope," he leaned close, "if you wanted to resemble a boy, then you should have procured trousers that don't wrap around your legs like that."

Her lips parted. Closed. Parted again. "I'm seated."

Reaper whistled, plopping in a chair across from them. "*Frère*."

Maxen pulled back, a vein ticking in his jaw. She swore the tips of his ears glowed red. "Forget I said anything."

Come to think of it, last night he'd covered her with his coat. Was that the reason?

"Yes," Reaper chirped. "Stare at each other. We don't exist."

Calliope averted her gaze. Stars, now she didn't know where

to look. Vexing man.

Dagger entered through the door of the tavern, his long, heavily weaponed coat swaying, followed by Saint. The latter disappeared though the back door while the former claimed a chair. She hadn't been formally introduced to any of these men, but they didn't treat her as a stranger. She rather appreciated that.

"What did I miss?" Dagger asked.

"Trust me, *frère*, you do not want to know."

Knight, still behind the bar, grunted. "Allegedly, he laughed, too."

Dagger arched a brow.

"Why is that such a shock?" Calliope asked. The man wasn't a statute that didn't possess the capacity to laugh.

Reaper leaned over the table, eyes gleaming. "This one never laughs, *petite souris*."

Calliope didn't miss the look of death Maxen shot his brother. She grinned. "What a charming brood all of you are."

Maxen's gaze moved to her, and her lips lifted at the corners at the consternation gathering between his brows. How had he ever appeared terrifying to her before? A remarkable thing, time.

Maxen's stare lingered on her too long, too heavy, until her grin faltered. She shoved another spoonful of stew into her mouth. "Stop staring at me as if you're waiting for me to do something foolish."

His voice dropped, dangerous-soft. "I am."

She shot the man a hot look.

"For hell's sake, one of you kiss the other before we all suffocate," Reaper muttered.

Maxen's snarl shut him up fast, but Calliope nearly choked on her stew, caught mid-swallow at the sudden gripe. Could these men stop saying such things?

Calliope almost groaned. Why did he have to reinforce *that* image in her head! Would she even get any sleep tonight?

MAXEN COULDN'T HELP himself. His eyes didn't obey the curses spewing at them in his head. They and a complete will of their own. And they wanted to stare. Her lips were curved in a cheeky little half-smile as she pursed. Her hair still tumbled over her shoulders like this morning—a magnificent, maddening, silken temptation. He wished she'd pin it up so the sight was his alone.

She was a vision. Continuing to wear breeches like she hadn't just set half his logic ablaze. Speaking to his brothers like they weren't dangerous men.

Unbothered.

Staggeringly breathtaking.

Calliope set her spoon in her empty bowl that she'd been diligently focusing on. It was already bad enough that his brothers were staring at him staring at her, but at least he'd refrained from following the spoon to her lips, tracking the small ripple of her throat as she swallowed.

She looked over at him. "I forgot to ask, how is your brother doing?"

"He's been through worse," Maxen said.

"Do you believe Mr. Peregrine is doing this?"

"Uncertain."

"We need to determine Peregrine's whereabouts." Maxen said to Dagger.

"What I would like to know," Dagger said, looking at Calliope "is how you met him last night."

Maxen hadn't even thought about that. He'd warned that blackguard to stay off his territory time and time again.

"He happened upon me in the street."

Reaper snorted. "Seems Maxen isn't the only one fol—" He shoved his boot into his brother's leg to shut him up. "Bloody hell, *frère*."

"What?" Calliope asked. "What were you going to say?"

"He's just speaking nonsense again," Maxen muttered. "But it is suspect that Peregrine just happened to be there when you left."

"What exactly happened?" Calliope asked. "You still haven't told me."

Maxen hesitated. He didn't want her bolting in alarm again.

"Two fires were set on our properties," Reaper answered. "Burned to rubble."

Damn it.

Her eyes flew wide. "Are they connected to the intruder in my shop?"

Maxen sighed. "Seems that way, unfortunately."

Her eyes narrowed. "How can I help you catch this enemy?"

His whole body went cold. His eyes locked on hers. "No."

"But—"

"No."

Her brow furrowed. "You didn't even let me finish!"

"I don't need to."

Dagger sighed and lounged back in his chair. "Just let her help, Max. She's in this whether you like it or not."

"She can help by staying put."

Calliope turned to glare at him. "In that case, I can just stay put in my shop."

Maxen cursed. "And how exactly do you plan to help us? This is dangerous, Calliope."

"However I need to."

"By that description, you only need to hold your position here."

"But I can be of value. And before you question my value, I do have value. You believe Mr. Peregrine has something to do with this, right? I can confront him."

"Absolutely not." Did the woman want to shave ten years from his life? "It would be too coincidental. We need a plan."

"Not much we can do but wait for now," Dagger said. "We have positioned scouts all over."

"Well, I might not be big and scary," Calliope pointed out. "But I am quite clever."

Reaper barked out a laugh. "Well, then let's hear this cleverness, *petite souris*."

"Well, whoever plots against you has resorted to using me as well." Her eyes met Maxen's. "So to catch them, let's set a trap."

She sounded a touch too eager for his liking. "Like my brother said, we already have scouts. Nobody moves without us knowing."

"But you can still set a up a thing of sorts and lure the enemy to you."

Reaper chuckled. "Set up a thing of sorts. I like this plan."

"I don't like it." Maxen held her gaze. Of course, this had crossed his mind, but no trap came without great risk, and after what happened to Serpent, he wasn't prepared to expose any more of his family. "We don't know who we are up against and already we have a man injured."

"I'm not saying we do something elaborate," she offered. "But we can try to use me to catch whoever sent that note to meet them here. Think about it, they might even already know I'm back at the tavern. What if we make them believe I'm being moved somewhere else?"

"Might work," Dagger said thoughtfully.

Maxen wanted to argue. "I don't like it."

"Hate to say it, *frère*, but it's not a bad idea. We might catch the enemy's messenger. Perhaps even who betrayed us."

Maxen dragged a hand down his face. "It's not a *bad* idea," he admitted reluctantly, "but this plan relies on too much luck. What if no one takes the bait?"

"Then we lose nothing," Calliope pointed out. "Except, perhaps, your patience."

Knight snorted behind the bar.

Reaper gave a lazy nod. "She's not wrong, *frère*. And no one's saying she walks out the front door with a bloody sign around her neck. We can make it look like she's being moved—carriage, decoy trunk, a bag or two—while the real mouse stays put."

Dagger scratched his jaw, thoughtful. "We've got that carriage Drake bought gathering dust."

Maxen looked at each of them, irritation a constant burn beneath his skin, jaw flexing. He hated that they were right. "And who exactly is meant to be in this decoy carriage?"

"I vote to do away with the decoy and just use me," Calliope said.

"When hell is cast in ice."

"Tighten the ship, remember?" she challenged.

That fire in her eyes—he didn't know if it made him want to pull her closer or lock her in her bloody chamber.

Knight cleared his throat. "We could use Ben."

Maxen turned. "The boy?"

"They're about the same size. No one would know the difference unless they got close."

Calliope stiffened beside him. "No."

"It's safer," Dagger said. "Cleaner. We draw them out without risking her."

"No," she repeated. "What if they see past the ruse?"

Maxen's gaze drifted back to her, noted at once the stubborn tilt of her chin, the tension in her shoulders, the quiet tremor in her fingers that she probably thought no one noticed. She was shaken. But she was also determined. Brave. He didn't have the heart to bluntly refuse. "I'll think about it."

Calliope's gaze narrowed. "That's not a no."

"It's not a yes either."

She shrugged with a smile. "But it's something."

Maxen had the distinct impression she would make sure his consideration would become more than a mere something.

She winked at him.

God. Winked.

Something deep in his chest crumbled.

Even here, she wasn't as safe as he wanted her to be. But damned if she wasn't braver than most men he knew. And he was starting to think he might be the one in most danger.

Chapter Eighteen

CALLIOPE BLINKED AFTER Maxen as the door leading to the back swung shut behind him. He hadn't said a word to her before he left. He just gave her a long look, something unreadable flickering in those stormy, dark eyes and a strange connection that slipped away along with him.

Had she said something wrong?

She exhaled, quietly. Not a sigh, precisely. A mere . . . release.

Reaper leaned back in his chair like a man born to slouch and smirk. He gave the impression of supreme laziness, but she knew, with those sharp eyes, nothing about this man was truly at rest. He was a wolf acting the sheep. Lord. And he put kissing images in her head, and she quite resented him for that!

Shameless.

"Is it always like this?" she asked him.

Reaper quirked a brow. "Like what exactly?"

"Secrets. Shadowy schemes. Brooding." Her gaze drifted to the exit again. "Silent storms."

Dagger arched a brow. "That wasn't a storm. That was Max being . . . Max."

"Right." She tilted her head. "And what, precisely, does *that* mean?" Max being Max could mean a million things.

Reaper grinned. "It means he broods better than the rest of

us. Saint is close second, Knight the third."

"Serpent comes close."

Reaper nodded. "But *frère* has the full 'smite-your-enemies-and-glower-while-doing-it' look perfected."

She had to agree there. "What was he like as a boy?" That, more than anything, piqued her curiosity. What kind of boy became a man like that?

"You should ask him that," Dagger said simply.

Right. Of course.

It was easy to imagine Maxen as he was now—powerful, unreadable, impossible to ignore. But she couldn't picture him with bright eyes and lanky legs. Couldn't picture him with scabbed knees or laughing until he hiccupped. *Had* he ever laughed like that? Had anyone ever tucked him in at night, or made him hot milk when he was sick, or told him he was loved or adored?

She doubted it.

There was a hardness in him, a kind forged by hellfire and held together with sheer will. But under that was something bruised. Something buried. She had glimpsed it in the way he touched his brothers, in the rough tenderness he tried to hide. And last night, when he'd looked at her like she was something he wanted and didn't know how to hold onto. Well, she might have very well imagined *that*, but still.

What had shaped him? What had hurt him?

What had he lost?

For all his moodiness, the man wasn't just danger and command. He was loyalty. He was protection. He was silent storms and deep oceans and things that made her insides ache without reason. And maybe—perhaps maybe—if she could understand the boy he'd once been, she might make sense of the man who had somehow taken root beneath her skin.

Something familiar in him stirred something within her.

When had he slipped past her defenses? She couldn't even name the moment. Perhaps it hadn't been a moment at all, but rather a steady erosion. Every glance, every broody word, every step wearing her down until she no longer remembered where her walls had stood!

She also understood his bone-deep determination to stay one step ahead of danger. It was the same with her and Duvessa. And the fact that he was a criminal? Stars, it scarcely seemed to matter. What did it say about her that she felt more at ease here in a tavern full of rogues than anywhere else? In a den of men the world would name villains.

Did that make her a villain by association?

Hah. If so, she would rather claim that title than the one she'd been born with.

Sorry, Papa. Mama.

This was not the fate they would have imagined for her—their daughter breaking bread with brigands. And yet, somehow, she didn't think they would fault her for her choices either. She might just have found the place she truly belonged.

Duvessa and her stepsisters would faint dead away if they saw her now. The thought of it brought a smile to her face.

She glanced at his brothers. "What about his stare? Has he always glared like that?"

Reaper flashed his teeth. "What do you think? Of course."

She nodded. "I thought so."

Reaper leaned forward. "What mischief brews in that head of yours, *petite souris?*"

Calliope glanced at the man. "What about his protectiveness? Has he always been this overprotective?"

Reaper shrugged. "I think you know the answer to that, *petite souris.*"

Dagger chuckled. "Or you can ask him."

Calliope groaned. "Oh, come on! You lot are impossible."

Reaper grinned, utterly unapologetic. "It's a rule. No gossiping about the each other, accept with each other. Certainly not to pretty little mouses he stares at like he's contemplating feasting."

Lord. More pictures of kissing flashed in her head. But! He stared at her like that? Her cheeks flushed before she could stop them. "He doesn't," she denied. "He doesn't look at me like that."

Two pairs of eyes burrowed into her.

Calliope almost threw her hands in the air. "Fine. New strategy. I'll ask about you instead."

"By all means," Reaper drawled, flicking his coin into the air at catching it again.

Calliope didn't waste time. "Why do they call you Reaper? Is that your real name? Sounds a bit grim."

He chuckled. "I earned the name."

"How?" she pressed.

The man stretched, like a cat. "Once upon a time, I may or may not have inspired a rumor that I don't leave anyone standing when I've got a blade in my hand."

Stars. "Is it true?"

"Now that, I can't answer." He winked.

Urgh. She turned to Dagger. "What about you? Is Dagger your real name or your nickname?"

He shrugged. "It's the one I chose."

So not the one he was born with. Come to think about it, did they all have the same mother? However, one glance at them and she refrained from asking. The subject might be too personal as of yet.

She glanced at Knight, the silent sentinel keeping his spot behind the bar. One could easily forget his presence. "Let me guess, also chosen."

He simply shrugged.

Reaper said, "That's his way of saying yes."

Calliope leaned back in her chair and studied them. "You're all the worst with driving conversation."

"Naturally," Reaper said easily. "Beasts usually are."

"They seem to hold grudges as well," she muttered. She'd hoped to glean a little insight into them, but all she discovered was they were utterly maddening. And their names were chosen by themselves.

Reaper just laughed.

Speaking of grudges, her thoughts drifted back to the slipper she left back in her living quarters.

Had Maxen found it? He would have said something if he had, wouldn't he? Was Maxen even his real name?

MAXEN CLOSED THE door to his chambers with a soft click, though the sound rang in his ears like a gunshot. He didn't move. He just stood there, breath held as if exhaling might crack the threadbare grip on himself he'd managed to drag upstairs with him.

He had almost kissed her right there and then.

In front of his brothers.

He yanked his shirt over his head in one rough pull, the fabric sandpaper against his skin. He needed it off. The shirt hit the floor with a muted rustle. He rolled his shoulders. The old wound on his side pulled tight. He rubbed a hand across his chest, the leather oddly soothing over the slashes that served as reminders of darker days.

Every word, every syllable of her voice dug into him.

He braced his hands on the edge of the desk.

The blood in his veins pulsed far too fast in his neck, and the skin beneath gloves itched. It was one of those days when all the scars on his body throbbed. Usually, they were triggered by phantom memories crawling along his bones. This time, only her face filled his head.

Damn Reaper.

The man was a blazing menace.

One by one, finger by finger, he peeled off his gloves. He only ever took them off when he was alone. Removing them also felt like laying down a weapon. He tossed them on the desk and stared down at his hands, flexing them once. Twice.

Scars mapped his skin, ridged in certain places, red and twisted in others, a patchwork of burns and cuts and memories he had no wish to keep. Tattoos that covered most of the obvious ones. Most days, he forgot they were even there. But today, they itched. Itched like the time they were still healing. He flexed again, watching the burn scar that cut across his palm like a jagged grin.

What the hell was he doing?

With a growl, he dropped heavily on the edge of the bed, his elbows braced on his knees, head bowed.

Too much.

Everything was too damn much.

The fires. Serpent's injuries. The unanswered questions stacking higher by the hour.

And her.

Bloody hell, her.

Calliope Turner had appeared in his world like a storm, and now she was wearing trousers tight enough to drive a man like him to prayer and had the grace to take space in his tavern as if she'd always belonged there.

She didn't. She couldn't.

Except, she did fit. Too well. Too damn easily.

And she wasn't afraid. Not of him. Not of his brothers. Not even of what Brighton could do to a woman like her. He rubbed at his face, dragging his hands down until his fingertips pressed into the muscle of his neck.

He needed sleep. A plan. Instead, all he could see was her. The way she'd spoken to his brothers. The light in her eyes when she challenged him. That smile she wore like a weapon—sharp and bright and utterly undoing.

He cursed under his breath.

She shouldn't be here. Shouldn't be involved. Shouldn't be looking at him like she saw something worth seeing. He didn't have the space for softness. He never had. Not since—

He clenched his fists. No. He wouldn't think about that now.

He got up, paced the room once, then went to the basin in

the corner and splashed cold water on his face. It did little to clear the fog.

What did she see when she looked at him now that she didn't believe he looked so "terrifying?" Still a beast? A monster?

He didn't know. He wasn't sure she did either.

And yet she returned without a fuss.

She made him forget. That was the danger. When she was near, things quieted. Enough to make him want more of what the devil would surely tear away from him later. And more was not something he could afford in this life of his.

Someone knocked on the door.

He turned, body tense, already half-reaching for the blade at his waist. No one ever knocked. Not that soft.

A note slipped under the door.

What the bloody hell was this now? He moved to pick it up and unfolded it, scowling.

Careful.

No name signed.

Who the devil would have the audacity to warn him to be careful? No one. No one with intentions he trusted. But whoever it was had reach in Fury's, where he employed several boys and a few others to see to the daily necessities.

Maxen didn't enjoy their flair for theatrics, whoever it was.

His fingers started to itch again.

He flicked the note onto his desk.

The itch over his scars intensified.

He was *always* careful. And thorough. And cautious. So excessively cautious, he made caution itself seem a reckless pursuit. He needed to vent. He reached for his gloves when another knock on the door came.

His eyes narrowed as he straightened. Was it another damn note? At this rate he would have to flog every boy in his employ.

But to his surprise, the door pushed open.

Calliope filled the frame.

Maxen froze. By God, she looked soft. Inviting. And those damn trousers.

Her gaze dropped—first to his bare hands, then to his bare chest. He saw realization dawn on her face as she took in all his scars.

Her eyes flew wide. "I-I'm sorry . . . I don't know what I was thinking. I shouldn't have just entered like this."

He let out a rough sound. Not quite a laugh. Not quite a grunt. He couldn't even find bloody words.

"Your gloves," she said, gaze flicking back to his hands. "You're not wearing them."

He flexed his hands, a reflex, resisting snatching his gloves up and tugging them on. "Not in my room."

"Ah." She hesitated, then stepped forward, only a pace, shutting the door behind her. Prince hovered behind her like a pale shadow, his head turning toward Maxen, watchful.

"You shouldn't be here," Maxen said.

Her eyes lifted to meet his. "I know."

Chapter Nineteen

CALLIOPE HADN'T KNOWN what to expect when the door creaked open. Well, fine, she'd expected something ordinary. Not *this*.

Maxen stood there.

Bare.

Bare. Chested. Bare chested. Bare hands. Her heart didn't just beat. It stuttered, then paused, then thundered like it meant to escape her entirely. Every rational thought fled as her gaze swept over him.

He was a *man* man.

Muscle and scars and muscle.

And stars save her, she wanted to press her mouth to every scar, trace every line with her tongue and ask the stories with her hands. Not a thought a sensible woman should indulge! But Maxen Fury didn't make her feel sensible.

He made her feel *wild*.

Broad shoulders, cut from some wicked sculptor's fantasy. The planes of his chest a canvas of sin, defined and dusted with a line of dark hair that arrowed down toward the waistband of his trousers. There was a scar just above his heart—red and angry— like he'd been stabbed. Slice marks adorned his ribs, his side, even his abdomen. Some clean. Some ragged. Each one a story she might never get to hear but was still dying to know anyway.

She swallowed hard.

If she'd thought him handsome before . . . This was *dangerous*, dangerous.

Every instinct screamed that she shouldn't be here. That she should turn around, close the door, pretend she hadn't come to him at all. But her feet wouldn't obey. Why had she come here again?

Oh, yes. Concern.

Yet, now, no words would form on her lips.

His brow drew together. "Is something wrong?"

Wrong. Hah. Everything about this moment was *wrong*. But somehow, also maddeningly, frighteningly right.

"No," she said, her voice oddly breathless. "I—um. No."

His gaze dropped to her hands, as if searching for signs of distress. Then his eyes rose again, calm, unreadable. But there was something there. A flicker of calculation. Something darker beneath the coolness.

She shouldn't stare. But her gaze dropped to his hands again. Big hands. Calloused and strong. But inked. The tattoos on his palms, black swirling lines that twisted into forms and runes she didn't quite recognize. Even his fingers were inked. She imagined one brushing down her cheek. She imagined all five pressing into her back.

Calliope!

Since when did you become a woman to have such thoughts?

She stepped closer without meaning to. "I mean . . . are those names on your fingers?"

He held out one hand, fingers curling slightly.

Yes, they were. Names etched deep into the skin:

Knight. Drake. Reaper. Serpent. Saint.

How extraordinary.

"They're your brothers' names," she whispered.

"Yes."

"You must love them very much." The intimacy made her

whole body clench. To wear his loyalty on his skin like that. His knuckles bore their names like vows—etched deep, permanent. No one had ever loved her like that.

His jaw worked slightly. "My family is my life."

She nodded, smiling. "I'm envious. That is something I do not have anymore. Family."

He stilled. "Is that the reason you came to Brighton?"

Calliope hesitated. Then nodded. "Yes. Amongst other reasons."

"Other reasons?"

"Curious, are you?" she countered, still smiling.

"You could say that." He looked down at Prince sticking to her legs. "You do have family, as unconventional it may be. He's a good dog."

"He is." Albeit a bit traitorous.

And she? She could still barely breathe. Because *he* was still bare-chested. *She* was still standing there. Because somehow the air between them had thickened. Her gaze dropped again. She couldn't stop staring at his hands, wondering what all the marks meant.

"The other is a compass," he said quietly, as if he could hear her thoughts. "A reminder to stay the course. The thorns represent obstacles. They cover the scars."

Scars? She hadn't even noticed the scars, too dazed by the black ink, but now she couldn't miss them. Cuts and burn scars. Her heart went out for the man. What a life he must have lived. "Did they hurt—the tattoos?"

He studied her. "Not more than what was already there."

She couldn't even fathom those words. She hesitated but finally asked the question that had been hidden in the back of her mind from the moment she met him. "Have you ever killed a man?"

His reply came instantly. "Not a man, no."

Oh.

"The act was one of mercy."

Oh. Well, that was oddly comforting. A non-bloodthirsty beast. "Right, you don't kill people. Rules like that start for a reason, correct?"

"To take a life," he said slowly, "you must first understand the value of one. We understand. So we don't take it."

Stars. This man was going to ruin her. "So you have different ways of taking care of your enemies?"

"There are many ways to ruin a man. Or woman. They don't require my hands."

Her gaze dropped to his hands again. "You hide them," she said softly. "Your hands."

He nodded.

She didn't know why that made her chest ache. "Then why did you let me see them now?" Her gaze lifted to his. "There are many ways you could have hidden them."

"I didn't *let* you." The corner of his lips twitched. "You walked in."

Her eyes flew wide. "Right! Intrusion! I seem to be excellent at that." Intruding in all sorts of situations.

"You are." His voice was soft. Deep. Almost amused.

No, most assuredly amused. Her cheeks warmed.

He stepped closer.

Calliope felt that one step in her weakening knees.

"You shouldn't be in my chamber."

Stars, forget her knees. Her whole body was in jeopardy here. "Because you are dangerous?"

"Yes."

Then why did that *yes* sound so inviting? The air charged around them. The moment before a storm breaks. She wanted to touch his chest, press her palm to that scar above his heart. Everything in her thundered to retreat—this man, this moment, this *feeling*—but her body had gone traitorous again, just like her dog.

Why had she come again?

Concern, yes. That was the excuse. But deep down, she'd

known. From the moment she heard him take the stairs, from the moment she'd told herself *don't*, she'd already decided *to*. And here he was in a way she wasn't ready for. Bare chest, ink, scars, and eyes that saw more than they should. He didn't hide the wreckage of his past. He wore branded into his skin. And maybe that's what shook her most.

She hid her past. Buried it as far as she could.

The urge to flee rose. "I should go," Calliope said softly.

His eyes—those dark storms—roamed her face. "Yes, you should."

Neither of them moved.

She squared her shoulders, refusing to give into habit. "You don't scare me."

His lips curved slightly. "You should be scared."

"But I'm not."

He leaned in, and her hands rose to his chest, pressing against the firm wall of him. He sucked in a breath, and the skin of her arms broke out in gooseflesh.

"You're doing it again," he said roughly.

"Doing what?"

"Stripping me of my power."

That was *promise*. A promise of power. And the promise made something in her break free. She wanted to taste that promise. To make those words real. To press her lips to something that felt like seductive truth. Before she could stop herself, she rose to her toes, fingers digging into his flesh, and kissed the beast on the mouth.

HER LIPS MET his, and the impact ripped the breath clean from his chest. Maxen didn't move. Didn't breathe. Didn't dare. She tasted like the sweetest damn hope he'd ever tasted, and everything he hadn't let himself want for too damn long. And then she pulled back, startled by her own boldness, her eyes wide like she'd just stepped off a ledge without knowing what waited below.

God. Not yet.

He reached for her, his hands coming up as if pulled by a force older than logic. One cradled her jaw, the other curved around the back of her head, fingers threading through the loose strands of her hair like he'd dreamed of doing it a thousand times. If he didn't kiss her again, he'd damn well explode into a million damn pieces.

His lips claimed her.

Calliope gasped against him, then melted, not holding anything back either. He kissed her like he didn't know how to stop. Like it hurt. Like it healed. Like bloody survival itself.

No finesse. Just pure want.

Her hands dragged down his bare chest, trembling slightly as they pressed against scarred skin. He broke the kiss only to drop another at the corner of her mouth. Then her cheek. Her jaw. The column of her neck, then the dip of her collarbone like each part of her held a secret he needed to learn. He curled a lock of hair around his finger and said hoarsely, "What the devil did you do to me?"

A shaky breath left her, one that was half-laugh. "I didn't mean to do any—"

"You don't need to mean it to do it."

She tilted her face up to his again, her lips a whisper from his. "Then kiss me again."

He pulled back a fraction to study her. Her eyes were dazed. Her lips swollen. Well, damnation.

He was lost.

So he kissed her again. This time slower.

One of her hands drifted to his shoulder, the pads of her fingers brushing the raised ridges of a scar. He hissed, the rush of being touched by her hands intoxicating. Being touched *softly*.

He didn't know softness.

But gods, he wanted to know.

She leaned into him to deepen the kiss, and he lost himself again—her taste, her scent, the answering willingness. Christ, he kissed her like he could convince himself he deserved her. And she kissed him like he already did.

Time stopped.

Or maybe time stretched.

He didn't know. Didn't care.

His mouth moved over hers again and again, until it was no longer just his hands memorizing her—but everything. His soul. His breath. His bones.

Her name—*Calliope*—lodged in his throat like a prayer.

He cupped her face, his thumb brushing across her. His other hand slid down to hers, gently lacing their fingers together.

Her breath hitched. "Your hands . . ."

"You've seen the worst of me," he said softly, reluctantly leaving her lips to press his forehead to hers.

She didn't answer with words. She leaned in and brushed her lips over his again. Soft. Certain.

"You've commandeered by mind," he said against her mouth. "What the hell do I do?"

She laughed. "To repeat my earlier sentiment: You kiss me again," she whispered urgently, "and you don't stop unless I do."

So bloody bold. "Christ, Calliope."

He gathered her closer but didn't dare touch anywhere below her shoulders. This wasn't about lust. It was about *touch*.

Desperate. Aching. Touch.

But everything else, her hair, her face, the fluttering pulse at her throat, he worshipped. He'd never been more terrified. And never more alive. It burned his soul—the touch of her fingers on his skin. His on hers.

Slowly, she broke away from his lips.

His chest rose and fell like he'd just finished a fight, but he didn't step away from her. Didn't tell her to leave again. He just stood there. Bare-chested. Bare-souled. Her hands touching both.

She stared up at him. "Is it too late to say I should go?"

He exhaled. Rough. "It's too late."

What the devil did a man do now? And what the blazes did he mean by saying that? He didn't know. But he couldn't stop himself either. *Promises were only as good as the people who made them.* But she made him want to listen to all her promises. She made him believe there was something left in him worth touching.

Worth saving.

Worth believing in.

But only for a moment.

A woman like her didn't really belong with a man like him. She lived in the light, while he lived in the shadows. She needed protection, while he still had to fight. Still had to find the rat who hurt his brother and set lit matches to his property. Used her to distract him.

"Why does this feel like something we can't undo?" she asked.

Because it was. "Nothing that's happened can ever be undone." Only forgotten. And even that was impossible in most cases. And if she walked away now, he'd ache for her in ways he didn't have language for. He didn't know how to do this. How to want someone with such force. How to be wanted by someone back.

Her thumb brushed along the scar that cut his lip. Maxen closed his eyes, letting the moment soak into him.

He hadn't been touched like this before.

Not ever. Not by someone who saw all the cracks and touched him so gently anyway. Who didn't flinch at his scars. Who didn't recoil at his truths. Not even in the moments he'd taken care of his needs. They were just impulses being dealt with. No need for real care.

He tangled their fingers together again, lifting their joined hands to his mouth. He pressed a kiss to her knuckles. If this was a dream, he'd rather die than ever wake up.

"I need you to be safe," he said, voice thick. He needed that more than he needed anything else.

"You don't have to keep me in a cage to do that."

Who said he couldn't do just that? "I'm not sure I know another way. And this is not a cage."

She smiled then. "Ship, then. I know you want to lock me up."

What could he say? It was the damn truth.

"You know," she murmured, "solutions that are found together obtain victory together."

Her words struck something deep inside him. They were true, but for one thing. Both parties must commit to the solutions or both risked losing out. This woman before him, she was the sort to commit.

Christ, he wanted to claim her lips again.

No, he *needed* to kiss her but . . . Could he keep his soul, his damn nerve, if he did? He didn't think he'd be able to stop if he did. If this continued, he would take something from her he could not return . . .

Maxen stepped back, his fingers curling into fists at his sides. The pained growl left him before he could stop himself. "You should leave."

Chapter Twenty

CALLIOPE SHOULD RUN. She most certainly should leave. So she just did that. What set him off, she didn't know, but his abruptness startled her into flight. She'd made it halfway to the door, Prince on her heels, before something had her stop, heart dropping to her belly then shooting back to her throat before dropping again.

Not something.

A name.

Her name.

Spoken like a curse and a plea all at once. A release of breath she wasn't meant to hear. Maybe it was the sting braided through each note, or the memory of his eyes, his hands, his kiss, all together.

Calliope turned back.

By the stars. No.

What did *she* do to *him*? Why did *she* have leave? How about the other way around? What did *he* do to *her*? Why did he not *leave*? She'd been sensible, to a degree, up until here. She had plans. A dream. Then he'd cast some sort of spell over her. She had actually kissed him. Without thinking, without planning. Without anything but pure, bone-deep, breath-stealing, brain-scattering want.

One step.

Then another.

His eyes bore into hers, and she could practically feel him assessing her behavior. Trying to make sense of what she was doing. He wouldn't get the answer. Honestly, she didn't even know.

Heat flushed low in her belly. A primal awareness.

Greed.

That was the word.

Not just for his mouth or his hands or that maddening scar above his heart, the one that split his lip. But for the way he looked at her. Protected her. Pursued her. She never imagined she'd feel this exposed.

Not after London.

Her pulse quickened as she stepped closer still, until she had to crane her neck to look up at him again, his scent enveloping her once more. She couldn't put a name to the notes—somewhere between wild and dangerous—but the spice was so blazingly heady she wanted to let her eyes drift shut and inhale deeply.

But that would break this spell.

Or enhance it.

She wasn't sure what would be more unnerving.

Her words came purposefully. "Don't ever command me."

His hand came up again. Slowly. Giving her time to evade. She didn't. He was cupping her face, firm and hesitant, thumbs brushing the arc of her cheekbones as if he couldn't quite believe he was touching her. The same as before yet somehow different.

How could she just flee from a moment such as this?

It was like he'd reached into her chest and found the wound still bleeding.

And then he swiftly let go. But instead of retreating to his side, that hand caught hers instead, and now that she was less dazed, she could feel the rough ridges of his scars against her skin.

"Why aren't you saying something?" she asked. "You're just

staring."

"So are you."

"We kissed." Was this the time to wonder what exactly that meant? As in *meant* meant? As in how to proceed in the future? Thinking about kissing and actually kissing, after all, were not the same. In fact, they weren't even in the same realm of realms.

His fingers tightened around hers. "I didn't mean to kiss you."

"I didn't mean to kiss you, either."

"Do you regret it?" he asked, a furrow appearing between his brows.

Did she?

Every part of her screamed no. But then uncertainty slithered in, cold and slick. "I probably should, shouldn't I?"

His jaw flexed, and he started to pull away.

She didn't let him.

"Wait," she whispered, keeping their fingers twined. Her father had once told her, *If you ever find yourself on the edge of a cliff, Calliope, look at the man who led you there. Does he want to push you off, or pull you back?* She hadn't understood back then. She was sure she never would. Now, she did. "I didn't say I did."

His eyes met hers again, and the storm in them settled. "You confuse the hell out of me."

She gave a breathless laugh. "We could start a club, then."

That startled a laugh from him. The rough sound hit her square in the chest. This man, he didn't laugh often. His brothers' teasing made that clear. But when he did, he was unfairly handsome. Less beast, more man. It made her want to kiss him again, memorize the way his mouth curved when amusement slipped past the shadows.

Just as quick, it was gone.

There he was again. All heat and shadows. All muscle and mayhem. Her insides twisted. She was in trouble. Deep, unholy, heart-thudding trouble. "My father would have liked you."

"I don't believe that."

"He would have," she insisted, tightening her grip on his

scarred hand. "He saw the best in people, even when they did not deserve it. Especially then. It was his greatest gift and his greatest undoing."

"What do you mean?"

"He trusted the wrong woman," she said quietly. "She . . . she wrapped her lies around him until he could no longer tell truth from poison. By the time he realized her poison, it was too late."

"Then he and I would not have gotten along. I don't much like poison, and I'm not fond of lies either."

"Some poisons are disguised prettily."

That earned her an arched brow. "Is that a warning?"

She laughed. "I'm much too simple for that."

"Says the rose."

"Why, thank you. I won't deny my thorns." Her mouth tilted. "And yet, you are the man of no poison, sitting at the center of Brighton's underworld. A little contradiction never hurt anyone, I suppose?"

His eyes flicked down to their still-twined fingers. "Contradictions keep men alive."

"So you don't like lies. Does that mean you never tell any?"

"Not to my family."

"Right, you just ignore them, I imagine." And she could also imagine he did it rather spectacularly.

"I'm not a whole man, Calliope."

"You look rather whole to me."

"You know what I mean."

She offered him a smile. She assumed he referred to his past. "A person's pain or past doesn't make them less of a whole person, Maxen. You're just a bit scratched. Possibly cursed. Slightly beastly. But not less."

He made a sound—half sigh, half groan—and dropped his forehead to hers. "You're not helping."

"Are you going to growl at me to leave again?"

His nose brushed hers.

Could they stay in this moment forever?

THE MOMENT CALLIOPE slipped out the door, Maxen snatched up his gloves and tugged them back on. A habit. A reflex. Something to do with his hands now that they weren't lost in her hair. And he didn't want the fading impression to vanish, so he'd trap them with his gloves.

You're a fool.

Fool or not, he could still feel her. The warmth of her skin. The beat of her pulse beneath his fingers. The unhesitating press of her lips against his, her touch leaving a mark on his damned soul. He couldn't shake the feeling that if he didn't *contain* this desire inside him, it might spread. Infect every thought. Every instinct. Every bloody plan.

An absurd, ridiculous sentiment.

One he couldn't stop.

He flexed his fingers, the leather biting into his knuckles, and staring at the closed door like it might spit her back out. But she didn't return. Of course she didn't. She'd kissed him, rattled him to his bones, and finally fled after she heard Reaper's voice in the hallway.

Sensible. Smart, even.

He wanted to go after her. Fortunately, he'd managed to stop himself. Monsters shouldn't want to want innocent angels.

The next tap on the door was too hard to be polite. Pushing it open before Maxen could answer, Drake stalked in, boots muddy and mood fouler than usual. "Serpent is awake, stubborn as hell and downstairs, dead set on hunting down his assailants."

Maxen cursed.

Naturally, his brother was already plotting revenge. The man had a dagger stitched into his soul and patience stitched nowhere at all.

Drake ran a hand through his hair. "He's bandaged and barely standing, but he won't listen to sense. Saint's holding him back for now."

Damn it.

Events were spiraling too fast, too personal. "Who the bloody hell could be hiding in the shadows?" Maxen asked. "The same ones who torched the warehouses or someone different?"

"The same," Drake said. "I'd bet my dagger on it."

"Then it's a message?"

Drake snorted. "More like a dare."

Could very well be. Enemies were nothing new. Rival crews. Smugglers with grudges. Aristocrats with their noses bent out of shape. But this? This felt different. Too precise. Too damn pointed. Fires, ambushes, shadows tailing Calliope's every step. This wasn't business. This was damn personal. As if someone wanted them all off-balance. And knew exactly which thread to yank to unravel him. And they were right.

There was a knock again, and Knight slipped in, face resembling a block of stone. "Saint wants to take a stroll tonight."

"No," Maxen said at once.

"He says it's the only way to calm Serpent's temper."

Maxen swore under his breath. "Knock Serpent out if you have to. No one is leaving Fury's tonight."

Knight gave a curt nod. "Reaper spotted a little tail through the window. Someone's watching the tavern. Could be watching us. Could be waiting for her."

A chill instantly spread through him. Maxen turned slowly to the window, but he didn't move. Waiting for her? They'd wait forever.

"Could be both," Drake offered.

Knight met his gaze. "She's the oddest piece on the board."

She was. She was the only thing here now that hadn't been here before. Maxen's hand curled into a fist. "We should delay fishing out the rat."

Knight's tone stayed level. "We can fish them out clean. Controlled. We set the trap, they come spy, we follow them back."

Maxen shook his head. "We don't even know who 'they' are."

"We will," Drake said quietly, "if they take the bait."

Maxen paced to the unlit fireplace, planted a hand on the mantel. His shoulders coiled tight, jaw locked. Whoever was starting fires was taunting them. They must be aware of Serpent's history, too. He felt it in his bones. And they were also using Calliope.

Unacceptable.

Both things. Every instinct in him revolted at the idea of putting her and his brothers in the path of a threat. Even in pretend. Even surrounded by every brother he trusted. Even if she *volunteered*.

Especially then.

He didn't like her eagerness to head straight into danger. This wasn't just about strategy. It wasn't even about the mission anymore. It was about *her*. At the same time, he didn't want to leave her alone at the tavern while they hunted. Didn't want her open to such risk. And damn him, but he didn't want her *far from him*, either. And he couldn't let his brothers do this alone.

Bloody everlasting hell.

"She stays close," Maxen growled.

Knight frowned. "Then we are doing this."

"We're not using her," Maxen clarified stonily. "We fake a move. A discreet exit. Whisper the details through the town's veins. Make it sound like we're whisking her off to a safe place."

"And when they bite?"

Maxen's face darkened. "We bite harder."

Drake folded his arms. "And where does she go?"

Maxen turned, eyes hard. "With me." As his side at all times.

Knight's brow lifted. "You think that's wise?"

No.

Moving forward with this might just be catastrophically unwise. But he couldn't do what his brothers wanted any other way. She'd already cracked open parts of him that hadn't felt anything in years. And after what had happened to Reaper at her hand, the night of rushing around searching for her, Maxen wasn't taking any chances.

He could even envision her. Calliope, stubborn as a mule, pistol hidden somewhere on her body, ready to act brave. His brothers would guard her well, but what if something went wrong and he wasn't close?

His gut stung at the thought, sharp and merciless. No. Not again. He'd let her run free once. He wasn't making that mistake again, not while an unknown enemy was circling her like a vulture. Not while blood had already been spilled.

"She'll be safer at my side than anywhere else," he said.

Drake didn't argue. Neither did Knight. They knew. Once he made that call, there was no recalling it.

"When?" Knight asked, his eyes twin coals of violence. "I'm in the mood to bite."

So was Maxen.

"Tomorrow."

✿❀ ❦ ❀✿

Chapter Twenty-One

CALLIOPE STOOD AT the bar, foot tapping while Reaper sat on a high stool a few feet away, coat hanging open, a coin flicking from finger to finger. Knight stood in the far corner, silent, arms folded, his gaze fixed on the street through the window. Dagger was there as well, turning a dagger lazily in his hand.

This morning, the tavern was cold, the kind of cold that crept under her jacket and settled there. Beneath, she wore a fresh set of shirt and trousers, this pair a soft brown. The place where fire ought to crackle was barren, which didn't help, but she suspected it best not to ask. Strangely, smoke still grasped at the interior. Not much, but enough to be noticeable.

Did Maxen smoke?

She'd never glimpsed him with a cigar, but the scent still clung to him at times. Speaking of which, where was the man? Every minute she waited for him to make an appearance, her nerves prickled more and more.

Waiting gave her mind too much time to think.

And, unfortunately, to remember.

The memory was a dangerous heat in her breast, one she kept trying to tamp down like an unruly fire. The moment kept replaying in flashes—the way his mouth had gone still, almost startled, before answering with something so controlled she almost wished it would snap. Well, for that man, control probably had snapped. There was even more than one kiss. And he kept touching her as well. But even his control snapping possessed control! Ah, sun and stars, the way his hands had held her face like they weren't allowed anywhere else.

And the way she had almost wanted them to be.

Foolish.

She had been utterly foolish. Kissing Maxen Fury, the dark Prince of Brighton, her landlord, her shadow in the Lanes . . . and she the lamb that had stepped with him into the night.

She had not meant to.

At least, not until she had.

But she didn't regret her decision either.

More curiously, she didn't mind the dark all that much anymore. Not when she was with him. Nevertheless, whatever had possessed her—defiance, gratitude, curiosity—she wanted a repeat. He was a man for kissing. He was also a man for traps, and apparently, that did not involve telling her the whole truth until it suited him.

She glanced at Reaper. He caught her look and grinned, the sort of grin that said he'd be just as happy to watch the world outside go up in smoke as lend a hand to save it.

"Stop fidgeting, *petite souris.* He'll be here soon."

"I am not fidgeting," she said primly. "And stop calling me that." *And* she hadn't asked. Was she that transparent, though?

"You're rattling in your skin," Reaper countered, the coin flicking rapidly between his fingers. "Nerves?"

"Impatience," she said, lifting her chin. "There's a difference."

Knight's voice came flatly. "Patience is virtue."

Said the outlaw.

Reaper chuckled. "There will be action soon enough."

"And what exactly will this 'action' be? No one has yet bothered to tell me what I'm meant to do besides sit in a carriage and look like bait."

Reaper exchanged a look with Knight—amusement meeting something sterner. That was her first warning.

"About that, *petite souris* . . ." Reaper said, drawing the words out.

Her stomach dipped. "About that?"

"You won't be in the carriage," Dagger tossed out.

There was a beat of silence. Calliope blinked at him. "I beg your pardon?"

"You'll be with Maxen," Knight said, as if it were the most reasonable thing in the world. "Holding back a few streets. Saint will take his place in the main carriage, with a runner dressed as you."

For a moment she thought she'd misheard. Then her spine stiffened. "A boy is going to dress as me?"

Reaper's grin widened. "Don't pout, *petite souris*. You've been dressing as a boy, and he's a quick runner if things turn sour."

"I'm dressed as a *man*." But that was not the point.

His brow arched. "Whatever you say, *petite souris*."

She could feel her pulse in her temples. "He won't need to run because no one will follow him! They'll take one look and know he's not me. And then your entire plan will amount to nothing!"

"It's safer this way," Knight pointed out.

"Safer?" And utterly pointless. "If you want to flush out whoever is following me, then you need to give them something worth following. They should know my face, my posture, the way I look out of a window. You think a street boy in a borrowed bonnet will fool them? They'll be watching for me, not an imitation."

Knight's face remained carved from stone. "It's our job to draw them out, not hand you over like a gift-wrapped parcel."

"Oh? And here I thought you were going to prevent that from happening. Seems I was mistaken."

Reaper shrugged. "Anything can go wrong."

Calliope leaned forward, hands braced on the counter. "If I'm not in that carriage, the whole scheme is useless. You're chasing shadows, and they'll vanish the moment they realize I'm not there. This is not the time for half-measures."

Reaper arched a brow. "Maxen dearest won't agree to it."

"Then I shall persuade him." She leaned against the bar and mimicked Knight's pose. "One way or another, if we are going to spring this trap, it *will* be real."

A shadow fell across the counter of the bar. The air shifted.

Speak of the devil.

Calliope didn't need to look to know it was him—her skin had already recognized him, the same way it always seemed to do. She was unsettled by how easily she noticed, unsettled by that knot of awareness.

Dark eyes met hers.

For a moment, something blazed in his expression, something that reminded her of the way his hands had held her face last night, careful, almost cherishing. But it was gone as quickly as it came, replaced by that steady, inscrutable mask. She hadn't even brought up the subject, yet felt the refusal like a door slamming. But if he thought that ended the matter, he didn't know her half as well as he believed.

Just you wait, Maxen Fury.

TROUBLE ALWAYS CAME in threes.

Maxen's morning had started with a throbbing headache and the sinking suspicion that a cycle was once again about to start. And he was right.

She was still wearing trousers.

Maxen growled, low and dangerous. "Why the devil are you wearing that again?"

She blinked at him from where she now leaned on the bar, wide-eyed and innocent, as if she weren't already a walking temptation designed solely to test his patience. "Are we going to rehash this again?"

Yes. Until she stopped wearing trousers.

He crossed his arms over his chest, trying not to let his gaze dip to where the "disguise" hugged her figure in ways that were nothing short of scandalous.

Her lips twitched, and he swore she was fighting a smile. "You'll just have to continue to suffer through my look."

Suffer indeed. He clenched his fists. All his hands wanted to do was *touch*. Her.

"Besides," she said. "It's more comfortable with this sort of business."

"Spoken like a true outlaw," Reaper muttered.

"It's practical," she replied, planting her hands on her hips. "Easier to move around, less restrictive than skirts."

Maxen pinched the bridge of his nose, counting to ten in a futile attempt to rein whatever was threatening to break loose. "Calliope," he began, his voice dangerously calm, "if you step one foot outside dressed like that with us, I'll—"

"You'll what?" she interrupted, arching a brow. "Forbid me? Lock me in your chambers?"

Maxen's eyes narrowed. "Don't tempt me." What he'd wanted to say was that if she stepped out with them, no one would believe her to be a boy. Though no one would believe it anyway. He looked at his brothers. "Are we ready?"

"We were just discussing how your mouse here thinks she should be the one in the carriage."

"No." She always took his white-knuckled control and made a wreckage of it, as if it were the most brittle thing in the damn world. As if last night hadn't already cost him more self-command than any brawl in the last decade. "You're not in the main carriage."

"I am." Her tone was soft and infuriatingly certain.

"It's too great a risk."

"And what will you do when no one follows? Tip your hat to boy in my place and say 'better luck next time?' They'll know it isn't me before the wheels have gone twenty yards."

His jaw flexed. "You don't know that."

"I do," she said, holding his gaze. "And so do you, if you're honest. If you want results, you need to make it real."

"You think I'd use you as bait?"

"I think," she said slowly, "you already are. The difference is whether it will work or not."

Maxen glanced at his brothers.

Reaper's grin sharpened.

Knight's arms remained folded.

Dagger said nothing.

"Saint rides in my coat," he said, clipped. "Hat down, head high. Tom wears a dress and bonnet and keeps his face down. They take the main way past the last houses, cut through the market, then out to the open road. The rest follow closely. You, Miss Turner, remain with me, two horses behind until we see who bites."

"And if no one does?" she asked.

"They will."

"Because you hope so?" she returned. "Or because you've done this before with a woman they already know?"

Damn it.

"Your boy will be a poor version of me. If your trap depends upon them believing I am in that carriage, then I must be in that carriage."

"You're not bargaining with me."

"You're right, I am not bargaining." Her chin lifted. "I am stating a requirement."

Reaper let out a low whistle. "The mouse comes with terms. This is why I avoid women."

Maxen shot his brother a filthy look.

"What?" Reaper slouched deeper, palms raised in mock innocence. "She has a point, *frère*. If you want a fox, you don't parade around a dressed-up dog as a hen and pray the fox is near-sighted."

Knight scoffed. "That is why women avoid *you*. Referring to them as animals."

"We don't know how deep the danger festers," Maxen said. "Which is why she stays where I say."

"Maxen." His name on her tongue did something fierce to him. His whole body clenched. "Would you have selected your brother to take your place if I weren't here?"

She stared at him. Calm, steady, stubborn as winter. The cap shadowed her cheekbones; a loose wisp of gold had escaped and brushed her jaw. Last night, his hands had fit there. Held, not claimed. A boundary he'd put on himself because touching her had already felt like standing at the edge of a cliff and choosing the drop.

He hesitated.

"Ha!" She narrowed in on him. "I'm right, aren't I? So why are you doing this now? You are not scared, are you?"

He almost growled.

"Compromise," Reaper offered, too damn cheerful. "Let her sit the first leg. We'll do the switch later if we must. There are plenty of spots. Tom takes over for the last stretch. If our rats haven't shown by then, they're not biting at all."

Knight's voice was cool. "Too many pieces in play."

"Pieces playing keep you alive," Reaper said without care.

"Stop speaking nonsense." Maxen's fingers itched. Itched to clench. Itched to throttle.

The routes unstitched in his head: corners, choke points, rooftops where men could sit without being seen. He loathed every version that ended with her in reach of a knife. A pistol. Eyes. He detested even more the thought of her walking out of this room angry and stubborn and straight into risk without his hand on the reins.

Could he even stop this at this point? "You ride nowhere without my order. Not one turn."

"Of course," she said with satisfaction. "I didn't expect any-thing less."

Maxen's mouth flattened. "I don't like it."

"I don't either," Knight said. "But I hate failing more."

"Then it's settled," she said with a nod.

"I'm not done," Maxen said firmly. "Your hair stays pinned. Your 'disguise' gets a coat over it. And you stay back from the window."

One corner of her mouth lifted. "Happy to oblige."

Reaper snorted.

Maxen stepped closer without thinking and almost wished he hadn't. This close, it was almost impossible not to reach out and touch her. "If I knock twice on the roof, you drop to the floor. If I knock three times, you get out and follow Knight. You do not wait, you do not ask questions, and you do not look back."

"And if you do not knock at all?" she asked.

"Then you stay where you are and let me bloody work."

She nodded. "Agreed."

Knight sighed. "Saint will complain."

"Saint can complain on the move." He looked to Reaper. "If anyone you don't recognize so much as blinks at that carriage, I want to be signaled before he finishes that blink."

Reaper flashed his teeth. "Of course."

He vanished through the back. Knight followed with a last hard look at Maxen that said he would hold him responsible for every hazard in this plan, and he would be right. He couldn't stop his gut from twisting, the kind of twists that came when men made choices they could not unmake. He had never intended to give in, yet something about the way Calliope defied him—chin high, green eyes ablaze—made him say the exact opposite of what he meant.

She seemed to have that way with him.

He shrugged out of his coat and covered her shoulders, his fingers brushing against the column of her neck before he retreated. A simple contact. It burned through every lesson he had ever learned about keeping a rein upon himself. "Remember the knocks."

"I will."

"Come. Let's set your trap," he said, guiding her where the carriage waited and, with it, whatever third trouble the day had saved for him.

✿❧ ❧✿

Chapter Twenty-Two

CALLIOPE SAT A hand-span back from the window, as instructed, her cap pulled low, while the carriage rattled at a steady pace. Rules. Always rules. She half-imagined him up there on the box, jaw set, eyes forward, reins held like he could muscle the world into obeying if it dared to veer off course.

These men lived by their rules the way other people lived by prayers. They might be outlaws, but they weren't careless ones.

But still outlaws.

She hoped this plan worked.

Then this chapter of her life would end as well.

She gripped the lapels of Maxen's jacket covering her and buried her face into the collar, drawing in a long breath. It smelled faintly, impossibly, of him—clean with that stubborn trace of smoke that never seemed to leave him. Solid. Male. Maxen.

How foolish you are, Calliope!

And so? A woman was allowed to be foolish once in a while.

She set her shoulders and let her head rest back on the cushion. But she should remain more alert. And remember the knocks. Two knocks—down to the floor. Three—out the far door and follow Knight's voice. Or was it Saint? If nothing . . .

Argh.

Something.

Well, it appeared everything might be going according to plan. No knocks were good knocks.

She lifted the hand that his had brushed earlier.

He wore his gloves again. He really never took them off. Well, not in public. Also not in front of his brothers. But that obstinate man hadn't covered his hands when she'd unexpectedly caught him without a part of his armor, and that made her feel things she ought not feel.

Maxen Fury . . .

Somewhere above and ahead, he sat, reins in his hands, the world in his keeping. The thought that this was supposed to end things—this day, this plan—flared sharp in her chest. Would she stay in Brighton? Start over somewhere new? But even as the questions came, so came the unbidden image of her dark landlord.

Maxen, up there on the box, not looking back.

She burrowed deeper into the seat. Leaning into the plush cushion might bring his voice through the wood and leather between them. Nothing came, of course. Only the pulse of hooves, the clatter of wheels.

It was almost worse than danger—the waiting.

A crack split the air. Distant, muffled.

Calliope shot upright. What on earth was that?

Another. Louder. Close enough to feel it.

Her spine went rigid, ears straining. No knocks.

Her pulse hammered. Was that good? Bad? Was *nothing* the signal to stay put or to move? What were the rules again? The team surged and the carriage rocked. She grabbed for anything, swallowing the cry that leaped to her mouth before it escaped.

Still no knocks.

Argh! What did that mean again? His voice filled her head.

Stay where you are. Let me work.

The roof gave a brutal thud. A man dropping his weight where no man should be. A second blow followed. Deeper, duller. The carriage shuddered as if the sky itself had stumbled. Then another sickening thud as something heavy struck soil beside the road.

Her mouth went dry.

No knocks.

Do not think, Calliope. Remember. Two means down. Three means out. None means stay.

The carriage lurched again.

Oh, lord. Was it over?

A blur streaked past the window—black, swift, unmistakably a horse. She jerked to the other side. Another rider there. Masks. Dark coats. Their movements were too smooth, too precise. Men drilled to breathe as one.

No.

No. No. No.

It *wasn't* over.

"Maxen?" she called, small and fierce, to the roof. No answer.

Her hand found the door-latch before pausing. Could she jump from a moving carriage? It hadn't picked up that much speed yet. What was she supposed to do? Hold fast? What would he do?

Just hold on a little longer.

She let out a shaky breath.

Would that phrase always cling to her? Always with a meaning of survival?

No knocks. The rules were simple.

But she could not abide them. Calliope flipped the latch, shoved her shoulder to the panel, and dropped from the carriage as it continued forward, refusing to think about anything else other than escaping. The road slammed into her, she into it, jarring her insides more harshly than she anticipated. White spots danced beneath her eyelids, and she rolled and rolled. The moment she came to a halt, she stumbled to her feet.

Unfortunately, she didn't get far.

A gloved hand closed over her mouth. "Easy now."

She tried to twist, to bite; a man lifted her clean off her feet as if she weighed no more than a shawl. A cap came down over her head, dark and tight. The world vanished. Sound crowded in— the thunder of hooves, voices, one last gunshot swallowed by the road—and then there was nothing but the quick, thunderous drum of her own heart.

Maxen was alive, wasn't he?

The alternative brought a chill to her.

Everything went black.

THE TASTE OF iron coated in his mouth.

Maxen opened his eyes to find himself flat on his back, the earth uncomfortably hard and the sky above unreasonably bright. A dull, insistent throb pulsed at the side of his skull—steady as a drum and promising to haunt him for the remainder of the day.

He rolled, spat red, and got to his knees.

He was going to kill someone.

He'd only ever killed one person in his life, and he vowed his hands—he clenched them into fists—would never take another life. But he was damn well willing to make an exception today.

He took in the scene around him. There was no sign of the carriage. Of Calliope. The earth showed only the rough churn of hooves and wheels, the track scuffed raw, and the bitter breath of gunpowder that hadn't faded.

No shouts. No answering thunder of hooves from the Fury line.

Where the devil were his brothers? They'd been following at a distance, Saint and Knight riding flank, Reaper holding the rear. They should have been here by now. Unless . . .

Bloody everlasting hell.

His jaw tightened. Unless those blackguards had struck them too.

Someone betrayed them.

There was no other explanation for what had happened here. He cursed again, his gaze hunting down the evidence layered in the tracks. Six sets of hooves' imprints came in together, close, tight, moved as one, then split like a forked stream. He glanced in the direction they moved. Damn it. If they hurt his brothers . . . if they hurt Calliope . . .

Their world would burn.

The ground beneath him swayed, but he forcibly held himself upright by sheer willpower and rage. Hoofbeats approached, and through the haze of red hurtled Reaper, his black gelding slick with sweat, nostrils flaring. His brother swung down before the horse had even fully halted.

"*Frère.*" His gaze swept the road. "Where is the mouse?"

Maxen didn't answer.

Reaper's jaw worked before his eyes narrowed on Maxen's temple. "You're bleeding."

"Not enough to matter." A little blood wouldn't stop his fury.

Knight arrived, galloping over, his coat streaked with mud and his pistol drawn, a fierce scowl in place. "Where is she?"

"Gone," Reaper answered for him.

Maxen just couldn't say that one word. Couldn't accept it.

Knight's gaze slashed toward the tracks before coming back to him. "Are you all right?"

Maxen gave a single, sharp nod.

Moments later, Saint thundered up the road, his eyes roaming over Maxen's face. "The girl?" he demanded before the horse had even stopped moving.

"Taken," Knight said, his voice steel.

Saint slid from the saddle. "You hurt?"

Maxen's hands curled into fists. "No," he said again, though the steady drumbeat in his skull disagreed.

Dagger and Drake arrived next.

"Calliope?" Drake asked.

Maxen shook his head.

Drake gave a curt nod, while Dagger's face turned thunderous. A woman had been taken on their watch. This wouldn't sit well with any of them.

"What the devil happened?" Reaper demanded. "*How* the devil did it happen?"

"Your boy," Knight said. "He betrayed us."

Saint swore softly.

"Impossible," Reaper snapped. "And he's not *my* boy. He's *our* boy."

"Knight is right," Drake said. "He is the only one who could have sold us out to the enemy. The only one besides us who knew."

Maxen turned to Reaper. "Wasn't he with you?"

Reaper scratched his head. "His mother has been sick. Perhaps he was lured over to the other side with promises."

"This should never have happened," Dagger said.

Drake nodded. "Agreed. We need to find the boy."

"Who would have thought we had beneath our nose the very thing we sought?" Dagger muttered.

Maxen's gaze swept over the road once more, the hoofprints, the splintered twig off to the side—anything that might tell him where they'd taken her. The sight of those tracks still made his gut twist.

"Find his mother," Maxen said. "Then we'll find him."

"Hopefully he can be convinced without blood," Dagger muttered.

Reaper scoffed. "You're too hopeful, *frère*."

Saint's lips twisted. "I'm in the mood to convince."

"No blood," Maxen said. "And we need a plan. If we move too soon, we lose them both."

Knight's brow furrowed. "Both?"

"Calliope," Maxen ground out, "and the blackguard who planned this."

Reaper let out a short, harsh laugh. "Your trap turned into a trap?"

"I think," Maxen said, meeting his brother's stare head-on, "someone went to a lot of trouble to show we are not untouchable."

Dagger's eyes narrowed. "Then they don't know you very well."

"Well," Reaper drawled with a sneer. "I hate to point this out, but we are not untouchable. And we were taken down shamefully easily."

Knight nodded.

"We were betrayed," Saint said.

Yes, and that should never have happened. Betrayal was unacceptable. Loyalty was above all else. Tom had to know that he'd be outed the moment their enemy struck. Which meant he was either extremely desperate, or their enemy was more convincing than they thought, or Tom had been loyal from the start, but never to them.

A little rat.

A little spy.

And he'd been in their house.

But his mind circled back to the irrefutable truth—she had been taken on his watch. His. That was a failure he could neither forgive nor forget.

"Reaper, Drake," Maxen said. "You follow the tracks with me. Knight, Saint, find the boy. Dagger, they might have a decoy."

"If they have, I'll be happy to deal with them." Dagger's lips lifted like a hound scenting blood.

Saint strode over to swing onto the back of Knight's horse, nodding Maxen to his own. "Don't lose him too."

Reaper whistled. "Poking the bear already."

Maxen glared at his brothers. However, some of the tension left his body, replaced by determination. He strode over to the horse and swung into the saddle, the movement sending a fresh pulse of pain through his skull. He ignored it and fixed his eyes on the narrowing strip of road ahead.

"Let's move," he ordered.

Mud flew under pounding hooves, the wind biting at his face, the world reduced to one single thought. He would find her. Every yard he covered was one less between him and the woman who'd slipped—no, been ripped—out of his reach.

They would pay for taking her.

Chapter Twenty-Three

AWARENESS RETURNED IN hazy flashes.

The first thing Calliope registered was smell. Old mold, at least she thought that's what it was, and something damp rotting somewhere. Second was the pain. *Never jump from a moving carriage again, Calliope!* Though, she ached less than she thought she would. Small mercies. Only then did she notice the sound of breathing. Most decidedly not hers. Or perhaps it was. At that point, anything was possible.

Her eyes flickered open.

The room was dark, light filtering only through narrow cracks between planks nailed across the windows, and for a moment, panic slammed into memories from the past and flashed through her head like nightmares.

Was she back in the attic?

Had Duvessa and her uncle found her?

How was that possible? She'd changed her name. She'd been so careful.

Calm down, Calliope.

She shifted and felt the pull of rope at her wrists, securing her to a chair, much as she'd tied Reaper, only her bonds were much more experienced. This must be penance for what she'd done to him.

A cough rasped from the far side of the room.

Her gaze snapped toward the sound, heart kicking against her breast. A shape hunched in the corner, knees drawn up, coat rumpled.

Sun and stars! "Mr. Rollings?" Relief surged so quickly it startled her, followed almost immediately by a pinch of guilt. She'd quite forgotten about the man. And from his state, he'd been here for a while!

He lifted his head. The shadows did little to soften the pallor of his face or the bruising that spread from his temple down the side of his face. One arm rested in a makeshift sling, and blood coated his cravat. "Ah, Miss Turner, you are finally awake."

"How long ago did I arrive?" She must have been dead to the world if she had slept through being strapped up like this!

"About an hour or so, I believe."

"I—" Her throat caught, but she had to dislodge this uneasiness from her heart once and for all. "I'm sorry. For that night. I was there, I saw them hit you, but I ran away."

"You did the right thing, Miss Turner." His lips twitched in something that might have been a smile, though it was gone too quickly to name. "John would not have forgiven me if any harm had befallen you. He might have my head anyway. I should never have requested you to meet me at such an ungodly hour at such an ungodly place."

"Why did you?" she asked softly.

"I wasn't thinking straight." He leaned his head back against the wall and sighed. "I thought I was being followed and didn't want to lead them to your shop. Things went wrong, nevertheless."

"An understatement."

He chuckled. "I overheard three men looking for a girl. They asked about a woman with fair hair. They mentioned you by name." His gaze found hers. "Your real name."

Calliope swallowed a gasp. "Mr. Fitz told you."

He nodded. "Rest assured, I shall never betray his confidence.

But I'm getting too old for this." His mouth quirked in a humorless way.

Cold prickled at the back of her neck. It could only have been Duvessa's men, couldn't it?

"Do you know if they are still in town?"

Mr. Rollings shook his head. "If they haven't found you yet, they may have moved on."

A girl could hope.

She forced herself to search the room they were being held in. Rough plank walls. A single door. No visible guards. But they *were* there. She could feel them. The masked men. Maxen's enemies.

She tested the ropes securing her wrists, grimacing. She wouldn't be able to break free on her own.

Rollings caught the motion. "Don't," he said quietly. "They'll hear."

"They?" That was hardly reassuring. She drew a long, steadying breath. "Someone will come, Mr. Rollings. In fact, they may be on their way already." Maxen. He'd come. If he was still alive, he'd come.

Mr. Rollings coughed again. "Ah, Miss Turner. Do not tell me you believe in knights on steeds?"

"Not knights, no." Though one of them was literally called Knight. "The Furys."

That earned her an incredulous, almost pitying look. "Fury? Then you have met them?"

"Maxen Fury is my landlord." Amongst other things.

The comical look that passed across his features almost made her laugh. "Then it must be fate. You put your faith in him?"

"I do." So blasted much.

Another sigh. "I wish you had heeded my warning."

"About the beasts that patrol the streets of Brighton?" She refrained from pointing out that Mr. Rollings asked her to meet in the very streets they patrolled. Instead, she said, "Perhaps you are right, Mr. Rollings. Fate had other plans. And they have been nothing but kind to me."

"To Calliope Turner, yes. Not Calliope Balfour."

"What do you mean?"

"How do you imagine they'll react once they discover your blood is just as blue as the people who tortured them into becoming the beasts they are today? My advice, Miss Turner: run. If we survive this, if we escape here, run as far from Brighton as you possibly can."

"Torture? You mean how they were treated by nobles?"

"Precisely that, Miss Turner."

Would they truly shun her if they discovered the truth?

The ropes at her wrists suddenly felt too tight, the room closing in with the heaviness of his words. *Calliope Turner. Not Calliope Balfour.* The name struck like the edge of a blade she had thought long blunted.

And Maxen? His brothers? Surely they weren't tortured in the literal sense? She thought of all their scars . . .

Her pulse thundered in her ears.

If Maxen learned the truth . . . would he cast her aside? Would he see her not as the woman who had escaped a nightmare and built a life from nothing, but as a reminder of the very world that had broken him?

"No, he—they—aren't like that." But could she truly claim that?

"Beasts are beasts."

He couldn't know what he was saying, could he? He couldn't possibly understand. And yet, the way his gaze held hers, almost sorrowfully, told her he knew precisely what blade he had just twisted.

No.

Maxen *couldn't.*

Wouldn't.

But doubt, that sly devil, slithered into her heart. She couldn't recall any disdain from him for nobles, but then, why would he discuss such things with her? They weren't amongst nobles here.

Would he lump her among them the instant he learned her name? Could she ever reveal her true identity now?

"Perhaps you are right, Mr. Rollings. However, beasts are often misjudged by us. They are, after all, humans too."

Somewhere outside, a laugh cut through the air, followed by footsteps and the door unlocking. Light flared as it swung open, making her squint. A figure stood framed against the doorway. Tall, blond hair neatly arranged, eyes locked on her.

Mr. Peregrine!

Memory surged. His voice leaning into her . . . his hand covering her mouth . . . words she had dismissed as nightmare when blackness claimed her. So it had been him all along!

His mouth curved into a smile, almost pleasant, but his eyes—cold and flat—betrayed whatever mood he tried to create with that grin. "So we meet again, Miss Turner."

Words lodged in her throat.

"You should have remained at Talon's, where I left you. Then it might not have come to this."

"Something tells me it would always have come to this."

"Perhaps." Then, with chilling ease, he pointed the black barrel of his pistol level with her heart. "Unfortunately, I've been instructed to take your life."

"What?" Calliope managed, her gaze flicking between him and the pistol. "By whom?"

"It's nothing personal, Miss Turner. Someone wants to teach Maxen Fury a lesson. You, it seems, are the means to do it."

"So I am to die here today. And you are to kill me." A strange calm settled over her. One she hadn't thought possible in the face of this situation. If she were to perish at this moment, she would perish only with one regret. That Maxen's was not the face she'd take to the afterlife.

"I ought to do just that, but I confess, I find the task rather distasteful."

Calliope blinked. "So you don't intend to steal my life?"

His smile turned sharp. "Now, now. I didn't say that."

VVIOLENCE RAGED IN his blood.

He couldn't remember the last time he'd been so furious. Perhaps the day he'd tried to kill his father but had got beaten to within an inch of his life instead. But he couldn't recall such bone deep rage in his memories.

Killing rage, perhaps.

But not this deep, burn-this-damn-island-to-ash sort of rage.

The rain had thinned to a cold mist that slicked the earth as they reached a run-down cabin where the tracks stopped.

"Something's off," he said, and swung down before his gelding had settled. Everything was too quiet. Too abandoned.

Reaper and Drake dismounted beside him.

"I agree," Drake said, dismounting.

"A trap?" Reaper asked, following suit.

Not a trap, but he felt it in his bones—the wrongness. "She's not here."

"You can't know that, Max," Drake said.

"I know."

"Well, what now?" Reaper asked. "Do we still go in?"

Maxen's jaw tightened, nodded. "Round the back."

They slipped along the wall. The place looked unlikely to withstand a proper storm in its present state. Even the back door seemed tacked on as an afterthought, its planks swollen with damp, a rusted hook-latch the only thing tethering it to a warped post. Drake pressed it with a finger. The wood moaned in protest.

"This can't be a hiding place, can it?" Reaper muttered. He shifted to shove the door open, but Drake's hand shot out, clamping his wrist. Drake inclined his chin toward the base of the door.

Well, hell. A wire, thin as thread and taut as a violin string, ran along the sill and climbed the hinge. It vanished into a crack.

"Blackguards," Reaper mutter. "Do you think someone is

here?"

Maxen's lip curled. "Let's find out." He pushed the door open and a glass shattered to the ground.

"What the devil are you doing?" Drake snapped.

"They'd have heard us approach on horseback."

Drake grunted.

Maxen slipped a double barrel flintlock from his trousers and stepped over the threshold inside, his brothers at his back. Inside, the air hung heavy with age. However, there were other unmistakable scents. Sweat. A hint of cologne. Subtle, but he caught them nonetheless.

People had been here. And recently.

The cabin also wasn't very big. A table and two chairs, which, by the looks of it, hadn't been used in years. Dust coated all the surfaces, and yet no footprints. His gaze fixed on the only other room within.

Calliope.

It hit him like a fist square chest.

There. She'd been there.

He closed his eyes, only long enough to master the rage boiling in his blood. Then he strode forward and stepped inside, gaze sweeping the chamber. In the center stood a single chair. A coil of rope lay at the base of it.

Maxen clenched his fists.

"Two," Drake said behind him. "Two people were held here."

Maxen followed his brother's gaze to the corner, where an iron ring had been driven into the wall at shoulder height. Another rope lay discarded there, stained with smudges of blood.

He advanced to the chair and dropped before it. *She sat here.* His gaze hunted for even a drop of blood. A note was left on the seat. One word was scrawled across it.

Talon's.

The same stroke as the note slipped beneath his bedchamber

door. That wretched bloody miscreant. "Peregrine."

Drake stepped up to the chair, retrieving the note. "This damn fool."

"Is he brave, or does he have a death wish?" Reaper asked darkly.

"Why would they keep her here?" Drake asked. "It couldn't have been that long."

"To switch her?" Reaper suggested.

"And then tell us to find her?" Drake muttered. "Does that even make sense?"

"They wanted me to see their strength," Maxen said, certain. "They wanted me to feel how they could touch me. That our walls aren't impregnable."

Drake cursed.

"Damn rats," Reaper muttered.

Maxen took one last look at the chair before striding from the room. He passed the table he hadn't given much attention to earlier and halted. There, pressed into the dust, lay the clear shape of a hand.

He set his own beside the imprint, his dwarfing it.

Hers. She had braced herself here. Left a clue.

That's my girl.

She probably hadn't known about the note Peregrine left.

Maxen slipped back out with his brothers. Rain fell as Maxen swung up on the gelding and gathered the reins tight.

"Talon's," Reaper repeated. "They want us out of our territory."

Drake scoffed. "Fool's thinking."

"If it's not ours, then we take it," Maxen said. "We take it all."

Chapter Twenty-Four

CALLIOPE PERCHED STIFF-SPINED on the bed, every muscle pulled as taut as a bowstring. She ought to have learned how to use a bow and arrows and insisted on bringing them. Perhaps then she wouldn't once again be in such a helpless position. She might even have put a few arrows through a few men's hearts. At this point, why even own a pistol? Precious little good it had done her!

It would appear the Furys were leaving their mark upon her.

She hoped Maxen found the print she'd left behind. A reassurance that she was alive. Who knew what the man might be thinking, and she hated that she might be the cause for his worry. She shouldn't have insisted on taking the boy's place. Then none of this would have happened.

She sighed softly.

Beyond the chamber, rain ran in slender streams down the window glass, and she couldn't help but muse how the world had decided to match her mood. Across from her, Mr. Peregrine lounged as though they were old acquaintances sharing a cup of tea. So this was what he considered stealing her life? He really ought to be admitted to Bedlam. This must have been the least polished she'd seen him in their encounters. His mask had finally slipped.

And it had slipped far.

The smile that had once appeared amiable now bore a cruel cast. That, perhaps, was the greatest alteration in him. She hadn't quite noticed at first it in the place she was kept with Mr. Rollings, but now she couldn't miss it.

"Where is Mr. Rollings?" she asked. She hated that she could not quite stop her hands from twisting in her lap.

Peregrine waved a hand as if brushing aside an unimportant matter. "Oh, don't worry about him. Worry for yourself."

Her stomach clenched. "You didn't kill me."

"No." He smiled faintly, though it didn't reach his eyes. Not even close. "I didn't. Nasty business, killing."

"You have poked the wrong beast, Mr. Peregrine." She made her voice stronger this time, even if her pulse thundered against her throat. "Maxen is not an enemy you want."

The man chuckled. "What a straightforward, yet innocent thing to declare. Yes, Miss Turner, I am aware. But our confrontation has been inevitable for years."

"Why? What did he do to you?"

"Let's just say it's not what he did, but what he didn't do."

Calliope arched a brow. Not do? "He didn't cut you into a business deal? Profit margins? Some form of haul?"

The man laughed at that. "Ah, no. It's something much more precious than that."

"And what is that?"

"His empire."

The man was mad. "Well, if that is what you want, then you should just give up now."

"Perhaps."

His answers were even more infuriating than Maxen's brooding. "Why did you approach me anyway?"

Mr. Peregrine shrugged. "Ah, that. Well, what I wanted was beneath your shop. You were just an added reward."

Beneath her shop? Why was she not surprised there was something beneath her shop? However, "I'm *not* a reward."

"I beg to differ."

"Just what do you think is going to happen, Mr. Peregrine? Are you going to use me to negotiate a piece of the empire? I'm not worth even a sliver."

"Well, we shall see just how much you are worth soon, won't we?"

Her whole body stiffened at that. She'd like to believe she was worth more than six months' rent, but an empire? No. All this for power? It couldn't be that simple, could it?

"Tell me, Miss Turner, how much faith do you really put into your gutter-borns? Fury runs in their blood, sure, but blood alone doesn't make a man loyal. Just look at me."

"What are you saying?" Calliope asked. He wasn't loyal to his family? "By the by, those gutter-borns, as you call them, would never betray each other."

"It's a figure of speech, Miss Turner."

"Nevertheless, you don't know Maxen very well."

He cocked his head with a smile. "Neither do you, I imagine."

"Perhaps, but he has been nothing but good to me."

"You are one of the lucky few, and I can count on my hands how many that is."

So could she. "Let me guess: six."

"Seven, eight with you."

Calliope's brows furrowed. "Who is the seventh?"

"Another scarred rodent."

Another brother? Maxen was only ever loyal to his family. "Aren't *you* a rodent by your definition?" she shot back, annoyed.

He tapped a finger against the armrest of his chair. "I'm one that rose from the gutters, too."

"Like them."

"Well, I'll argue I rose without gruesome scars."

Calliope scoffed. "Just because you don't bear physical scars, that doesn't mean you don't bear scars at all."

"Spoken like a truly educated woman."

She shrugged. "I have sense at times."

"Just not enough not to fall in with that lot. They would sell their own children if it meant it would save their skin."

What rot! "Nonsense! Not one of those men would commit such atrocities!"

"Can you say that with complete certainty?"

"Yes." Because she had come face to face with such a monster before. Lived in her house for years. Was about to be sold to an old man as a wife. But she wouldn't give this coxcomb the satisfaction of an explanation just for him to twist her words.

"Do you know why you're still breathing, Miss Turner?"

Her heart lurched. "Why?"

"Alive, you have value. Dead, you are only a message."

"You broke your word to whoever gave you that instruction, so that doesn't make you the most loyal person to trust, does it? Anyway, what gives you a right to what they've built?"

"In this world, Miss Turner, no one gives you the right to anything. You take it."

The philosophy of a blackguard. Fabulous.

Her hands fisted in her trousers. It would be best if Maxen didn't come. But she knew as clearly as the image of his dark eyes blazing with fury filled her mind that he would come. She quite imagined that when he raged, the world would either bend or break to his will. She didn't know if she should be comforted by that thought or terrified for him.

She chose the former. "You will regret this when he arrives."

Peregrine cocked his head, studying her as one might study a puzzle. "There will be no regret when I see the look on his face when he realizes he cannot win against me. Ever."

Her throat went dry.

He's baiting you, Calliope.

His eyes glinted, like a cat toying with its prey. "Your heroes are such fragile things, Miss Turner."

Her lips parted, scathing retorts burning on her tongue, but she never had the chance to blast them.

A loud crash came from outside, followed by splintering

wood, a blistering curse, the unmistakable thud of fists striking flesh. The beat of boots, a table toppling. Calliope didn't need to see the storm breaking through the inn's walls. She knew it in her bones.

Maxen had arrived.

The world might not be breaking today, but this inn just might.

"Fragile?" she taunted.

Peregrine's smile didn't falter as he lazily laid his arm over the armrest of the chair and pointed the pistol at her.

"We'll see about that," she finished.

THE DOOR GAVE way beneath Maxen's boot with a splintering crack. Wood tore from its hinges, and he stepped into the chamber, eyes finding Calliope instantly. Peregrine rose to his feet, the pistol in his hand snapping to him.

Maxen paid him no mind.

He saw only her.

"Calliope."

She sat on the bed, her posture proud, defiance flashing despite the pallor that robbed her cheeks of color. A smile lit her face when their gazes locked. The very sight of her rent him asunder.

He strode across the room, lowering onto one knee before her. He clasped her chin between two fingers, tilting her face left then right, hunting for any signs that she'd been harmed.

"Did he hurt you?"

Her throat worked. "No."

"Did he touch you?"

She shook her head, hair brushing against his hand. He almost pulled off his gloves so he could feel the slight brush.

Good. Then on to business.

He started to rise but paused when his gaze was caught on her wrist—by rope burns. Thunder roared in his skull.

Peregrine, this bloody blackguard.

Slowly, he rose, framing the space between her and the man across from them. A pistol trained on him, almost making him laugh. Did he believe that would stop him? Make him hesitate?

He stepped up to Peregrine and grabbed him by the collar with both hands, hauling him up from his seat and slamming him back against the nearest wall with a force that rattled.

"Maxen!" Calliope cried out in alarm.

"It's all right, love. He won't kill me." The barrel of the pistol pressed against his chest, the hard mouth of it finding his heart. Maxen looked down at it, then back at Peregrine's cold, infuriatingly amused eyes.

No, he was *toying* with him.

His brothers fanned out behind him, and Maxen could feel the wave of their agitation, their fury.

"Go on," he said softly to Peregrine. "Pull it if you dare. I will rise from my damn ashes like a demon and devour you whole."

Drake cursed. "Maxen."

"Well," Reaper drawled. "That escalated nicely."

"Let me put him down where he stands," Knight said.

Saint's voice was low. "Neck. Quick."

"Or slow," Knight said. "There's merit in slow."

Peregrine gave the barest twitch of a smile, pistol still steady. "One pull, gentlemen, and your mighty Fury King falls."

Drake's voice cut through, ever sensible. "Enough posturing. Kill him and you die. Simple math."

"Ah, so this what brotherly love feels like."

"What's your plan here, Peregrine?" Maxen snapped. Something was off. It was almost as if Peregrine wanted this very thing to happen. Expected it to happen. But what did the blackguard hope to gain? There was no winning this battle with them.

"Let's just strangle him with his own cravat and be done with him," Reaper suggested. "Slow or fast, doesn't matter to me."

"We don't kill," Drake pointed out.

Maxen's whole body was aware of the woman behind him, so he couldn't very well remove a limb or two.

Reaper chuckled. "I'd say Peregrine looks a little . . . uncomfortable. How's the cravat, darling? Tight enough? Shall I take over, *frère?*"

Maxen ignored his brother's taunt. He had eyes only for the man pinned in his grasp, only for the pulse beating just below his hands. He had thought only for that pistol aimed at his heart while Calliope's bruised wrist still burned behind his eyes. And Christ, for fighting the urge to do exactly what his brothers were taunting about.

"You put your hands on her," Maxen growled.

"I didn't," Peregrine answered, perfectly calm.

"You tied her."

"A necessary precaution. My fingers didn't even graze her skin."

Did that bloody matter? Maxen leaned in, his head a hair's breadth from Peregrine's. "Don't speak to me about necessary. That's a dangerous road. Fatal even. Just not by my hands."

The pistol pressed harder into his chest. Still, he didn't move. Didn't blink. Didn't give Peregrine the satisfaction of even a damn flinch. "You want my empire," Maxen said softly. "But all you've done is give me reason to burn you and yours—whatever pitiable thing it may be."

"Mine took you and yours out in seconds. You all could be dead now."

"A mistake we won't make again."

Behind him, the brothers closed the circle.

And Calliope . . .

Maxen pressed Peregrine harder into the wall, his fingers tightening on the man until the perfect cravat bunched and strained. The pistol's hammer fell into place with a sharp click as Peregrine drew the metal fully back.

Maxen chuckled.

A brutal, grating sound that cut through the storm outside and seemed to quiet the entire room.

"Well, hell and damnation," Reaper muttered. "Second time in my life I hear him laugh."

"First time," Knight muttered.

"That's not a laugh," Drake said.

"Do it," Maxen said. "Let my brothers cut you apart limb from limb before they toss you in a crate bound for China."

Reaper's smile sharpened. "I'll take an ear."

Dagger's knuckles cracked. "I'll take his hands."

Saint finally spoke, deep and cold. "I'll take his tongue."

Knight nodded once. "And his eyes."

Drake sighed, and Maxen imagined him pinching the bridge of his nose. "We should still take him back."

"What if that's what he wants?" Dagger said.

"Good catch," Reaper said.

Yes, good catch.

Still wouldn't stop Maxen from dragging him back to the tavern. The dungeon.

The pistol never wavered. Maxen's grip never slackened.

"Maxen," Calliope called his name.

He heard nothing else. Not the storm outside, not his brothers shifting closer, not even Peregrine's breath in his face. The instant he loosened his grip, Saint was there. Silent, efficient, his hand slamming into Peregrine's wrist, pistol clattering across the floor. His brother had Peregrine disarmed and on his knees, his arm twisted back at such an angle that bone snapped.

Knight crouched to retrieve the fallen weapon, weighing it in his palm before tucking it into his belt. "One less toy for him."

Reaper smirked from the doorway. "I still vote for death by cravat strangulation."

Maxen finally exhaled. Turning, he went to Calliope, and in one swift moment, he scooped her up and marched from the room.

Time to go home.

Chapter Twenty-Five

CALLIOPE COULD STILL feel him.

He had carried her as though she weighed nothing at all, his chest a wall of heat and steel against her, the steady beat of his heart pounding against her ear as if it belonged to her. And only her. He hadn't let her go until he stopped before her chamber door at the tavern, and she hadn't asked him to. And lord, the imprint of his arms . . . his body lingered on her skin. In fact, she swore the raw scent of him had sunk straight into her veins.

Madness!

Utter madness!

Now she stood at the center of the room, Prince sprawled at her feet, staring at him while he remained stiffly in the doorway as though he had no intention of moving farther, broad shoulders shadowing the light behind him. His scarred mouth was a grim line, arms crossed over his chest, hands curled into fists.

He hadn't spoken since setting her down. He simply stared.

It was unbearable.

Unnerving.

Pulse-fluttering.

Each time his gaze flicked over her and her wrists, only slightly reddened from the rope and the faint scrape on her cheek from where she'd leaped from the carriage, her scalp prickled. His gaze traced every visible mark with ruthless intensity.

And yet he said nothing.

The silence that stretched caused a full force of prickles to erupt all over her body. She wanted him gone. She wanted him closer. Stars, she wanted to be in his arms again.

Her fingers twisted in her jacket. "If you mean to stand guard, Maxen, at least step inside." And he could close the door before he attracted the attention of his brothers!

His jaw flexed, but he still did not move. "I can't."

That gave her pause. "Well, if you can't, then can you go?"

His eyes bore into hers. "I can't do that either, Calliope Turner."

Lord. This *man*.

How had he the ability to melt and freeze her at the same time?

His eyes shifted to the bruise on her wrist again.

She had been carried from an unknown threat to safety, but safety was not what throbbed through her veins now. Oh, no. Need was what throbbed. A need for something in its truest form. Her lips confessed before she could stop them. "Turner is not my name."

The words dropped between them like stones into a still pond, sending ripples she could not call back. Her nails bit into her palms. She had not spoken that truth aloud in the months since she started to use her mother's name.

Maxen's head lifted, eyes narrowing.

"I—" She swallowed. "I needed something else when I came to Brighton. A name that did not carry . . . everything from the old one."

His eyes flashed, before he said. "I understand."

"You do?"

"How do you think I and all my brothers, half brothers, bear the same name? We left behind our old lives to step into this one."

Right. She'd almost forgotten about that. "A better one or

worse one?"

He pushed off the doorframe, kicking the door shut with his boot, stalking up to her, each step purposeful, a predator closing the distance. His eyes burned into hers, black and searching, and she had the strangest impression that he could see straight through her, down to the marrow where she had buried every secret.

"That depends on who you ask."

He stopped before her, the air crackling with danger. A danger she was more than happy to not run from this time. "You should not give me truths, Calliope." His voice was a low growl, hoarse. "That will only make me want more."

Her heart broke out in a little dance. "Can you handle more?"

"I don't know."

A muscle ticked in his jaw. His hand lifted, then dropped, as though he warred with himself.

She reached out to trace the scar on his lip. "I don't know anymore either."

With a curse torn from somewhere deep in his chest, he seized her by the wrist, dragging her up against him in one swift motion while be arched his head into her palm, brushing his lips against the red marks. Her gasp caught in her throat, but it was swallowed the next instant as his mouth crushed against hers.

Sun and stars!

The kiss was nothing like the first ones. That had been reckless, impulsive. This was ruinous. A storm breaking its banks. Wildly welcome. His lips almost bruised hers in their claiming, his hand fisting in her hair, tilting her head back as though he could devour every tremor of breath she had left.

Calliope loved it.

She clutched his coat with both hands, holding on as if the world might vanish beneath her. His body pressed into hers, big and bulky, and yet she felt safer there than she had anywhere else.

The taste of him was desperation, anger, relief.

It matched everything she felt.

She had meant to confess, to explain, to offer him truth. Instead, she was drowning in him, in the fury and the hunger and the terrible, impossible comfort of being wanted this way.

He tore his mouth away with a ragged curse. His chest rose and fell, harsh and uneven against hers, his hand still a brand at her wrist. She expected him to step back and put space between them. He did the opposite. His forehead pressed to hers, breath ragged, his words came like a vow and a curse both.

"Push me away."

"No." How could she do that when all she wanted to do was pull the man closer? Stars, at this point he'd have to stop her from scaling him!

"God help me, Calliope. Say it now or never say it at all."

"Is that a threat?"

"Yes. Hell. Yes."

She chuckled even as her belly twisted, a battle of uncertainty and need raging inside. But in that moment, with his arms caging her, his kiss still burning her lips, she did not want him to. And although a part of her feared him, feared this, she could not ignore the way her pulse quickened at his touch. How this man, seemingly obscured in darkness, chased away her own.

She wanted him. She wanted him more than she'd ever wanted someone in her life before. More than escaping that household. More, *perhaps*, even than her breath.

"I won't push you away," she whispered, her fingers clenching. "So don't push me away either."

"Calliope."

The tone of warning made her smile.

He cursed, and she yelped when he lifted her without warning and carried her across the chamber. The world tilted before steadying after he lowered her to the bed. He caged her between his arms as he stared down at her, looming over her. His hand lifted again, almost as if he couldn't help it, and tracing the bow of her mouth. The scrape of leather reminded her that he still wore his gloves. He was still hiding.

"Remove them," she whispered against his touch.

His brows crashed together, and his eyes flickered, startled, the muscles in his throat working as though she'd asked for something utterly intolerable. "What?"

"Your gloves," she repeated softly. She parted her lips against the seam of leather. "Remove them. I want to feel your hands."

He went still, utterly still, as though she had stripped him bare with nothing more than those few words.

"Is this your way of seducing me?" he said roughly.

"Yes."

"Christ."

For a moment she thought he would refuse. Then, slowly, like a man stepping into fire of his own free will, he tugged one glove free, then the other, tossing them aside.

How could her breath not catch?

His hands were scarred, inked, branded with violence. She was keenly attuned to his gaze on her as she reached out first, catching one in both of hers. She lifted his hand to her lips, pressing a kiss to the ravaged flesh.

He stilled.

Absolutely stilled. As though she had unlaced him with that single touch.

She kissed his hand again, letting her lips linger on the curve of scar tissue, on the dark sweep of ink that branded him as Brighton's beast. "These hands carried me to safety today," she murmured. "You don't have to hide them from me."

"If you'd been hurt . . ."

"But I wasn't. I won't be hurt with you here, will I? Although, you should probably deal with the wreckage that is Peregrine."

"Tomorrow," he said. "I'll deal with the wreckage."

"Well, in that case . . ." Calliope murmured, recklessly, bravely. "Wreck me, then."

A sound broke from him—half groan, half curse—and then his bare hand cradled her face. She leaned into it, closing her eyes, letting the touch sink into every hollowed, bruised place inside her.

And then his mouth found hers again, nothing held back this time. It was as though by kissing the beast's scars, she had kissed the man beneath them. She pushed her free hand into his hair. She welcomed the storm, the danger, the wreckage of it. Because in his scars, in his kiss, she had found something truer than any name she could claim.

She'd found herself.

EVERYTHING ABOUT HIM might be a monster, but those eyes of hers, from the very first moment they'd locked with his, they'd always had a way of fooling him into believing he could still be forgiven for everything he'd done.

But her lips? Her kisses?

They had the power to wreck.

And wreck they did.

His white-knuckle control shuddered apart inside him, the fortress he had built about himself proving nothing more than weathered ruin. There was nothing left to brace against—not when every single touch she gifted him came as a blow to his gut.

"I want you."

The three words breathed into him.

Three words that had the strength of a thousand lightning bolts. His entire life, no one had ever wanted him. What he could do, yes. What he could take, yes. But not *him*. He didn't know what a man was meant to do with such words—where to set them, how to hold them without spiraling into insanity. So he let his body answer for him and prayed she would hear what his tongue could not shape.

He could taste his absolute downfall on her skin. Her taste.

He kissed her harder, deeper.

He lifted his head a fraction, breath harsh. "Say it again."

The quiver that passed through her went straight through

him.

"I want you, Maxen."

The words tore something loose inside him, old and primal, and what replaced it was dangerous in another way his mind could not begin to grasp: a tenderness so sharp it nearly felled him. An overwhelming need to claim her roared through his veins, fierce as the very pulse that kept him alive.

She wriggled beneath him, lifting just enough for him to strip away her jacket and shirt, their urgency making the act clumsy, desperate, perfect. He flung each garment aside until only her stays remained, and he could no more keep from dragging his mouth over the swell of her breast than he could stop the moon giving way for the sun.

He wanted to mark her.

Leave proof of this moment. His teeth grazed her skin, and he clenched a fist to keep from biting down. She didn't deserve such animalistic behavior. He might be a beast. But with her, he could never be beastly. He could, however, be impatient.

He dragged his tongue over her skin. "I want you naked. Completely."

She laughed, husky, half-daring. "Are you asking for my permission?"

His jaw tightened, eyes burning into hers. "I'm telling you what I want." His thumb traced the curve of her breast. "Every inch of you bared to me."

Her fingers caught at his hair, tugging. "Greedy man."

"I am greedy. So bloody greedy."

"So am I." She bared her neck to him. "Aren't you a criminal overlord who takes what he wants? So take me."

Bloody everlasting damnation.

His cock swelled more painfully.

"You should be punished for those words," he rasped, pulling at the ties of her stays. His mouth followed, hot and unrelenting down her skin. "Punished severely."

"How?" She exhaled a small groan.

"With my lips. My body."

"I'll allow it, dark prince."

Her stays flew across the room. Damn. Damn. Damn. He lowered his head and closed his mouth over one peak, treasuring the gasp that tore out of her.

"God, Calliope," he muttered against her skin. "I could spend the rest of my life here." His hand cupped the other breast, thumb teasing, dying for every sound she gave him. "Sweetest bloody punishment I've ever delivered."

She arched, laughing breathlessly, tugging his hair. "You call this punishment?"

He lifted his head just enough to growl. "The night has only just started."

His hands dragged down to her breeches, working with more urgency than skill. He cursed, low and vicious. "These damn things."

"I quite like them," she teased.

"I don't," he ground out, yanking at the stubborn cloth until he could shove breeches and drawers beneath together down her hips. He hated that his brothers had seen her in them as well. Several times now.

She lifted her sweet derriere, wriggling to help him work them down. Her boots made it clumsy, however. Muttering another curse, he rose to his knees where he straddled her, and twisted around, tugging at the leather until he got one off, then the other, tossing them aside before stripping away the last of her clothes in one rough sweep. This was not the polished seduction she deserved. Just raw, desperate need, and while he knew she deserved so much more than this, Maxen didn't know how to be anything else. Fortunately, his luck must have been great in his past life, for this brilliant woman didn't seem to mind. "There," he said as he twisted back to her. "No more damned barriers."

"Now you."

"Happy to oblige, love." He tore his jacket from his shoulders, flinging it carelessly to the floor. Then he dragged his shirt over his head and threw it aside.

Her gaze locked on his chest in fascination. Something tender, hot, and dangerous to him. He paused before the corner of his mouth twitched. "Go on. You've already touched them."

She did. Her fingers traced the ridges, featherlight, and his whole body jerked as if she'd struck him. Breath slammed out of his lungs, chest drawing tight.

Had anyone ever touched him like this?

No. But then, he'd never revealed these scars to anyone but her.

Heat ripped through him, violent, scorching, worse than any blade he'd ever taken when she levered herself up to place her lips over one particular scar just above his breeches. His heart thundered. God help him, he wanted to snarl, to shove her away before she saw too much, but he couldn't. He couldn't move at all.

"Christ, Calliope, careful." If she kept looking at him like that, touching him like this, she'd undo every last bolt he'd hammered into place.

"How did they happen?"

"War." Probably not the kind she'd imagine.

She scoffed. "I should have known better than to ask."

His gaze pinned her. So bloody beautiful, her throat and body bared, her eyes on him as if he were worth looking at. He reached for the flaps of his breeches, jaw clenched, breath sawing, every nerve near to breaking. "I need to remove my—"

"No," she breathed, catching his wrists, eyes gone dark with urgency. "No time. I need you now, Maxen."

God save him.

The words punched through the last splinter of discipline. He fumbled the buttons and shoved the breeches over his hips, his cock freed, heavy, aching, and throbbing with the same need that wrecked him. But as much as he wanted her, he couldn't just mount her and have his way like a rutting dog. He lowered himself between her legs, lips scraping down her body until his mouth hovered over the place he wanted most.

She gasped, sharp and breathless. "Maxen, what are you—?"

Her words cut off the words just as he sealed his mouth over her core, claiming her there just as ruthlessly as he'd claimed her lips above.

Her cry nearly made him explode there and then, her taste burning into him like fire and absolution. He gripped her thighs harder, holding her to him, refusing to let her escape the truth of what he was giving her—the truth that he could worship, that he could destroy, and that she held the power of it all in the palm of her hands.

That she owned him.

Body and soul.

His thumb traced her nub while he pushed a finger into her, and her body answered him like the tides answer the moon, and the sound she made drove him to the cliff edge. And God help him, he would take it all, every gasp, every shiver, brand them onto his soul until he was ruined beyond saving.

But he was just a damn man.

He nearly lost it when she cried out his name, or perhaps it was snapped as a curse, he couldn't tell at this point. He could hardly hear anything other than the pulse in his damn cock threatening to explode. He clenched his jaw and forced his mind elsewhere. Horseflesh, the stallion coming up for sale in a month. Anything to keep from spilling like a green boy.

Hands fisted his hair and yanked.

Her look said it all.

Take me. Now.

Maxen chuckled, bending over her, bracing his forearm beside her head, his other hand sliding to guide his cock to her entrance. "Didn't you like that, love?"

She stilled. "It's not that I didn't, but shouldn't something else go there?"

Another chuckle as he teased the tip of her breast with nose. "My lips are still part of my body, is it not?" He nudged inside.

"It's different," she said. "I want to be one with you. Be one with me."

"Look at me," he whispered.

She did.

"Tell me you want me."

Her lips parted, before whispering, "I want you."

He pushed into her.

She clutched at him, and he bit back a groan that sounded so much like surrender. He sank deeper, and she rose to meet him, and somewhere in the meeting a piece of him he'd kept walled in for years broke loose and fled. When he reached a barrier, he pressed his mouth to the hollow at her collarbone, over the beat of her pulse as he drew back and thrust through it.

Boody *home.*

But the word wasn't big enough. Nothing was. He felt her open to him, stretching, reaching. She took him in as if the world had been arranged for this, and the feel of her around him—hot, tight, *his*—cut through every scar he'd ever worn.

"Christ." His head dropped to hers. "I can't lose this. I can't."

"Who says you will?" she whispered, the words a thread pulled straight from her core to his.

He moved, slow first, finding her rhythm, then faster as she urged him with hands and hips and those small, wrecking sounds he would hear in his sleep for the next thousand nights. She unfurled, stretching, reaching, embedding deep into his soul. And he was a man whose shadow could black out her stars.

Perhaps it would.

But she *was* the damn stars. He could never smother them. Not when she cast all her light on him. They burned too bright. She was the light that evaporated his shadow. He had no power to hide himself from her.

"I need—" His voice broke. "Calliope. I need—"

Bloody everlasting hell.

"Take it," she voiced on a sigh. "Take *me.*"

He set a hand beneath her thigh and hitched her higher and

drove deep, until she was shaking, until his own bones rattled from the pleasure. Every shudder, every gasp told him where to lead. His thumb found her, circling in the rhythm she set, taking his cue from the frantic dance of her hips, until she broke apart against his hand and his cock.

"That's it, love." He pounded harder. "Show me. Let me feel you."

"Beast," she said.

"I'm not a gentle man, love."

"I know," she croaked. "I chose you."

Something in him howled at that—something young and starved and damn unworthy. He was moving harder now, drowning in the heat and clutch of her, and still it wasn't enough. Nothing would ever be enough. He would spend the rest of his life trying to get closer and it wouldn't be close enough.

"Promise me," he said, the words ripped from some dark place. "Promise you'll never leave Brighton without telling me, Calliope. Promise me."

Promise you'll never leave.

"I promise," she murmured against his ear, and his whole body broke into shivers so violent he had to brace harder to keep from collapsing.

"Again," he said, because he was greedy, because he would starve without hearing it twice.

"I promise." Her lips brushed his jaw, his mouth, his throat—a litany of yeses.

He kissed her like he was a drowning man and her lips were air, then drew back enough to see her face as he drove them higher. She was flushed and wild and perfect, pupils blown wide, lips swollen with his name. He wanted to slow it, memorize every frame, but her hand slid into his hair and tugged, and that was the end of any thought of gentleness.

He felt the change gather in her—the tremor that began low and climbed, the way her breath caught and wouldn't settle. "There," he urged. "Come for me, love."

He felt her tighten and his vision went white with it, the world dropping away until there was nothing but the clench of her around him. She had gifted herself to him without defense, and he would give her everything that was left of his life in return.

"Promise me again," he growled.

She shattered on his cock.

He drove once more, twice, and the pleasure hit like a hammer, bright and obliterating. He buried his face in her neck and let it take him, every muscle strung and then undone, the release tearing through him with a violence that left him bloody shaking.

Like a damn youth.

He held there, locked deep, refusing to let the world back in. He didn't move. He didn't want to scare it away—the fragile, impossible peace of being where he'd never thought he'd belong.

"I promise."

Chapter Twenty-Six

CALLIOPE OPENED HER eyes to find another pair already on her. Lord. Those eyes. Dark, unblinking, unbearably intense. Maxen lay on his side, head propped in one hand, as though he'd been content to spend the rest of the morning simply watching her breathe.

A blush of heat spread through her whole body at his regard.

"Don't look at me," she squawked, her voice still raspy with sleep.

"Why not?" His mouth curved faintly. "You're so beautiful."

"No one is beautiful in the mornings."

"You are."

So beautiful. In a way that defied even beauty. Was this what happened when a man you desired so completely that you began questioning your whole being smiled at you in such a way? Her bones softened all at once. Perhaps peace was the biggest, most elusive, dream of them all. Always hoped for but never quite accomplished. Perhaps peace lived in a wild wilderness that was never meant to be tamed. Perhaps that was the allure of the hopeful understanding of peace.

He traced the curve of her nose with a knuckle. "How are you feeling?"

Embarrassed! "I might ask the same of you."

"My scalp is numb from all your yanking, but other than that, I've never felt better."

Her body burned hotter at the bluntness. "Why are you so honest in the morning? I think I much prefer the silent, broody you."

"I, myself, am surprised."

"What's the hour?" she asked, diverting the subject to a less embarrassing one. "Do you know?"

"Noon."

She shot upright, clutching the blanket to her body. "Noon?" Her mind leapt ridiculously to his brothers. What would they think? What would they say? "I need to return to my shop!"

His brow furrowed as he rose with her. "Why?"

"The threat is gone, is it not? I can't just abandon my shop. And you must have," she hesitated, "you *know*, underlord things to do."

"I don't." He drew her back lazily against him. "Stay for a little while longer."

"I *can't*."

"You can."

She blinked at him. "Is that a demand?"

He rubbed his cheek against hers. "No. Just a command."

She gave him a snort.

Hah! *Hah* . . . She could still scarcely believe this moment. She had—heavens above—slept with a man. In his bed. Joined bodies with him. With *him*. The very thought probably should have horrified her even just the slightest bit now that the adventure of the night had passed. Not now. She had done the most natural thing in all the world. Her body, her heart, her very bones had always known he was meant to be hers.

And she his.

Which was absurd, of course. Entirely mad. And yet . . .

Promise me.

Lord. For the love of wax, *Lord*.

She *had* promised. She'd made a promise! In her books, she

might as well have married the man. And she wanted nothing more than to laze in this bed, curl herself into him, and allow the day melt away. But she could not. Her shop called. Responsibility tugged. She couldn't let him sway her. Right?

Wait! Her dog! She glanced up at Maxen. "Where is Prince?"

Not even a pause. "Knight has him."

Wait . . . "*Knight*, as in your brother?"

"Is there another?"

Her face went hot. "Maxen! Does he know?" She motioned wildly at the tangle of linens between them.

A soft chuckle grazed her ear, unexpectedly wicked. "Feeling embarrassed?"

"Yes!" she hissed. She jabbed a finger at him. "Wouldn't you?"

He pushed into her, his lips brushing her temple, his breath warm and sure. "I could never feel embarrassed with you."

The words shot straight through her chest, as did the hardness of his body, leaving her momentarily speechless. What kind of man said such things after ruining a woman's every good sense? And worse, what kind of woman's whole body went weak at them?

Yours.

Hah!

Calliope, you harlot, you!

"Such deep words in the morning."

This time he hesitated before murmured lowly, but with conviction, "I'm not a man of depth."

She didn't believe that. But then, all people had multiple depths to them. "It's all right to have shallows as well. The ocean isn't all deep. It's shallow too. And the deep parts push out waves that roll out to crash onto shallow shores. They are all still beautiful."

"There is nothing beautiful about me."

"I suppose you are right. *Handsome* would be the better word."

A grunt-like scoff.

"But you know, you make me forget the world I left behind," she admitted, her voice barely above a whisper. "That cannot be a good thing."

"We all leave worlds behind. I'd like to believe that's a good thing." He pressed a kiss to the top of her head.

"Your past?" Calliope asked. That world, she could understand. Some worlds weren't meant to be carried forward. Others were meant to be loosened from the heart.

His lips brushed hers. "Past, future, everything except every moment with you."

He bit back a grin. "And you claim not to be romantic."

"Don't fool yourself." A sneer touched his features.

She chuckled. One fact stood above the rest: A part of her, perhaps the biggest part, *wanted* to be rescued. Not slay the villain herself. A part that longed to lay the burden down. Simply be happy. But him? In a curious twist of fate, she'd save him, even if it meant she perished in his stead.

Fanciful thoughts, no doubt.

"Nevertheless, I really must go."

"Why a candle shop?" he asked suddenly, his thumb idly tracing a circle on her skin as though the question were nothing.

Calliope didn't have to think to answer. "My mother. I used to sit with her while she coaxed light from wax. The motion of her hands. The puckered brow while she deeply concentrated on her task. Her smile when my father interrupted. Him joining their efforts. Starting my shop, it's . . . it's the only part of them I could keep alive."

"You are honoring them. Noble."

She smiled at him. "Noble, eh?"

"Noble." He shifted, hovering, no, *looming* over her, his arm braced in the pillows, caging her in with the sheer breadth of him. Her breath hitched as his shadow fell across her face, his eyes dark and determined, as though he'd read every frantic beat of her heart and had decided precisely what to do with it!

And she had a clue.

"Maxen," she whispered, nerves tangling with sudden want. "I really—"

Her words cut off as his mouth found hers. A slow, deliberate kiss that unraveled her protest before it ever formed.

Between breaths, she tried again, desperate for reason. "I—"

Kiss.

"Need—"

Kiss.

"To—"

Another kiss, harder, hotter, until her thoughts frayed completely.

"Go," she managed, though the word came out ragged, half-melted against his lips.

He claimed her thoroughly then, robbing her of all thoughts until there was nothing left but the feel of him, the taste of him, the wild certainty that she belonged here.

With him.

Her fingers curled helplessly in the bedding, the other slipping up to his chest. Stars, sun, and wax, his heart pounded beneath her palm.

"I can't stay," she whispered against his mouth, though her lips sought his even as she said the words.

"You can," he answered, his hand cupping her cheek, holding her still for yet another kiss. "And you will."

Her pulse rioted. "*Maxen*, for the love of wax, Fury . . ."

"Calliope, for the love of my sanity, Turner," he returned.

Her lips parted, but before she could say anything, he kissed her again, sweeping away all rationality until she was lost, wholly and completely, beneath the onslaught of him. By the time he drew back, leaving her dazed and panting beneath him, Calliope had forgotten every sensible reason she'd had to leave.

And stars help her. How was she supposed to care?

MAXEN LEANED OVER the desk in his room at the tavern, papers spread in chaotic disarray before him. Columns of figures bled together, black ink smudged by his restless fingers, the abominable accounts staring back like a damn battlefield. He had neglected them for days. Ever since Calliope had stepped, uninvited, into his world and left him unwilling to think about anything else.

Damn it.

He scrubbed a hand over his jaw, glaring at a ledger that stubbornly refused to make sense. It ought to have his complete focus. He was, after all, responsible for keeping order over a realm most men of his birth would never dream to rule. But numbers, profits, collections—all of it seemed a pale, bloodless thing compared to the warmth of Calliope in his bed this morning.

He leaned back in the chair and shut his eyes. He had not wanted to let her go. Hadn't wanted to leave her to her lodgings tonight, alone. The beast inside him had snarled at the very thought of it, urging him to keep her close, to keep her *his*.

And yet, urgent matters required his attention. Debts to tally, shipments to account for, men to pay. Losses to count. Retribution to plot. He told himself he would see to each quickly, neatly, so that tomorrow he might call on her with his conscience clear.

Tomorrow.

He shifted in the chair, eyes snapping open to slide to the clock. Four hours. It had only been four blasted hours.

That was enough time, surely. Enough time for her to catch her breath?

Or was it too soon?

Might she want more space? He thought of her blush this morning, her startled laugh, the way she'd clutched him as if her modesty might yet be salvaged. Or had that been a slap?

Regardless, she might prefer a night of peace. A night without him looming in doorways, stealing her protests with kisses.

His jaw tightened, hating the thought of separating even for a night. Should he wait? Could he wait? Was the threat truly over? He could use that as an excuse . . .

His eyes fixed once more on the clock.

Four hours.

Damnation. He was already halfway to the door when it swung open and Drake strode in. The arse didn't even bother with greetings. Just jabbed a folded parchment into his chest and crossed his arms.

Maxen arched a brow. "You look like you need a drink."

"You're the one who's going to need one."

No words a man wanted to hear. "Why? Did something happen with Peregrine?"

Drake shook his head. "He's still trussed up like a chicken in the dungeon."

"Good. Let him stew." He turned the paper over, examining it. "So what is it?"

"News from Dare. Came this morning."

Tension coiled. The Earl of Dare. Drake's cousin. Given his brother's face, this wouldn't be good. Still, he unfolded the parchment, eyes skimming.

And stopped.

Then read it again.

His eyes lifted to Drake. "What am I looking at?"

"The client list of the solicitor, Fitz."

John bloody Fitz.

"And?" There was no Turner. That didn't mean much. She could be someone's family. But he dismissed the idea as soon as it entered his mind. Who would send family off to live alone in a place like Brighton, running a candle shop?

"Balfour."

Maxen's gaze flicked to his brother before dropping to the last name on the list. He went cold. "It says here *Earl* of Balfour?"

"That's right."

"What's the connection?" *Don't bloody say family.*

"Daughter. But the late earl, not the current one."

Family.

Nobility.

Aristocracy.

A chill spread throughout his blood. "You sure?" His brother hesitated. "Since you didn't think to add your cousin's letter with this, just spit it out."

"The Earl of Balfour had a daughter named Calliope."

Maxen stilled.

"She went missing just over three months ago. Her step-mother has been frantic searching for her."

"Dare discovered this?"

"He has a man who is friendly with a household maid. The earl's daughter went missing before she could come out to society."

Maxen stared at the name like it might rearrange itself into something less disagreeable. Of course, it didn't.

"You good?" Drake asked.

He wasn't. Not in the slightest. "It might not be her." But even as he said the words, he knew they the question was shite. Hadn't she admitted her real name was not Turner? But then, she hadn't given her real one either.

You didn't want it.

Hell and damnation.

Drake blew out a breath. "You think she's here to spy?"

"No." Final. Absolute.

"Maxen—"

"I don't know what she's doing here," Maxen snapped. He tossed the list back to his brother. "But she's not a damn spy."

"I don't need to remind you what happens when we cross paths with aristocracy. Or have you forgotten our father? Or uncle? Or the Duke of Mortimer?"

Maxen sneered. "You don't have to bloody remind me of

that." His own mother had been the third daughter of an earl, cast out after her affair with his father and birthing a child out of wedlock.

Drake sighed.

"Balfour," he repeated under his breath, like the syllables themselves were poison. "She's a bloody lady."

"A runaway lady, if it makes a difference."

"It doesn't." His chest was tight. Hell, his whole body was. He couldn't bloody breathe. "She was supposed to be a girl with a shop and a dog and a secret. Not this."

Drake didn't say anything. Just leaned against the edge of the desk and waited.

Maxen's jaw ached from clenching, temples starting to throb. The gloves were too tight. His clothes were too tight. His damn skin.

She'd been in his home. In his arms.

He'd kissed her like she was his.

A blue-blooded noble.

Christ.

It meant disregard. It meant games. It meant the kind of people who stepped over bodies in the street and still made speeches about order.

His hands curled at his sides. "She might not be like them." Bloody hell. Even he could hear the desperation in that. He was done for. Damn well done for. Because while he hated the fact that she was part of that life, he didn't hate her. He could never hate her.

He bloody lo—

"You look at her like she'd just handed you your heart back."

Maxen froze.

"I don't." Look. Like that.

He thought of the way she'd looked at him—wide-eyed and flushed, lips parted. Like *she* hadn't meant for that night to happen but still decided to claim it for herself. Like it undid her as much as it undid him.

She hadn't seemed like a lady then. She'd seemed like a girl on the edge of something thrilling and petrifying. Just like he was.

"Maybe she's hiding," he muttered. Clinging. That was what he was doing, was it not? Clinging. He rubbed the back of his neck and turned away. Damn Drake for witnessing him like this. Damn himself for letting *her* get close enough that the truth now almost tasted like bitter betrayal. A part of him didn't want to care. Not about her reasons. Not about her past.

But that didn't change what was already unfurling in his damn chest.

"What else do we know?" he asked, voice rough.

Drake nodded toward the letter. "Not much. Balfour hasn't filed anything. No bounties. No inquiry. But Dare says the girl was supposed to marry some viscount."

Maxen's head snapped up. "She's betrothed?"

"Don't know, but whatever it was, the match fell apart with her disappearance. That's the last known detail."

He pressed a fist against his chest.

Christ. A lady. One with secrets and a fake name and damn it. He still wanted to kiss her again. Claim her again.

What was he if not a fool?

She wasn't just a woman with a hidden past anymore. She was *everything* he'd been taught to hate growing up. And she still looked at him like he was worth something.

Him.

A monster.

But still he wanted her. Wanted to understand her. Wanted to know why someone with titles and wealth and whatever privilege came with being a bloody earl's daughter had ended up hiding behind a shop. He wanted to believe that their night together hadn't been a mistake.

But was it?

Everything he felt for her—this confounding longing, need, protectiveness, want—felt like a betrayal of *his* world. Of children born in gutters. Of men and women who starved while nobles grew fat off taxes and tariffs.

She was one of them. Even if she didn't look like it.

"So, what now?" Drake asked.

Maxen didn't answer.

He didn't know.

He hated lies. Deception. And he didn't want to believe her capable of either. But promises were only as good as the people who made them, so he couldn't rule out betrayal. He only hoped to God he was wrong. He *needed* to be wrong.

Chapter Twenty-Seven

*F*IE. *FIE. FIE.*

Only a few hours had passed but already Calliope wanted to abandon the shop and hurry back to the tavern. That, however, wouldn't do. So she changed into her plainest dress and scrubbed at the shelf in brisk circles. First the shelves. Then she could entertain thoughts of Maxen Fury.

Hah. An impossible feat, that.

Cleaning was always accompanied by thinking. And all her thoughts circled back to him. His bed. His heat upon her skin. Her lips still swollen from those persistent kisses. Marked. Thoroughly claimed.

And the promise.

Oh, the *promise!*

Had that been wise?

At the time, it had seemed simple enough. She wasn't planning on leaving Brighton. She might have entertained the thought after she'd met him and the first time she'd slipped away, but not anymore. However, what if the choice was stripped from her? What if Duvessa found her?

Should her stepmother even still matter at this point?

A grin stretched her lips. Last night, she'd been thoroughly ruined. She would be of no more use to Duvessa.

That's right!

She was of no more use. How absolutely freeing. Still, a pinch of guilt entered her heart. Should she tell Maxen her true identity? Would he cast her aside if she did? Was there anything to cast aside? She'd like to believe there wasn't, but her landlord-man was different.

He saw the world differently.

What if, when her lease ended in six months, he refused to renew?

Urgh!

She pressed harder at the shelf, scrubbing as if she could rub away the discomfort in herself. She didn't believe Maxen to be that way, but apparently he loathed the aristocracy. Enough to regard her with contempt if he discovered she was born into the very world he despised? She couldn't say. She could only hope *not*.

She was still at a loss as to how to broach this.

He deserved the truth. The promise she had made—was it not already broken, keeping this part of herself hidden? Well, if she were being philosophical and all that.

She paused mid-scrub, the look on his face that morning flashing across her mind. *Past, future, everything except every moment with you.*

Her throat thickened.

She wanted to believe him. Wanted to believe he could see her, not the origin of her name. That he might understand the years she had spent surviving, enduring, hiding. But to confess was to risk everything. Her freedom. Her heart. Him.

"Stars, help me," she whispered, leaning her forehead briefly against the shelf. She straightened almost just as fast, smoothing her skirts. Not today. Not yet. She needed one more hour, one more day of this happiness before facing whatever the truth might bring.

Tomorrow perhaps she would tell him. Tomorrow she would be brave.

Or perhaps the day after that.

Or perhaps *after* she extended her lease.

For now, she had shelves to wipe. And a heart that refused, no matter how she lectured the thing, to stop missing him.

The bell above the shop door chimed.

Calliope's brow furrowed. It was late afternoon, and her shop was closed, so she must have forgotten to lock the door. She turned, her smiling freezing when she came face to face with three large men.

Prince started growling.

Stars, preserve her.

Just by one look she could tell these weren't Maxen's men.

"Easy," she murmured, putting a smile on her face. "Gentlemen, I'm afraid I'm closed for the day."

No one moved.

Prince padded forward, hackles bristling. He planted himself between her and the men, his growl deepening.

"Fine beast you've got there," the one to the right drawled. "Shame if something were to happen to him."

Calliope's hand clenched tighter around the rag. "What do you want?"

"For you to come with us willingly," the one in the center said.

"Who sent you?" It couldn't be Mr. Peregrine. The Fury brothers had him. She doubted these men worked for him either. A cold suspicion formed in her heart. Could it be Duvessa? No, Calliope refused to believe it until she saw it with her own eyes. "If you think I'm coming with you, you are sadly mistaken, sirs."

"Don't know who, missy. Just paid us a nice penny to deliver you to them," the one to the left said. He also pulled out a pistol. "Unharmed."

Her whole body went cold.

He pointed the pistol at Prince. "They didn't say anything about a dog."

"No!" Calliope cried out. She threw her arm out as if she

could shield him from an oncoming shot. "Don't you dare!"

"Then will you come with us willingly?" the man in the center asked, lifting a brow.

"Yes," she said quickly, "if you promise you will not harm him. I'll go quietly. Willingly. But not a single hair on his body must be harmed." Prince barked once, sharp, savage. "Don't worry," she murmured to try to ease him. "Boy, we will be fine."

"Agreed," the center one said, clearly the leader of the trio.

She forced herself to stand straighter, though her knees had started to tremble a bit. "You came for me, not him. Hurt him, and I swear you'll have trouble worse than me on your hands. He also belongs to . . ." she bit her tongue before Maxen's name could slip out. Stars, she couldn't drag him into this. Not if these men weren't already his enemies. But she wanted to reaffirm her stance in some way, ". . . to a man you do *not* want to cross here in Brighton."

"Put it down," the leader ordered his man.

Relief nearly staggered her as the man tucked his pistol away. Even Prince settled, sensing part of the nightmare had been averted.

He came to her side and sank to the floor.

"Now then," the leader said, "shall we go?"

Her stomach lurched, but she nodded, and Prince, senses sharp, rose to his feet again.

"The dog stays here," the one who'd brandished the pistol said.

"Fine." She'd rather him be safe here anyway.

"Prince," she whispered low, careful. "Stay. Guard the shop for me." The dog whined, pressed against her thigh. Her heart nearly split. She bent quickly, wrapping her arms around his neck, burying her face in his fur. "Good boy," she breathed. "Wait for me."

She rose, lifting her chin. *Be brave, Calliope.* "Let's go."

The man on the right stepped forward and seized her arm, rough fingers clamping around her elbow. His grip was iron, and she had to force herself not to resist, not to fight. She glanced back as they escorted her out. Prince stood in the middle of the shop, ears pricked, body rigid. She pressed her lips together, swallowing the lump in her throat.

Her gaze darted to the empty shop next door.

Afternoon shadows stretched long, and for a wild moment she imagined Maxen striding from one of them, dark coat flaring, eyes blazing, come to sweep her out of these men's clutches. But the lane was empty save for three horses.

She thought of her promise.

Maxen wouldn't believe she'd abandon him, would he? Not with Prince still here. Knowing him, he would suspect something amiss. The man's senses were sharper than a hawk's. She would bide her time, keep her wits, and pray her beast discovered her absence quickly.

Rough hands lifted her onto a horse. She shot a glare at the man swinging into the saddle behind her, but he didn't so much as spare her a glance.

The leader of the three tossed a cloak at her. "Cover yourself."

She dragged the coarse thing over her shoulders and head, stealing one last look at her shop. Her heart plummeted.

No! Prince!

These villains hadn't even shut the door.

Horror numbed her as Prince padded out, those loyal eyes fixed on her. The man spurred the horse into a trot, and she swallowed her protest in fear that they might go back on their word and kill Prince.

Pure hopelessness enveloped her.

Bad people, it seemed, had a way of finding her, no matter how fiercely she tried to avoid it. And danger, it seemed, was an ever-present shadow, no matter how meticulously she safeguarded herself.

MAXEN STOOD IN the middle of Calliope's lodgings, clenching and unclenching his fists.

She was gone.

So was her hound.

Other than that, nothing had changed much since the last time he'd been here. She hadn't cleared all her belongings. Hadn't cleared her candles or the stock at the back. It was as if she'd left in a hurry like the last time she'd tricked his brother. The door had not even been locked. It was so bloody similar he wanted to punch a hole in the wall. But instead of his brother being duped, this time it had been him.

She'd left.

Again.

She'd promised . . .

And? Who are you to have asked that of her in the first place?

He was nobody.

Just some beast.

Maxen cursed.

He hadn't inherited his place in the world. Every scrap of authority had been purchased with cracked bones. Whatever authority he possessed did not extend to her. He had no right to her at all. Except the rent of her shop. And he wanted all the rights. That made him greedy. impatient, and impulsive. All the things that got men like him killed.

His gaze swept the room once more, inventorying what was there and everything that wasn't. Had she thought him comical when she'd said yes, she promised to tell him before she ever left? Had she smiled into the dark and let him have his pretty fancy because it cost her nothing in that moment? Or had she regretted it the instant light returned, when she saw him as he was in daylight—too large, too rough, too much of the wrong world?

Don't bloody spiral, you fool.

Too bloody late, he returned to himself.

Maxen's fists curled tighter, the phantom pinch of old violence burning in his knuckles. He could see it—hell, he could taste it—the urge to tear the whole place down. Smash her candles into wax-splattered shards. Shove the shelves until they split in pieces. Grind every shard of broken wax further into paste beneath his boots. Reduce her pretty little shop to rubble.

Like she had reduced him to wreckage.

He saw another room then, his mother's, all those years ago. He had wrecked that place, too. After her body went slack beneath his hands. His fingers remembered the tremor of death, the convulsion, the desperate clutch at his wrists as she fought for breath. He remembered the madness that told him the ending was a mercy, an to end her suffering.

And when it was done—when the last breath left her broken body—he had laid waste to everything within reach. Tables overturned. Chairs splintered. Curtains ripped from their rods. He'd smashed his head into a wall until blood ran hot into his eyes. Because he couldn't bear the silence that followed. Couldn't bear what he had done.

That same madness whispered now. *Slaughter this place. Tear it apart so there's nothing left to remind you she was here.* If he destroyed it all, maybe he could purge the hollow she'd left behind.

His hand twitched toward the nearest shelf. He could already hear the satisfying crash of wood and glass, smell the explosion of scent, and all the bloody things she'd bottled and created with her own hands. He wanted to ruin it. To prove she hadn't mattered. That none of it had mattered.

But there was no mistaking the truth.

The image of her face, eyes bright, lips curved in that stubborn little half-smile, rose unbidden. He'd cupped her cheeks more times he could count, carefully, as if she might vanish beneath his touch. That same hand now curled into a fist, because the beast inside him only knew two hungers: to cradle or to crush.

And God help him, he didn't trust himself to know the difference at the moment.

He wrenched back from the shelf with a growl, shame searing his chest. He would not destroy her place. Not as he had destroyed *hers*. Not as he had destroyed his own mother. He could not destroy that. He would not.

Because if he did, he would prove every fear true. That he was nothing more than a monster in a man's skin, doomed to strangle out anything good the moment it came within reach.

He felt the surge of anger rise—fast, hot, riddled with those old contempts. But a quieter, stubborn truth tugged at him. *Calliope was not like them.* She was . . . sunlight dressed in boy's clothes who did not back down from a challenge. So he would not wreck this place. He would not wreck her memory.

Not yet.

He shut his eyes against this last thought and opened them at once, angry with himself for the weakness. His world had room for facts, not fancies. Fact: she was not here. Prince was not here. And he might have believed she'd run out for an errand had he not been standing in this very position for three hours.

Three hours of thinking. Of cursing. Of intolerable numbness.

She wasn't coming back. Fact.

His jaw locked until something threatened to crack. "Damn you," he cursed into the quiet.

The instinct was immediate, bone-deep: hunt. Track her as he would any debtor, any enemy who thought to cross him. He could follow the smallest trace. Brighton bent when he wanted it to. She could not vanish from him, not if he didn't allow it. Not without any trace.

His fists flexed.

A part of him already saw the path, already planned the questions, the threats, the coin to loosen tongues.

But damnation. What then? Would he drag her back if he

found her? A woman who had already chosen to walk away. A noble, bred for another world, who had humored him with promises she could never mean. He'd be chasing nothing more than an angel he could never truly catch. Never truly hold onto.

The thought lodged bitter in his mouth.

He had chased enough illusions in his life. He would not chase another.

Maxen slowly forced the tension from his jaw.

No.

He would not hunt her. He wouldn't chase what didn't want to be kept. He turned on his heel and left the shop without a backward glance.

Calliope Turner belonged to the past now. And he would leave her there.

Chapter Twenty-Eight

"G o," ONE OF the men barked, shoving Calliope toward a carriage that rattled to a halt only yards away from where they'd been waiting for an hour or so. She thought the ride to this location took about the same time, but she couldn't be certain. Time moved differently when one was in a state of panic and frantically thinking of ways to escape. Fortunately, they never once showed any interest in her after she'd been apprehended.

She stumbled to the carriage step, her wrists chafing raw from where they'd tied her hands. Prince's absence rubbed raw as well, a hollow ache that grew sharper with each passing mile she was dragged from him.

And not to even mention her Brighton Beast.

But she couldn't think about him right now. She might just go mad from it.

The carriage door opened and Calliope stopped short.

Duvessa.

The nauseating sweetness of her stepmother's perfume struck first, the same scent that had haunted her childhood. The woman sat with imperial composure, hands folded in her lap, a faint, but mocking, smile playing upon her lips as if she had been expecting this scene all along. The months apart had certainly not softened her stepmother. If anything, time had carved her sharper, more harridan than lady, every inch of her draped in silks, a sight that was both familiar and sickening.

She had thought—hoped—Brighton would be far enough. That last night's ruin had freed her from this specter of her past.

But here she was.

"Well, what are you waiting for?" Duvessa snapped at the men. "Untie the poor thing. We're not barbarians."

The man who had pointed the pistol at Prince stepped forward and wrenched at her bindings. The rope fell loose, leaving angry marks she rubbed without thinking. Another shove sent her stumbling again. She caught herself, glaring at him with what defiance she could muster, before stepping into the carriage to face her stepmother.

The man shut the door and rapped on carriage, and with a lurch, the carriage rolled forward.

"We meet again, my dear. Did you truly believe I'd never find you?"

She'd certainly prayed so. "*How* did you find me, stepmother?"

"It took some time, but then I recalled that your mother was prone to that place."

She was? Calliope hadn't known. But perhaps her heart did. Perhaps that was what had attracted her to Brighton. A moot point now. "Why come for me at all? I am old enough to make my own choices now."

Duvessa's smile did not falter, though her eyes hardened. "Old enough? You ungrateful child. I secure you an advantageous match and you run away? No matter what you do, you are a Balfour, whether you wish it or not, and Balfours do not shirk their duties."

"Duty! I refuse to marry a man thirty years older than me!"

"You will do what you're told."

"I am no one's pawn," Calliope shot back, though her voice trembled despite her effort to steady it. "Not yours. Not anyone's."

"Your uncle, the current earl, has agreed to the match."

"*I* have not agreed."

"Calliope, stop. You've had your moment of freedom; now you have to do your duty."

"And what of you? My uncle is the earl now. What do you have to gain from this match?"

"That is between me and your uncle."

"So nothing good."

Her stepmother glared. "Bravery suits you ill, my dear. You may imagine yourself free, but blood binds tighter than rope. And your blood is worth more than you comprehend. Honestly, child, I am doing you a favor."

"I want nothing from you," she managed, fingers curling into her skirts to hide their tremor.

Duvessa's faint laugh slid like a blade into her gut. "No, but I will take everything from you, nonetheless. And you will give it— willingly or otherwise."

That chilled Calliope. She had to escape. If she didn't . . . Duvessa's games always ended in bruises, and this time Calliope sensed the pain would be greater than ever before if she didn't find a way out. "You will not get away with this."

"On the contrary, my dear." The woman studied her. "How did you manage your little escape? That's the one thing I haven't been able to deduce. You must have had help."

"I'll never tell you."

The woman shrugged. "Well, where you are going no one will help you this time."

Her heart stuttered. "What do you mean?"

"We will be heading straight to your wedding."

The words struck like a blow, knocking the breath from her lungs. *Her wedding.* The very sound of it made bile rise at the back of her throat. She had fled that fate once, sworn she would never again be shackled for another's gain, yet here it loomed once more—closer, more suffocating than before.

Her pulse battered in her ears. Images flitted through her

mind: a stranger's ring upon her finger, vows forced upon her, her cage snapping shut. No shop in Brighton. No Prince. No Beast. Only Duvessa's cold hand steering her life as though she were a puppet dangling from rotten strings.

"No," she whispered, though the word tasted brittle. "You cannot force me."

Duvessa's smile only deepened, as though Calliope's rebellion amused her. "Child, you mistake me. I *will*."

Terror knotted inside her, but with it came a spark—small, defiant, furious. She pressed her nails into her palms until she felt the sting. *I won't let her win. Somehow, I will break free.*

Her gaze flicked to the carriage door, to those outside, to the blur of the country beyond. Panic threatened, but she seized the spark instead. *There must be a way.*

She could jump. Again.

But it would prove as futile as the first time. No, she'd need to bide her time.

Perhaps where they stopped for the night.

As if reading her thoughts, Duvessa said. "Oh, and do not get any ideas. We shall not be stopping."

Calliope kept her features schooled. She refused to show her nervousness. "You think you know every thought in my head." She forced the words past the lump in her throat. "But you don't know me at all."

Duvessa's eyes glittered. "I know you precisely. You are still that foolish little girl who believes she can outrun her fate. You mistake this stubbornness of yours for strength."

"I call it endurance."

"That is what all cornered creatures call it, I imagine." Her stepmother's smile curved upward. "But order is kinder than the wild, child."

"I will never agree." Not even in death. Not even in the next life!

"One day, you will thank me for saving you from your own silliness."

Hah! Who was being silly now? "You will wait forever."

"Forever?" Duvessa sneered. "Child, eternity bends more easily than you think."

"Well, I'm honored you came all the way here to collect me yourself."

A scoff. "You are quite slippery."

Calliope drew a slow breath, forcing her shoulders back. It would be easier facing Maxen's enemies than holding a conversation with this woman! She had been kidnapped before, so she'd learned not to make a hasty decision. She'd strike when the time was right. All she had to do was to appear small and unthreatening as much as she could.

Which was extremely hard. She worried about Prince. Was he hurt? Had someone gone back and shot him? Her heart gave a painful twist. And Maxen? By now he would have found her gone. Was he angry? Would he try to find her? Would he even know where to start?

"You will learn your place," Duvessa said softly, mistaking her silence for surrender. "It is the only way your life will show you any kindness."

Wrong.

Her stepmother was so wrong. Life will show you precisely what you allow it to show you. Her nails dug crescents into her palms, but she refused to respond any longer.

I shall show you exactly my place, stepmother.

THE HINGES SHRIEKED as Maxen slammed the door of the dungeon wide. He glared at the man bounded and gagged on the floor. They hadn't even provided him a chair. Everything, even the table, had been removed.

Good.

This man was not to be underestimated.

Maxen stalked forward, Drake slipping in behind him with a

torch held high, its light slashing across the damp walls. Peregrine shifted, dragging himself upright against the stones. His face was a ruin of bruises, one eye swelling shut, yet that damned cocky glint still clung to him like a fool.

His hands flexed open and closed, as though eager for a throat.

"So you are the enemy in the shadows. I should have bloody known." He crouched before the man, yanking the gag that covered his mouth down. "I just didn't think you to be this damn eager to be shipped off."

"Fury," Peregrine drawled. "What a pleasure. If I'd known you were coming, I'd have ordered better accommodations."

"Mocking me won't work. Who are you working for?"

Peregrine grinned. "You don't think I'd take you on alone?"

"*Who*," Maxen's eyes bored into Peregrine's swollen face as he repeated, "are you working for?"

Peregrine spat blood to the side, sneering, "Working for. You make it sound as though I take orders like some common thug."

Maxen's hand shot out, fisting Peregrine's cravat and jerked him forward so violently the man finally grimaced. "Answer me."

"I don't *work* for anyone."

"You think me a fool? You think I don't see another's hands in this?"

Peregrine's eyes flashed. "I should think you see very little, Fury, with that storm cloud forever across your brow. And yet here you are, gnashing your teeth at me like a beast with no prey left. Has the girl got you so on edge?"

The mention of her was the spark on dry gunpowder.

Maxen flung him back against the wall so hard Peregrine coughed, still laughing even as the stone knocked the wind out of him. "So you fell by the hand of a woman."

Maxen's boot came down hard on the Peregrine's ribs.

Peregrine grunted in pain.

Served him damn right.

"You think this is amusing?" Maxen leaned in, eyes burning.

"You think a thousand men haven't tried to claim our throne? You breathe because I allow it. And right now, I'm less inclined than I've ever been."

"Kill me, then." Peregrine spat blood to the side. "It would at least prove you can do something besides brood and bark."

"Maxen," Drake warned.

He needn't have bothered. "Death is mercy. I don't deal in mercy. I deal in absolute ruin."

"You should thank me," Peregrine with a grin. "I spared her life."

The next punch split his lip. "Spared? Don't talk to me about spared."

"You are quick to temper. Like him."

Maxen froze. A muscle ticked in his jaw. "Like who?"

Peregrine's grin widened, grotesque with blood. "The man who sired you."

Drake cursed behind him. "What the devil are you saying?" his brother demanded.

"Haven't you guessed? I've the same bastard blood running through me as you and you."

Maxen shot to his feet and took two steps back. "Impossible."

"There it is. The look I've been waiting for. The one where you realize you can never win against me. Your brother. Your family."

"Don't be so sure," Drake said darkly.

"You think you're the only bastards that man sired? The late Duke of Crane planted his seed far and wide."

"I hunted down all his offspring."

"You missed one."

Bloody hell, *no*. Maxen refused to believe it. Granted, he wasn't naïve enough to believe there weren't any more. But Maxen had found all the ones who'd been disregarded. All the ones struggling to claw their way out of misery.

"How old are you?" Drake asked.

"Why, the ripe old age of thirty."

Maxen's mind raced. They were thorough. They had men all over Britain keeping score on that filth's affairs. Serpent had been the last sibling they'd tracked.

"You said you spared Miss Turner. What did you mean by that?" Drake asked.

"It means someone wanted her dead."

Maxen's hackles rose again. "I thought you said you weren't working for anyone."

"I'm not." Peregrine spit more blood to the side. "I'm working with him. Or was. I draw the line at killing, too, you know. But our uncle has quite the bone to pick with you lot."

Bloody everlasting hell.

Uncle.

"Let me guess, you're the reason he's returned," Maxen growled. "We missed you and you went to him? Why the devil didn't you come to us?"

"Because I didn't know you existed!"

"Maxen," Drake said, shaking his head. He turned to Peregrine. "How old were you when our uncle found you?"

"Seventeen."

So thirteen years ago.

"He got to you before we could," Drake said. "He must have erased all trace of you."

What the devil was this? What was he supposed to do with this claim? Could he even believe a word from Peregrine's mouth? How many times had they been deceived by him over the years? And all this while knowing who they were. That they were blood. This could be another damn farce. A trap. "You expect me to believe a word from your tongue? You reek of lies."

Peregrine chuckled. "Believe me, don't believe me, it changes nothing. Blood tells, Fury. You cannot scrub it away, no matter how many thrones you build in England's gutters."

Drake stepped closer, torchlight casting long shadows across his brother's scarred face. "If you share our blood, why side with him? Why the devil would you cling to our uncle? You must know what sort of man he is."

"Why, to get your attention, of course."

"Attention?" Maxen bristled. "Stabbing from the shadows?"

"You yourself know what man he is. Appearances must be kept."

"And he ordered you to kill Calliope."

"He did."

If he were to ever break their number one rule, it would be for his uncle. "Where is he now?"

"I don't know."

"You're lying," Drake accused.

"I'm not. Why do you think I allowed you to catch me?"

Maxen barked out a laugh filled with fury. "Allowed us? Such a damn show you put up. Why not come to us from the very start? When you first learned of our uncle's temperament?"

Peregrine's bruised mouth curled. "Because he offered me a place when the rest of the world offered only a noose. He gave me a name to wield, coin to spend, and men to command." His face turned mocking. "I just didn't know what price I would pay."

"And what price is that?" Maxen asked.

"My damn soul, brother dearest. My damn soul."

Maxen surged forward, his grip crushing as he grabbed Peregrine by the coat again. "Do not talk to me about your soul. I made something from nothing. And if you are truly one of us, you might have had the same had you not chosen the viper's den again and again."

For a single second, Peregrine's grin faltered. Then he lifted his chin, blood streaking his teeth. "Ah, kill me, ship me off, I'm dead anyway, and so is your little bird if *he* finds her."

Maxen was about to drive his fist into Peregrine's face again when the door creaked open and Reaper's voice cut through the chamber.

"*Frère*, we have visitors."

Maxen's head snapped over his shoulder. "Who?"

"A lady with some blasted flower's name, a marchioness, and

her bloody marquess husband."

"So handle them," Maxen snarled. "I'm busy here."

"Can't," Reaper said grimly. "They claim your little mouse has been kidnapped."

$$\text{Chapter Twenty-Nine}$$

MAXEN SHOVED THROUGH the door with his brothers on his heels, his gaze instantly landing on the trio standing near the entrance of the tavern, as out of place as lilies in a field of ash. Bloody aristocracy. However, he recognized the women instantly as two of the ones who had visited Calliope's shop the day after the scuffle with the intruder, who was now on his way to the nearest docks, awaiting his fate.

Saint, Knight, and Serpent, who had apparently kept watch over them as they waited, said nothing. Only Dagger was absent.

Maxen didn't bother with niceties. "Where is Calliope?"

The man with the women scowled thunderously. The blonde woman at his side turned to him. "Ah, so I was not mistaken, at least. We've come to learn that she might have been kidnapped."

Might have been. So they were not certain. "From whom did you learn this?"

"A boy who distributes pamphlets for me," the red-haired woman said. "I'm Violet, by the way. I've just opened a flower shop."

"When was this—the supposed kidnapping?"

"About four or five hours ago."

"And you're only coming to me now?" Maxen snarled before he could get a grip on the raging fire that flashed through him.

"How did the boy know she was kidnapped? Was she in distress?"

"We were out," the blonde one said. "We only just found out. My husband, Warton, tracked you down. We didn't know who else to turn to, and well, you seemed rather protective of her that day we visited the shop."

Of course. "The gothic hero."

The blonde's cheeks reddened.

"Did the boy say what happened?" Maxen asked.

"Three men came into her shop, and she left with them," the man, Warton, said. "They made her cover herself in a cloak, but the boy said she looked panicked."

Maxen's jaw flexed, teeth grinding. Three men. A cloak. Panic. He could all but see it. A storm thrashed inside him. He caught the twitch of Drake's head as his brother moved in closer, Reaper at his side, both silent pillars.

Drake broke his silence. "What did these men look like?"

The red-haired, flower-named woman frowned in thought. "The boy said they were not Brighton men. How he could tell, I'm not sure."

"Oh, they can tell," Reaper muttered darkly.

Outsiders.

Bloody hell. His fist curled. He'd known from the start she wasn't an ordinary woman. The way she carried herself, the refinement beneath her stubbornness. And then Drake had gone and confirmed it with Dare's information—daughter of an earl, apparently engaged. A runaway lady.

He stared at the trio. One of *them.*

Did that mean she was kidnapped or merely collected?

"Will you save her?" the blonde asked. Her eyes narrowed. "Or was I mistaken in thinking that you care?"

Maxen's teeth bared in something like a snarl. Care. The word burned. "She is my tenant. That is all."

Reaper gave a soft, derisive snort, but didn't speak.

Drake sighed.

Violet stepped forward. "Tenant or not, she needs help. Will you give it or not?"

His temper spiked. "Her matter seems to be a family matter."

Drake's warning slid into the moment. "Don't make a mistake here, Maxen. *Matters* might not be what they seem."

Maxen forced a breath. "If it was her family, then it is no business of mine."

Reaper snorted. "No business of yours? That's not what I heard—"

"Reaper," Maxen growled.

"What?" his brother challenged. "You're just going to let her go like that?"

"What the devil do you want me to do? Steal her back?"

"Do you want to steal her back?" Knight asked.

Yes, damn it. He hated the image of Calliope living any sort of life without him. A noble life. But, "If she is a lady, then perhaps she belongs with them. Perhaps I've been a fool for thinking otherwise."

The blonde gave a most inelegant snort. "Let me assure you, sir, as a marchioness, that line is the most nonsense I've heard in an age! Love is love! It transcends class. Only *fools* believe otherwise."

"I think she just called you a fool, *frère*."

Maxen's eyes cut to Reaper, but the arse only grinned, dark challenge glinting in his eyes.

The marchioness folded her arms. "Well? Will you sit and sulk, or will you act? A woman's future may hang in the balance."

"She is not a woman," Maxen snapped, and the woman's husband took a protective stance. "She is a lady. A runaway. And I've no place meddling in the affairs of the nobility."

"Seems to me you've meddled plenty," Drake muttered.

Warton spoke again, steady as stone. "If you do nothing, she may vanish forever. Her family, or whomever these men are, will spirit her away, and she will have no voice in the matter. Is that truly an outcome you can live with?"

Were these people really nobles?

Maxen's thoughts churned. Their words scraped at him, each one lodging like a thorn. No matter how he told himself it was none of his business, that she had all the trappings he despised, the picture of her, her laughter, her smile, her sparkling green eyes, rose unbidden. She had chosen Brighton. She had chosen freedom. Damn it, she had chosen him, in her way. Could he stand idle while others stripped her choices from her?

Dagger entered, Prince trotting at his side.

"Cock on a duck," Reaper muttered.

Maxen's whole body went cold at the sight.

"Found him outside the tavern," Dagger said, the lines between his brows furrowed deep.

The tavern seemed to shrink, every sound muffled but the low whine Prince made as he darted forward, sniffing at his feet. The dog's white fur coat was muddied, his nose nudging insistently toward the door as if demanding that Maxen follow.

For a moment, he couldn't breathe. The dog had been with her, almost always at her side. And now here he was, alone. "She . . ." He bent, hand sliding over Prince's coat.

Maxen straightened, fury exploding anew, his hand still buried in Prince's fur. The air burned in his lungs, every heartbeat a drumbeat of rage.

What the devil was wrong with him? Why was he standing here debating this? Questioning this? He truly was a damn fool. They'd taken her, stolen her from under his roof, from her shop, from him.

She hadn't broken her promise.

"Have you come to your senses, *frère?*"

No one stole from him. No one stole *her*. The thought came torn from somewhere deep. His chest felt caged, his blood roaring.

She'd undone him. Remade him.

"I think he has," Drake noted.

"I'm saddling my horse."

His words snapped like a whip, jerking the room into motion.

Drake gave one short nod, already turning for the door. Reaper grinned, wicked and savage, his knuckles cracking like he'd been waiting for this since Maxen had returned after finding her gone.

Dagger only exhaled, tension draining from his stance, and muttered, "Thought you'd never bloody say it."

The other three merely stepped forward silently.

The marchioness nodded. "At last, sir. A sensible decision."

Maxen shoved to the door, Prince trotting at his heels, the tavern door slamming wide as he strode into the night. The storm inside him broke loose, a beast unchained.

They thought to take Calliope? They would learn what it meant to steal from Maxen Fury.

CALLIOPE SWORE HER limbs were about fall off by the time the carriage lurched to a halt. The door opened to reveal a house she never thought she'd ever set foot in again. Memory crashed over her, swift and merciless. She was a girl again, clutching her books to her chest, hoping for a smile from her stepmother that never came. Her father's voice, always so gentle, reassuring her by quoting Shakespeare. Rare jewels she had polished over the years in the hope they would shine brighter than the darkness.

A hopeful sentiment.

What lingered was sharper. Duvessa's voice dripping venom. The attic. The mocking laughter of her stepsisters. But then at the same time more rare jewels in the servants who had helped her.

Just a little longer.

She shouldn't be here. . . Didn't belong here . . .

She belonged in Brighton. She belonged with *him.*

Her fingers curled into her skirts. *I escaped this place once. I can escape it again.* "I thought you said we weren't coming back to the house."

"Oh, did I?" Duvessa arched a brow. "I meant the wedding

would be here. All troublesome servants have been dismissed, of course, but there will still be a wedding tonight. Though we have to get you cleaned up first. Can't have you sully the family name."

So she had lied. Amused herself at Calliope's expense.

"Out," one of the men barked, and Duvessa motioned her to exit first.

Calliope stiffened, her body aching from the long confinement, but she forced herself to move slowly, with dignity. She would not stumble on these steps, not when they led to her prison.

Two silhouettes spilled from the doorway, and Calliope's breath stilled.

Her stepsisters. Morgana and Victoria.

Morgana's shrill laughter pealed first. "Well, well, look what the tide dragged back. I thought Brighton had swallowed you whole."

Victoria's lips curved into a poisonous smile. "She looks half-swallowed already. Just look at those clothes. How dreadful. You're certain she isn't some common beggar Mama picked up along the way?"

Calliope glared at them. "At least I did not waste my days growing cruel and idle."

Morgana gasped, hand pressed theatrically to her breast. "Cruel? Idle? You wound me, *sister*. But my, you have grown bolder!"

"Stepsister," Calliope corrected tightly.

That earned another titter. "Where's your mongrel? They didn't kill him, did they?" Morgana taunted.

Calliope refused to answer as she was herded inside by the three ruffians.

Morgana leaned close, her voice a hiss. "No matter, your husband might buy you another. If you beg."

"When have I ever begged?"

That drew a sneer. "You've always fancied yourself clever,"

Victoria said. "Clever enough to run away. And now look where it's landed you, dragged back home in rags."

She would rather wear rags and live in Brighton with Maxen than wear pretty dresses and be shackled to misery. Even the darkest corner in Brighton wasn't as dark as this house and these people. Brutish, brooding, impossible Maxen. He was no gentleman. Yet in his presence, she had felt more alive, more seen, than in any other moment.

And she still had that card up her sleeve.

She was no longer chaste.

If she revealed that at the right moment, surely no man would take the chance to marry her? Let them believe they'd won. Let them think her spirit cracked. They would never know that her thoughts, her heart, had already escaped beyond these walls. Now, she would only have to escape with her body.

"Where is my uncle?" Calliope asked. "If I am to be forced into this farce, should he not be here to deliver me into it?"

Duvessa's lips curved. "So demanding, child. You'll see him soon enough. He is out with your betrothed. They are finalizing arrangements."

Morgana giggled, looping her arm through Victoria's. "How quaint, that your fate comes down to coin."

"Coin and convenience," Victoria added smoothly. "A lady who runs makes her family look desperate. Better to tie her down quickly, before gossip turns into ruin."

So this was about money?

Calliope's nails bit her palms. "You speak of ruin as though it is not already here. If Papa still lived—"

Duvessa's eyes hardened as she shot a glare at Calliope. "If your father still lived, your fate would not have been any different."

"That is a lie," Calliope shot back, her temper sparking. "Papa never would have sold me to the highest bidder. He believed in honor, in choice."

Morgana clapped her hands together. "Oh, how charming!

Our Calliope still dreams of hopeless fantasies."

"Dreams are for children," Victoria agreed.

Calliope scoffed at them.

"Silence," Duvessa said coldly. "Your fate has been sealed, child."

Calliope refused to respond to the taunt. She should try to find a way to get word to Mr. Fitz. She was afraid, however, she wouldn't be given a chance.

Morgana laughed. "Yes, fate brought you back where you belong. The attic still waits for you."

Vile.

Victoria smirked. "Yes, we've prepared it for your return."

Duvessa silenced her daughters with a flick of her hand. "Enough. Take her upstairs. We've wasted too much time already. The earl and her betrothed shall return soon, and I expect her to be prepared. There will be no more theatrics."

One of the men grabbed her arm and led toward the stairs. Calliope lifted her chin, refusing to be dragged like an animal. Every tread stirred old shadows—the attic's cold drafts, the sting of laughter in the corridors, the loneliness that had once smothered her.

But she was not that girl anymore.

She had tasted freedom. Brighton's salt air still thrummed in her veins. Maxen's fierce gaze, his impossible presence, his body against hers burned hotter than these walls could ever contain.

They thought her cornered. They thought her caught. But she had claws now, sharp enough to draw blood.

Her stepsisters followed, whispering gleefully behind their hands. The house had once threatened to swallow her entire being.

Not this time.

E VERY EYE IN the room turned to Calliope the moment she stepped through the doors flanked by the three men who had taken her from her shop. She ignored those stares. Chin lifted. Shoulders squared. Let them look. Let them wonder if she was the same girl they'd once scorned.

Because she wasn't.

Not anymore.

And she wasn't going to cower for anyone. Not again. Especially not for Duvessa.

She had, however, been surprised at the quality of the gown. She wore a gown of flowing white, matching gloves that came to her elbows, and pearls in her hair. Her stepmother had even dressed her in a pearl necklace, which of course, to her, felt more like a collar than anything else. Even so, appearances had to be kept up, she supposed.

All eyes turned to her.

Her uncle, the Earl of Balfour, had finally arrived and stood by the window with a drink in his hand. He was heavier than she remembered, his once-dark hair now a thin, silver crown around his head. His belly strained against his waistcoat, and his lips pursed with disapproval. He spared her but one glance before averting his gaze.

She could scarcely believe she shared this man's blood!

Beside him stood another man, dressed in lavish gold. Too much gold. Age had not been kind to him. A wide belly, even wider than her uncle's, sweat gleaming at his brow despite the cool of the room, piggish eyes that raked over her as though she were cattle at market. She just had to look at the greed in his gaze when his eyes fell on her to know he was the betrothed, Lord Flemmington.

With them was a corrupt officiant, she presumed. How else could he allow a woman to be forced into a union against her will?

Her stepsisters hovered by the piano, tittering and giggling, but still only the second most annoying sight of the day. Duvessa, she took the top spot. The woman seemed to have had a sculptor carve a look of smug victory into her face. Most annoying.

Calliope couldn't deny the apprehension that stole over her as to whether she'd be able to fully escape, but she *was* determined to remove that insufferable gleam from all these people.

"Well," the earl said into the air, "my niece returns."

"I was kidnapped back," Calliope pointed out.

"Semantics." He waved a hand. "You have caused trouble enough."

It appeared her betrothed knew of these troubles and had still decided to go through with the wedding. Her plan might not work.

Lord Flemmington made his way to her, his gaze openly sliding down her bodice. "She's thin," he muttered. "But serviceable."

Revulsion crawled up Calliope's throat. "I am not a broodmare to be inspected."

Morgana giggled, clapping her hands. "Oh, how bold! Brighton gave her a quite the tongue."

"Pity it didn't give her sense," Victoria added.

Duvessa raised a hand, silencing the jabs. "Calliope knows her duty. She will comply."

Calliope laughed. "Comply? Is that what you call kidnapping now?"

Lord Flemmington's face mottled red. "Girl, you will not shame this family again. We shall be married tonight. The paperwork is ready, the vows will be spoken, and you will cease this insolence."

"I will not," Calliope said flatly.

"Defiance," Duvessa purred, circling closer. "How tiresome. You ought to thank us for taking you back at all and for setting this match for you."

Were these people addlebrained? "Taking me back? I have known nothing but your cruelty at your hands! This is no different."

The stepsisters gasped as though offended. Morgana pressed a hand to her breast. "Cruelty? What nonsense!"

Lord Flemmington grunted. "I paid a hefty price for this union, so shall we get on with it?"

Calliope's heart pounded, the walls closing in. So it *was* money. All this was done for *money*. Her nails bit her palms.

Now's the time.

She lifted her chin, bracing herself. If she shocked them, she might be able to dash past her guards. She knew this house like the back of her hand. She could disappear for hours before they found her. "You would wed a girl already ruined?"

Duvessa's sharp eyes whipped to her. "Do not listen to her."

"Listen to me?" Calliope challenged. "I wonder, did you sell me or my maidenhood? For I don't possess that any longer."

The room froze.

"That's not true!" Duvessa exclaimed.

"Oh, it's very true, stepmother," Calliope said, an undercurrent of mockery in her tone. "Used goods. Bedded. By an outlaw, no less. Albeit a handsome one."

The words landed like a cannon blast. Gasps, sputters, outrage.

"You lie!" Duvessa snapped, her eyes narrowing. "You dare

speak such filth in this house?"

"Yes, lies," Victoria hissed. "She says it to escape her duty."

But Calliope did not waver. She looked her uncle dead in the eye. "Examine me, then. Summon a doctor. You'll see the truth. I am no innocent. I am ruined. Worthless to you."

Lord Flemmington bristled. "What is the meaning of this, Balfour? You promised me she would be chaste!"

The earl's hand drink scattered against the wall. "You dare shame this family with such depravity?"

"I dare speak the truth," Calliope declared.

Morgana's face twisted. "Who? Who touched you? Name him!"

Calliope's lips curved, cold. "A man you'd spit at in the street. A criminal. A beast." A lovely, gentle, broody beast.

"Enough," Duvessa hissed. "You weave lies. She is untouched. She must be. She will be examined, and the truth will out."

Calliope's chin lifted higher. "Do what you must, the outcome will not be changed."

"Fetch a physician," Duvessa said. Calm voice. Cold eyes. "Now."

One guard moved for the door.

"Wait," the earl snapped. "We'll not have the neighbors talking. Send for Dr. Pritchard. Quietly."

The guard nodded and slipped out.

Lord Flemmington said, "If she's spoiled, I'll not take her."

Thank stars!

However, her plan to dash off was felled by her uncle.

"Hold her." The earl pointed at the guards who remained. "I won't have her bolt."

The corridor beyond the doors erupted with noise. Shouts, cursing, a cry of pain, and an all too familiar crash of something shattering against the floor.

The room froze again.

"What is that?" Duvessa snapped.

A laugh bubbled from Calliope even as one of the guards caught her arm.

The drawing room doors blew inward.

Their reckoning had come.

Maxen filled the doorway, eyes cold, flanked by Reaper and Drake. He looked like dark, avenging angelic beast. So did his brothers. In fact, they looked positively menacing.

A part of her hated that he now knew. Hated that he saw what her life had been like. But stars, she also wanted him to keep seeing. Because someone was angry *for* her. Furious, even. His eyes burned into her. And he didn't look away.

No one had ever burned for her like that before.

The man gripping her arms tightened his grip, and she flinched. Not missed by her beast's sharp gaze.

He all but snarled, "Hands. Off. My. Woman."

EVER SINCE PEREGRINE had taken Calliope from under his nose, Maxen had known fury in a dozen shades. Nothing, absolutely nothing, compared to the rage he felt at the sight of the scene before him. He'd never seen Calliope look so damn beautiful, but at the same time, one sweep of the room, at what was being forced on her, and he wanted to rip the dress from her body and burn it. He'd rather endure the torment of her striding about in trousers than see her in what was meant to be a wedding gown for another man.

"Who the blazes are you?" an older woman demanded, two young women pressed close to her skirts.

"The last man you should have crossed." He crossed the floor in three strides, slammed his fist into the man holding Calliope, and in the same motion seized her waist, dragging her against him. The man dropped like an ox, both hands flying to his bloodied nose. He rolled, groaning, spitting crimson. His partner shifted as though to lunge, but Reaper's pistol cocked with an audible click. The second man froze. Drake leveled his on the man on the ground.

The world righted. Most of his fury bled away now that his woman was back in his arms. Where she damn well belonged. "I've come to collect what was stolen from me."

Maxen didn't spare them another glance. His arm tightened around Calliope, and bright, sparking eyes stared up at Maxen.

"How did you find me?"

He smiled. "Did truly believed I wouldn't?"

"Well, London is rather large."

"Not large enough."

She grinned at him.

"And he had me," another voice cut through the room. Two men entered, and Maxen scowled. Never mind that he'd vowed to never set foot in London again, but he'd had to stop and ask for directions, and help from Drake's cousin, the Earl of Dare, who had also come along.

"Mr. Fitz!" Calliope exclaimed.

The man inclined his head. "Lady Calliope."

"So that's how you fled," the older woman sneered. "Fitz. Such elaborate schemes."

"I've always had Lady Calliope's interest at heart," Fitz said. "Even now. You are aware you cannot force anyone to wed without their consent?"

"This is a family matter," a grey, old man snapped.

"Ah, Balfour, Countess Duvessa," Dare said. "You are quite right. Since it's a family matter, you should allow your niece and the Furys to sort out *their* family matter without interference."

"So this is the ruffian you bedded?" Balfour snapped.

Calliope coughed, her face reddened. "I had to do something," she said by way of explanation.

Maxen arched a brow, but satisfaction filled his entire being. "I'm a man who values family. I shall take full responsibility."

"You'd wed a lady?" Doubt flickered in her eyes, and he hated it. That she might think he believed her unworthy in some way. She must have heard about his aversion to the upper class.

"I'd wed Calliope."

That earned him an even bigger beam. "Then I'd happily wed a beast."

"You harlot!" the woman, Duvessa, cried.

Maxen almost lost his damn tempter and punched a woman. "Madam, if you ever call her anything but an angel again, I will destroy every single thing you hold dear."

"How dare you speak that way to your betters!" the old man in gold snapped with indignation.

This was why he'd had to become stronger, wealthier, more powerful. So not even a tip of their fingers could ever hope to touch you. And they couldn't touch him. "How dare *you*? A man who would bind a woman to his will with force has forfeited the right to call himself anything but coward. If you ever come near Calliope again, I will break every bone in your body."

The stepmother stepped forward. "Do no think for one second we're scared of you, you brigand?"

"Allow me, *frère*." Reaper, with the devil's own grin, changed the aim of his pistol.

Maxen covered Calliope's ears just before the crack of the shot exploded against the floor at the women's feet. The three screamed, collapsing into a heap of wails.

How bloody satisfying.

His arm tightened about Calliope, sheltering her in the cage of his body. "You bloody menace," he muttered at his brother.

Reaper only laughed. "They'll live, but they should be very, very afraid."

Drake gave an exasperated sigh but did not lower his weapon. Neither Fitz nor Dare seemed all that startled.

Maxen turned back to the pale visages of Balfour and whoever the old man was. "Hear me well. Calliope belongs to no one but herself. She chose to stand with me, and I with her. You come for her, you come for me. That is all you need remember."

Duvessa's fan snapped shut with a crack. "You will never be able to enter society after this!" Duvessa cried from the floor.

Calliope lifted her chin. "I belong in Brighton with my beasts, anyway."

Pride swelled in Maxen's chest so sharp it near knocked him senseless. For a man who'd been called monster more times than he could count, the words struck like salvation. He did not want to stay any longer. He bent, swept Calliope into his arms as if she weighed no more than a feather, and strode for the door.

Fitz and Dare stepped aside, the former grave as a judge, the latter with infuriating amusement dancing in his eyes.

"Drake," Maxen growled, pausing only a heartbeat. "Round up those two and find the other one."

"Why?" Calliope asked.

"They touched you. Took you from your shop against your will. They're going to the dungeon."

Her lips parted, but before she could speak, Reaper chuckled. "I'll collect the other one, *frère*. You go make up with your lady."

Christ yes. He was about to do just that.

Chapter Thirty-One

CALLIOPE'S RETURN TO Brighton had been a whirlwind of dazedness, kisses, and untimely interruptions by Reaper. So much had happened that she could scarcely wrap her mind around it all. Prince had found the tavern in her absence, and Holly, her husband, and Violet had also sought Maxen out since her kidnapping had been witnessed. Due to being away on business, Mr. Fitz never received any news until the day Maxen, his brothers, and the Earl of Dare showed up on his doorstep.

Mr. Rollings was apparently alive and well. Retired.

And Mr. Peregrine was Maxen's half-brother!

And his uncle had ordered her death simply in an attempt to bring Maxen to his knees. Perhaps that would have been more shocking if she didn't have an evil stepmother. However, the threat of his uncle still loomed over them.

If that did not mean she'd been well and truly claimed by Brighton's underworld, nothing would.

She could scarcely believe she was back in her shop, and this time with no fear of being dragged off to her old house. That chapter had closed. Nothing else had changed here either. Well, except for one glaringly obvious thing: Maxen Fury had moved into her lodgings.

Speaking of the man . . .

She padded upstairs, Prince faithfully at her heels. "You and I, Prince," she murmured, "we have come a long way, haven't we?" He wagged his tail. "We are not alone anymore."

She was, however, alone at the moment. The rooms were quiet, and Maxen was nowhere in sight.

Her gaze fell on an unassuming little chest set neatly beside the bed. Curious, she crossed the room, lifted the lid, and gasped.

Sun and stars!

Her slippers lay nestled inside, the very ones she had all but forgotten in the chaos of events. So Maxen had found the other one that day she'd left. He hadn't said a word. Her heart filled with inexplicable sentiment.

He had kept them. As though they were some cherished relic.

"Stars," she breathed, stroking them. "You ridiculous, impossible man. Who keeps slippers?" she whispered to Prince. "And how am I supposed to resist that?"

She fell even more in love with the man.

Beside them rested a dagger. She traced a finger over it before moving to the final item. A ribbon, worn and faded. She touched it lightly, then lifted it from the box.

"It was my mother's," a voice said behind her.

She started, turning to find Maxen leaning against the doorframe.

"I killed her."

The words should have chilled the air, and Calliope blinked, but she had learned enough of this man to know there was far more to that admission than those three, terrible words.

"Why?" she whispered.

"She was in pain. Beaten near to death by my father, the late Duke of Crane. The doctor said a bone had punctured her lungs, and there was nothing to be done."

Her heart twisted. "You ended her suffering."

"Some would not see it that way."

"I am not some." Her gaze dropped to his hands, still gloved. "Is that why you keep your hands covered?"

"They have her death on them."

"They have mercy on them," she countered. She placed the ribbon back inside. "You are a good man."

He arched a brow. "As good as a monster can be?"

"If you're a monster, then I'm the daft girl who keeps wandering into your lair."

His mouth twitched. "Not daft. Brave."

"Brave enough to love a monster? Does that make me one, then? I don't believe that. You're not a monster, Maxen. A beast perhaps. My beast. My Beast in Brighton."

He pushed back from the door, and with slow, deliberate steps, he closed the distance between them until nothing remained between them but clothes.

He kissed her, softly at first, testing, then deeper, his fingers weaving in her hair as if it were their most beloved place. He pulled away slightly. "I love you."

Stars, the man new how to stun a woman senseless! "I love you, too."

"You can't just say it," he pressed, eyes burrowing into hers. "I'm not a man who lets things go. I can't bear to lose you."

"Fortunately, I'm not a thing. And you won't lose me. Ever."

His smile was slow in coming. But when it came, it stole her breath.

And her knees.

And her sanity.

Maxen reached out, brushing his knuckles against her cheek. "You've no idea how dangerous you are to me."

"Likewise." She suddenly chuckled. "So, I belong to myself, heh? You don't own me?" She wouldn't mind being owned every second by this man.

He nodded. "I don't own you, love, but you very much own me."

"Such a silver tongue! Kiss me again, this time . . ." she grinned, "just a little longer."

He kissed her again, and while this was certainly not the first time, he'd never kissed her with the whole of himself pressed into the space between them like their souls were merging, never with every vow he'd never dared speak sliding from his mouth to hers.

He picked her up and carried her to bed.

A laugh tumbled from her throat. "It is broad daylight, Maxen! Entirely scandalous."

He laid her down, covering her with his body. "I've found myself rather partial to daylight recently."

Heat rushed to her cheeks, though her heart throbbed sweetly. Once, she had loathed darkness. Now—even in the blaze of noon—she felt safe in the shadows he cast. She realized something she had never thought possible.

Calliope loved the night.

MAXEN STOOD WITH his palms braced upon the counter in Calliope's shop, sleeves rolled, jaw unshaven, some candles lit to give some light. casting enough light over his brothers who gathered around, every single one of them restless. Upstairs, Calliope was sleeping, Prince had joined him downstairs.

"Only you would move simply move in with a woman in such a fashion, *frère*," Reaper said.

"She didn't want to leave the shop," Maxen said simply.

"You good?" Drake asked.

"I have never felt alive in my own life," Maxen said. A part of him had awakened from the dead. "Until her." So yes, he was good. More than good.

"She ours to protect now, *frère*, which brings us to the matter of business for the night. Do we ship him off?"

Him as in Peregrine.

Their newfound brother.

"Far." Serpent said with a scowl. "Anywhere with a great deal of water between him and us."

"No," Maxen said. That arse had been right. He'd said they could never win against him because he was family. He was right. He'd never harm a brother. Had he found his brother before their uncle had, things might be different. "He's family, whether we like it or not."

Drake's lip curled. "I don't like it."

All his brothers concurred.

"He kidnapped your woman," Knight said.

"Don't bloody remind me." Maxen scowled. "And he got his arse beaten for it."

"What is he actually after? Blood? Or revenge?" Dagger asked.

"Perhaps family," Saint suggested.

That was Maxen's guess, too.

"Lovely," Reaper drawled. "Let's knit him a blanket and send him on his way."

The memory of Deveraux Peregrine's smile didn't sit well with him. "We can't let him out of our sight."

"So we keep him with us," Drake concluded.

"It could be a trap," Knight said. "To integrate into our family and ruin us from the inside."

Dagger tapped the counter. "Savage."

"Trap or not," Serpent said, "we are fools if we forget the spider who spun it."

"Sirius Faiththorne," Saint announced the name no one wished to utter, and the name went through them like a cold draft.

Drake's jaw ticked, the only sign of the fury.

Reaper's usually upturned lips turned down.

Serpent muttered, "Poison wears his face."

Knight's voice was blunt: "He should've stayed gone."

Dagger scowled.

So did Maxen. They could no longer deny his existence. "He'll want revenge for us shipping him off."

"He'll want revenge for many things," Drake muttered.

"He'll want Brighton," Knight said.

Dagger nodded. "Every coin we took from him."

Reaper flicked a coin between his fingers. "He'll want her, *frère*. More than anything now that our newfound brother betrayed him."

Maxen felt old and new fury resurface. But beneath it something else lurked. Shame. Bitterness. They'd all been fools once. "He took from all of us, but he won't again."

"The shop might not be safe," Drake pointed out.

"We tighten the ship," Maxen said. "Ship as in Brighton. We clear it of any rats not loyal."

"Can't find them all," Knight pointed out.

"Then we make better examples of the ones we do find," Maxen said darkly.

Reaper clicked his tongue. "And we cut all his little ties one by one."

"We cannot cut what we cannot see," Serpent said.

"Then we smoke him out," Dagger offered. "Spiders hate smoke."

"That's hornets," Saint said.

"Peregrine might be useful in that regard," Drake said. "He should know Sirius better than us, at least."

Maxen nodded. "We can put it to a vote when he proves himself. Agreed?"

Everyone nodded.

Reaper sighed extravagantly. "We're having a very *principled* night. Fine. I will abstain. I shall not pull all his teeth."

"Your restraint humbles us," Dagger said dryly.

Reaper grinned. "Doesn't it just?"

"Uncle has ears everywhere," Serpent said. "He'll know if Peregrine has turned."

"Then let him bloody know," Maxen said. "If he's willing to harm Calliope, I won't be polite with him anymore. God help him or anyone who tries to touch her again. I will end them. Not words. Not threats. An end."

"I like the sound of that," Reaper said with a grin.

Maxen nodded. "Then let the hunt begin."

Epilogue

SIRIUS SWEPT THE papers from his desk in a fit of rage. "Those bastards!" he snarled. "I will have them beg for the mercy they denied me yet!"

THE END

Thank you so much for reading Maxen and Calliope's story! Writing their journey was an absolute joy, even if it was a bit tough at times. They had minds of their own! But I hope you loved watching these two hearts find their way to one another.

If you're curious about Maxen's world beyond Brighton, you may enjoy reading about his elusive duke half brother in *Beauty and the Lyon*, where another brooding hero is drawn out of the shadows by a rose brave enough to see his heart.

Thank you for stepping into Brighton with me. There are always more beasts lurking in the wings . . .

XO
Tanya

Award-winning and bestselling author Tanya Wilde developed a passion for reading when she had nothing better to do than lurk in the library during her lunch breaks. Her love affair with pen and paper soon followed after she devoured all of their historical romance books!

When she's not meddling in the lives of her characters or pondering names for her imaginary big, white greyhound, she's off on adventures with her partner in crime. Wilde lives in a town at the foot of the Outeniqua Mountains, South Africa.

You can connect with her at www.authortanyawilde.com.

Instagram – instagram.com / tanyawilde
Facebook – facebook.com / authortanyawilde
BookBub – bookbub.com / authors / tanya-wilde